T0193699

THE EDGE

Also by Bill Noel

Folly
The Pier
Washout

THE EDGE

A Folly Beach Mystery

Bill Noel

iUniverse, Inc.
Bloomington

The Edge
A Folly Beach Mystery

This is a work of fiction. All of the characters, names, incidents, organizations, and dialogue in this novel are either the products of the author's imagination or are used fictitiously.

iUniverse Star
an iUniverse, Inc. imprint

iUniverse books may be ordered through booksellers or by contacting:

iUniverse
1663 Liberty Drive
Bloomington, IN 47403
www.iuniverse.com
1-800-Authors (1-800-288-4677)

Because of the dynamic nature of the Internet, any Web addresses or links contained in this book may have changed since publication and may no longer be valid. The views expressed in this work are solely those of the author and do not necessarily reflect the views of the publisher, and the publisher hereby disclaims any responsibility for them.

ISBN: 978-1-936236-38-1 (sc)
ISBN: 978-1-936236-39-8 (ebk)

Library of Congress Control Number: 2010917730

Printed in the United States of America

iUniverse rev. date: 1/3/2011

CHAPTER 1

The monsoon-like rain snuck between seams in the tin roof and cascaded into the two garbage pails I'd placed in the living room. The floor vibrated; the tall, ceramic lamp rocked precariously on the edge of the table. One-hundred-mile-per-hour winds ripped three of the six screen panes from the enclosed front porch. My ears ached from the wind's roar combined with the whistle of air pushing effortlessly through the gaps in the window frame. Water seeped under the front door. I was losing the battle against Mother Nature. Frank had come to visit—Hurricane Frank.

For most people, Frank would be filler on the morning news, sandwiched between a cat being rescued from a tree and the escalating price of gas. My retirement cottage was two blocks from the Atlantic Ocean. Frank trumped felines and petroleum.

I had watched television coverage throughout the night until the electricity succumbed to the storm's intensity around 9:00 a.m. Frank was expected to hit land somewhere between Kiawah and Savannah in the next couple of hours. I distinctly remembered the confident weather forecaster saying not to worry because Charleston was on the northern edge of Frank's coming ashore. He also kept reminding his viewers that Frank was "only" a Category 2 hurricane. On the scale of five, Frank was small, with evacuation optional. Winds could cause damage to doors, windows, and roofs. I laughed when he said that mobile homes *could* suffer damage. With airtime to fill, dumb things slip out.

I was standing in my rustic cottage, fewer than ten miles southeast of Charleston. My legs were shaking as much as the lamp. I pressed my palms against my ears but failed to block the screeching sounds of the tin roof peeling back. Water was everywhere; there was no electricity. My mind raced. I stared at the leaking ceiling and then at the walls. "You've survived worse storms over the decades!" I yelled. "Tell me you'll pull me through this one." My hands were balled into fists like I was ready to strike out at the wind.

The walls didn't answer. Maybe I should have promised them a fresh coat of paint.

If this was a small hurricane and I was on the northernmost edge, God help those in the midst of its fury. The saving grace was that I was two rows of houses and numerous trees from the beach—enough, I thought, to protect my domicile from the brunt of the storm. I was thankful that I wasn't in a mobile home.

I paced from room to room, surveyed the increasing damage, and prayed.

For my first six decades, hurricanes were things I experienced secondhand from television reporters leaning into the wind, palm branches and roofs blowing past in the background, and humongous waves dwarfing nearby piers. Tornadoes were the natural disasters that threatened my previous home in Louisville, Kentucky.

I'll mark September 4 as my first experience on Folly Beach with an angry Mother Nature. That is, if my house is still standing and I can find my calendar after Frank moves inland.

*   *   *

The deluge stopped as quickly as it had begun. The winds slowed to thunderstorm intensity. My well-worn hardwood floor was covered with water, but it had pooled in the center of the living room and kitchen; sagging floors did have a virtue. The water hadn't ponded around the edges, and thus, the drywall was spared. Water from the ceiling had dwindled from a steady pour to a continuous drip. Every towel, washcloth, sheet, and sweatshirt I owned was scattered around the house; and doubled-up at the front door to stem the literal and figurative tide of rainwater coming from the porch.

I took a deep breath and sat in one of the wooden chairs at the kitchen table. My hands shook, my head throbbed, and my heart bounced off my rib cage. I was terrified.

It took an hour for my heartbeat to return to normal. I heard less of the howling wind and more sirens from the Folly Beach police and fire vehicles as they crisscrossed the small barrier island to aid residents and vacationers. Dogs crawled out from whatever shelter they had huddled under and barked for food and attention—or simply rejoiced in being able to howl.

The house was tiny so it didn't take long to survey the damage. The computer and television appeared unaffected, although I wouldn't know for sure until power returned. Most of the furniture was dry; only one chair felt the wrath of the initial roof leak. I had pushed the chair aside and slid a trash can in its place, but its future looked short-lived. I didn't have any antiques or family heirlooms, so it didn't matter. I was thankful to be alive.

I cautiously pulled the trash containers to the back door and emptied them into the yard. The rain had stopped. It was going to get hot, and steam was already curling up from standing water. I squeegeed as much out as I could and propped the door open so the brisk wind could evaporate the rest.

I slipped into my retirement clothes of choice—a short-sleeve, faded, red golf shirt, cargo shorts, well-worn deck shoes, and my canvas Tilley hat—and followed the pails into the yard. I had a better view of the roof from the side yard and was surprised to see how little damage there was to the tin roof. There were three spots where the wind had peeled the tin back. With some luck and a couple of dry days, I could bend it back in place, drive a few roofing nails into the durable, metal covering, and caulk around the edges. I had never been on the roof and hoped I wasn't overly optimistic about my roofing skills. A good friend, Larry LaMond, owned Folly Beach's only hardware store and could tell me the error of my optimism.

I wasn't as optimistic when I got to the front of the faded blue, weatherboard cottage. Three wooden frames holding the front porch screen had been ripped off and were leaning against the front door, twisted with the wood shattered—far beyond my carpentry abilities. The screen door was torn from one of its hinges and dangled precariously by the intact hinge. No brilliant repair plan came to mind, so I turned my attention to my seven-year-old Lexus parked at the curb. A large branch had blown across the street from a neighbor's oak and bashed in the passenger door. The dent was deep, but the door opened with only a groan.

Railroad tie-sized branches and uprooted trees were everywhere; my street was blocked at both ends. I was only two blocks from Center Street, the main street of commerce and the only street connecting Folly Beach with the rest of the United States. The police and fire sirens brought more howls from the island's substantial canine population as the vehicles weaved around limbs, ponding water, and debris. Residents began surveying the damage, first in their yards and then venturing farther from home.

Folly Beach was returning to normal. Or so I thought.

CHAPTER 2

My professional life had centered around an international health-care company in Louisville; the last few years before retiring, I was stuck in its human resources department. My true passion had been photography. I opened a small photo gallery in the main business district when I moved here three years ago. Business had never been great, and with the slipping economy, sales had declined to a notch slightly north of nonexistent. A couple of successful real estate ventures, an early retirement package, and a lot of luck allowed me to financially handle retirement, but I wasn't flush enough to keep subsidizing Landrum Gallery, creatively named after yours truly.

The gallery was in a row of old—some have noted ancient—stucco and concrete buildings on Center Street. It was farther from the beach than my house, so I doubted Hurricane Frank had caused significant damage; but I wanted to check. I chose to drive the relatively short distance. Besides, I wanted to check on a couple of friends, and cell-phone coverage was as dead as the electricity.

The two-block drive to Center Street was like navigating a massive maze. I moved a half block before having to drag a branch out of the way. Bert's Market was in the same block as my house. Everyone who had ever been on the half-mile-wide, six-mile-long island for more than fifteen minutes had frequented Bert's, a local landmark.

Good to its slogan, "We may doze but we never close," the store was open. A rippling, windswept puddle covered the few parking spaces in front of the store, but the door was propped open with a concrete block. The interior was illuminated with lanterns, and the beams from flashlights were visible as they weaved through the narrow aisles. I love stability, so Bert's warmed my innards.

My innards continued to be warmed when I found my gallery nearly untouched by Frank. I swept the small amount of water that had burrowed under the front door to the sidewalk. Shops on either side of me had suffered significantly more water damage. I credited the new front door for sparing the gallery—the door I had to buy after the police splintered its predecessor last year. I couldn't blame them since they were nabbing a killer at the time and saved the building from exploding—with me inside. The door was an excellent investment.

Friday was traditionally a good sales day, but I suspected Frank would keep the vacationers out of a photo-buying mood. Instead of opening, I drove my newly remodeled car to Charles Fowler's apartment.

Charles was one of the first people I'd met when I arrived on Folly Beach. We're as opposite as two humans can be; he's as quirky as they come, and that's saying something on Folly Beach. I had met him just after I had found a body in a desolate area of the small, unique island. He started following me around, and for a couple of weeks, I had suspected that he was a killer and was out to erase me from the earth. He's now my best friend. He's also my unpaid sales manager, confidant, chronicler of everything important and irrelevant, and self-anointed partner in our unofficial, unregistered, and unapproved C&C Detective Agency that occasionally rears its naïve head.

"Hey, Mr. Photo Man," Charles yelled the familiar moniker he had used with me since the day we met. He was in front of his small apartment as I walked across the ground-up seashells and gravel covering his parking area. "Enjoy the shower?"

He was sweeping water out his front door, so I assumed the "shower" had visited his apartment. Charles lived on the marsh side of the island on Sandbar Lane and was as far from the coast as possible and still be on the island.

"Yeah," I said as I peeked around him to see how much damage there was in his apartment. "I have four showers in my house—three aren't over the tub. Everything here okay?"

"Just water," he replied and kept sweeping. "A few wet books; nothing bad."

Charles's entire wall space and most of his floors were covered with books. The interior of the tiny, first-floor apartment took on the appearance of a book-cave; books of every genre, shape, size, topic, and several languages, lined the walls from floor to ceiling. He claimed he had read all but the cookbooks. I doubted it, especially the books in other languages, but couldn't prove or disprove his proclamation. Besides, I didn't care.

"If you're here to move in, we've got a problem," he said.

"Why?" I replied. "If you moved those three hundred and fifty-seven books from the couch, I'd have plenty of room to sleep."

"Not going to happen," he said and continued to push the water from the living room. "Any damage other than extra showers?"

"The front porch has been rearranged a little, but I'm lucky." I pushed past him to see what I could do to help make his apartment less waterlogged. "It doesn't look bad in here," I continued. "You were lucky."

"I didn't expect things to turn out well—seldom disappointed that way. As your good buddy, George W. Bush, once said, 'I'm the master of low expectations.'"

Charles has the uncanny, sometimes irritating, and often entertaining habit of quoting U.S. presidents.

"Heard anything about other damage?" I asked.

"The power's out, the phone don't work, I'm standing in my living room, and not a single carrier pigeon has arrived. How would I know about damage?" He sighed and pointed his broom out the door and moved it around like he was blessing Folly Beach.

"Hmm," I said, "I figured you knew everything about *your* island."

"Good point." He leaned the broom against one of the cinder blocks and pine-board bookcases. He grabbed his ever-present, handmade cane, tapped it on the floor twice, and said, "What are we waiting for? Let's check it out."

Charles had lighted on Folly Beach twenty-four years ago after "retiring" from the world of work at the ripe old age of thirty-four. Before I had arrived, he worked off-the-books, odd jobs. There was always a construction company looking for day labor or a restaurant wanting him to help clean up after hours. He even made deliveries on

Folly Beach for the local surf shop and restaurants that catered to shut-ins. His main mode of transportation was an immaculately-maintained 1961 Schwinn bicycle. He had a twenty-year-old Saab convertible, but it spent most of its time sitting in front of his apartment while the tires dry-rotted.

What Charles lacked in an eight-to-five job, he made up for as the consummate collector of gossip and trivia.

He closed the door, said something about the mess would be there when he returned, and walked to the parking lot. Despite the rising temperature, he wore a long-sleeve University of Colorado T-shirt and cutoff shorts. A Tilley hat I'd given him after he had lusted after mine covered his thinning, gray hair.

To the left of his gravel parking lot, I noticed several moored small boats slowly bobbing on the Folly River. I grinned at the serene sight.

"So," he said, "want to hop on the bike or take your car?"

The first no-brainer of the morning. I grinned and headed to the car. Very little was beyond walking distance on Folly Beach, but given the choice of walking or riding, I'd be the first to the car. Experience had convinced me that exercise was two, four-letter words.

Lack of sleep and the constant drumming of the overnight rain on my roof were taking their toll. My head throbbed, and my muscles screamed for a rest. But I knew if I was with Charles, I would have to work through it.

"Where to?" I asked as I slowly slalomed around branches and puddles in his parking lot.

"Larry's. I'd say he's already at the store and left any damage at home for later."

Larry's house, more accurately, his rental house since his house was the victim of a crazed arsonist last year, backed up to the still, mysterious marsh and was three blocks from Charles's apartment. Charles kept the window down and yelled greetings to residents who were in their yards assessing the damage or just lounging against their paper boxes and sharing hurricane war stories with their neighbors. He wanted me to stop so he could talk to each one, but he knew Larry's house was our focus.

Larry's rental was average size by Folly Beach standards; that meant small. It was similar to mine—well-aged and had survived many storms, hurricanes, and eccentric renters. Other than a couple of cosmetic bumps and bruises, it looked intact. Charles, the ever-curious (nosy) friend, insisted we walk around it to make sure we hadn't missed anything. Fortunately, we hadn't.

Our next stop was Pewter Hardware, Larry's pride and joy. Larry had owned the store for several years and didn't know the origin of the name; even stranger, neither had the previous owner, who had called it his business for a couple of decades. Rather than investing in new signage and stationery, and confusing the residents, he stuck with the old name.

A small lot in front of the store was jammed with pickups, vans, and a beat-up, rusting Honda. We parked across from the store and stepped over a section of a privacy fence that had blown into the middle of the street. Of course, Charles wouldn't let it lie; we had to drag the fence back to the yard where it had recently stood vertical.

Pewter Hardware was huge compared to Charles's apartment, but for a retail business meeting the hardware needs of an island, it was miniscule. Its three aisles were wide enough for one medium-size person to maneuver; this morning the only space to turn around was in the lot. Brandon, Larry's only full-time employee, stood at the door and was losing the battle to direct customers to the appropriate section. We didn't need anything, so we told Brandon we were checking on Larry. He pointed toward the chest-high counter, with a cash register and two oil lanterns providing illumination. The top of Larry's head was barely visible. Larry was, as my friend Bob Howard was prone to say, a "shrimp-squirt, vertically challenged sad sack." To others, Larry was five feet one inch tall, weighed slightly over a hundred pounds in a winter coat, and was in his mid-fifties. Larry was also tough as the anvils he sold, extremely proud, and too stubborn to replace the high counter with one more proportioned to his low center of gravity.

A line of customers snaked around two aisles, their arms juggling blue tarps, lanterns, candles, buckets, and mops. Larry barely had time to wave, much less talk to us, so we waved back and left him to meet the clean-up needs of the islanders. We crossed the lot, and Charles helped two strangers lift five sheets of plywood over the tailgate of their truck.

"Nothing like buying closing-the-gate-after-the-horse-escaped plywood," he mumbled to no one in particular.

Along with uprooting trees, ripping out sections of fence, and mangling my screen windows, Frank had sucked the clouds and rain off the island as it moved inland. The sun brought much-needed illumination and hope.

Charles had volunteered to ride home with me and try to repair the screens. We'd borrow my neighbor's ladder—if it hadn't blown off-island—and Charles would venture to the roof to see what needed to be done.

We turned left off Center Street onto Ashley Avenue, the home of Bert's Market and the lesser-known location of my cottage. The street was blocked a couple of hundred yards past the house by two white Crown Victoria units from the Folly Beach Department of Public Safety—known as police cars to everyone else. I assumed the street was closed because of the downed power lines or debris.

My headache was about to reach earthquake proportions.

CHAPTER 3

"Whoa!" said Charles as I stopped in front of the house. "The black van behind the roadblock is from the coroner's office."

As luck—all bad—would have it, we were familiar with the vehicle you never wanted to see on your street. "We're going to see what's going on, right?"

"You bet," said Charles, who was already out of the car and using his cane as a walking stick. He rushed toward the action. I followed.

Officer Allen Spencer met us as we approached the first police car.

"Good morning Chris, Charles," said Spencer. "Your houses okay?"

"Yeah," I said. "A little water; nothing bad."

Spencer had been on the force for more than three years but still appeared about the age of box wine. Charles and I had way more encounters with him than anyone should. We had been in some tough situations over the years, but he had come to trust us; and, despite my concerns over changing his diapers, I respected his skills as a police officer.

Charles was right about the van, and now that we were closer, I saw three more police cars and two of the city's fire engines. Several public servants were gathered around something in a vacant lot on the far side of the street.

"What's going on?" asked Charles.

A good question, I thought. I had never heard of a coroner's visit to a dead power line.

"We've got a 187," Spencer replied.

"In English?" asked Charles.

"Murder," said Spencer.

Hadn't Frank imposed enough devastation on Folly Beach? "Who? What happened?" I asked.

"Don't know," he said as he shooed a couple of curious neighbors walking their dogs. "We just got here. Chief Newman and Officer Robins are by the body." He nodded in the direction of the gathering. "The coroner's office had a run just off-island and came right over. The Sheriff's Department has been called, but their detectives are busy with hurricane stuff. They won't be here for a while."

"Who?" I tried again.

"Robins said there wasn't any ID. He didn't recognize him."

"Chris, Charles, over here."

We turned from Spencer when Chief Brian Newman yelled for us. The chief was tall and trim, and stood with the confidence of a former military officer, which he was. He stood out among the group gathered around the body.

"Be my guest," said Officer Spencer. He lifted the yellow crime scene tape for us to walk under and waved his hand toward the activity in the field.

Chief Newman and I had become friends. I had stumbled onto a few murders and had become a thorn in his side as well as an extremely lucky citizen who helped him catch some killers.

"Morning, gentlemen," he said as we approached. "Any damage to your houses?"

There was something comforting about his concern in the midst of a horrific situation, reinforcing why I loved the fascinating island. We told him everything was okay and waited for his lead.

"You live close," he said as he looked at me, and then turned to a covered mass about twenty feet from the road. "Maybe you can identify him. He doesn't look familiar."

My head felt like it had a bowling ball rolling around in it.

The three of us stepped around puddles in the waterlogged field and approached the body. "You know the drill," said the chief. "Don't touch anything; don't get too close."

Charles and I were intimately familiar with "the drill."

Newman nodded to the middle-aged, bored-looking man from the coroner's office, and the two of them lifted the lightweight tarp from the body.

I fought my instincts and looked.

The victim was in his late thirties or early forties. His hair was long and pulled in a ponytail by a rubber band. He had a three-day beard and was dressed in a mud-stained, white T-shirt covered with drying blood. I thought he had on dark blue shorts but couldn't tell for sure; all my attention was focused on his upper torso. After all, how could I not focus on the colorfully striped, aluminum arrow protruding from his chest?

Charles gasped. "Holy Robin Hood," he mumbled.

The body looked familiar, but I couldn't remember from where. I shook my head no and swiped away a couple of flies from my face. Countless more swarmed closer to the body.

Charles had taken a couple of steps back and turned to the chief. "Les Patterson … that's Lester Patterson."

"Sure?" asked the chief.

"Yeah."

"Let's go to the car," said the chief. He nodded toward the unmarked, black Crown Vic. "It'll be cooler, and we can get away from the flies."

We didn't argue.

"Okay, Charles," said the chief as the air conditioner strained to blow as hard as it could. "What do you know about him?"

The chief and Charles were in the front seat, and I leaned forward from the back to hear over the air conditioner.

"I didn't know Patterson that well," started Charles. "I saw him in Bert's; we talked a few times."

"That's where I'd seen him," I said. "We never spoke."

Charles wasn't about to let me hog in on his story.

"He was a strange one," he continued. "The few times we talked, he rambled on about flying saucers, the Loch Ness Monster, and how his apartment was haunted."

"Know where he lived?" asked the chief. He was fiddling with the air conditioner knob to turn it down so we could hear better.

"The Edge," said Charles.

"Where?" I asked.

"The weird boardinghouse on Arctic, ocean-side," answered the chief before Charles could unload some trivia on me. "Old Mrs. Klein's place."

"Cindy Ash lives there," added Charles.

"Oh," I said, "that's only two blocks from here. I didn't know it had a name."

"Okay, Charles, what else?" The chief clearly didn't care what I knew about the boardinghouse.

"Like I said, Les was strange, but he wasn't a washout." Charles stared out the window toward the body and continued. "He worked for an air-conditioning and heating company on James Island—Coastal Heating and Air, I believe. I never saw him at Bert's—day or night— when he wasn't buying a twelve-pack of beer. HVAC must be seriously dehydrating work."

"I'll check with Officer Ash. She may know something," said the chief. "Anything else?"

Charles rubbed his chin. "Well, not to speak unkindly of the dead, but you wouldn't have a good chance of finding him sober on the weekends."

"No longer a problem," said the chief, showing a rare glimpse of gallows humor. "He must have handled it well. If he hadn't, I would have made his acquaintance."

The chief was distracted when a dark blue, unmarked Crown Vic pulled up next to his car. "It looks like the all-knowing killer-finders from Charleston have arrived."

Two detectives exited the vehicle like they owned the world. I didn't recognize them. The Folly Beach Department of Public Safety did what it could for law enforcement on the island, but murders were investigated by the Charleston County Sheriff's Department. They were on the same side as the local police, but in the eyes of most local law enforcement officials, the side was wide and each was on the far opposite end.

"Thanks, guys," said the chief, "I'll tell our new arrivals what you said." He opened the door and waved to the detectives. Charles and I slipped out the passenger side and headed to my house.

As we walked up the porch steps, Charles said, "You're amazing. You've been here, what, three years, and you've already found a murdered developer, proved a suicide wasn't, saved Larry's life, and in the last ten hours brought us a hurricane—and now we're involved in a Bambi non-look-alike up the street."

I stopped and stared at Charles. "Involved in!"

He nodded.

"No way," I said.

Charles grinned.

CHAPTER 4

I opened my eyes to the amber glow of the bedside clock flashing 12:00 and the sound of my stomach growling; power was restored sometime during the night. The short walk to Folly's supermarket was inevitable.

The demise of Les Patterson and Hurricane Frank was the buzz at Bert's Market. Customers ranged from neighbors I recognized to vacationers who would have stories to tell their grandchildren about how they lived through the "hurricane of the century." Time will increase the intensity of the storm; and, technically, Frank was the first hurricane to hit Folly Beach this century, so they would be accurate. I hoped that would still be true for the next thirty years or so.

The outsiders were oblivious to the killing that had taken place within sight of where they were shopping, but the natives—especially those who had survived other hurricanes—were more interested in the murder. Word had spread that Charles and I had been in the presence of the police, so two of my neighbors, people who normally ignored my existence, were quick to pelt me with questions.

"Yes, it was Les Patterson," I said.

"No, I don't have any idea who killed him," I said, with my patience still intact.

"Yes, he was killed by an arrow," I mumbled.

"No, Charles was not arrested," I said. My tone bordered on irritation.

Folks I had never seen before were gathering around. We were blocking others from doing their post-hurricane grocery shopping, and the milling crowd was loud enough to get the attention of Mari Jon, my favorite clerk. She had come from the storeroom in back. Mari Jon was five foot ten and could see over many of the customers. She was in her late twenties, beanpole-thin, and had such an endearing smile most people overlooked her beaked nose and acne-scarred face.

"Morning, Chris," she said. She kept the smile on her face and nudged the others out of the way. "Can I help you find something?"

I knew that wasn't her intent. I had been in Bert's hundreds of times and could find most everything with my eyes closed. Mari Jon was extracting me from the center of attention. She made a production of helping me find three items located exactly where I knew they'd be and then slowly walked with me to the checkout counter.

"I knew Les since he moved here four years ago," she said.

No surprise there. Mari Jon knew most of her customers, called them by name or nickname.

"He was a bit peculiar." She smiled. "Was always talking about UFOs. His latest kick was that he kept hearing someone, or something, as he put it, digging in the sand around the Edge."

"Did he see anyone ... or anything?"

"Said no," she whispered as she rang up my box of cereal, Milk Duds, and six-pack of Diet Pepsi. "He did say he could 'feel them' outside, whatever that meant."

There were already five people and two dogs in line behind me, so I didn't want to monopolize her. I thanked her and turned away from the counter.

"Chris," she said before I was out of earshot, "Les was a nice guy; he didn't deserve what happened."

Who did? I wondered on my short walk home.

The phone was ringing as I juggled my groceries and key to unlock the door.

"Crossbow! Shot with a damned crossbow," the voice of Bob Howard bellowed from the earpiece. "What the hell have you got yourself into now?"

"Hello" and "good morning" weren't in Bob's vocabulary. He's a Realtor with Island Realty, or as he describes it, "the second largest of the three small realty firms on Folly Beach." We became "odd couple" friends when he helped me find my house. He's a year shy of his seventieth birthday, blustery, with facial hair too short to be a beard, too long to be neat. He has a huge heart if you can work your way through the blubber, profanity, and attitude.

"Crossbow," I said. "Where'd you hear that?"

"None of your damned business," he said.

I didn't respond. My way of giving him a second chance to fess-up.

"Louise, if you must know." He couldn't stand silence.

Louise was Bob's eighty-something-year-old aunt, who worked at Island Realty and spent most of her leisure hours listening to the police scanner. She had missed her calling to be either a cop or island busybody.

"Figures," I said.

"I hear you were nosing around the crime scene—actually, meddling, according to my dear sweet aunt."

I enlightened Bob about why Charles and I were asked to be at the scene. He responded with a gruff "hmm," and then the phone went dead. "Good-bye" wasn't in his vocabulary either.

CHAPTER 5

I was to meet Charles for lunch at the Lost Dog Café. My kitchen is the most underused room in the house, so the Dog was my adopted dining room. Between Bert's Market and the Lost Dog Café, I don't know which was the most recognized—and admired—business on the island. The Dog got my vote. First, because it served the best breakfast and lunch on Folly Beach. It didn't serve the best supper because it closed after lunch. Second was because it employed Amber Lewis, the best waitress in South Carolina—and better yet, the lady I have dated for more than a year.

The Dog was in a one-story concrete block building six blocks from the house and catty-corner from Landrum Gallery. The building enjoyed an earlier life as a Laundromat and, according to rumors, a bingo parlor. The formerly bland structure sported a colorful front porch and a second outdoor seating area on the side that faced a small pocket-park and the town's community center and library. A life-size, concrete dog statue welcomed guests at the door, and the rails around the patio were carved in the shape of dog bones. If there was doubt about the owner's love of canines, they were dispelled when one stepped into the rustic, inviting restaurant. The cream-colored walls were covered with framed photos of dogs—big and small dogs of all races, colors, and moods; smiling, yawning, sleeping dogs … dogs, dogs, dogs. I'd often wondered why cat lovers didn't run screaming from the restaurant.

I heard Amber greet customers at a table near the door before I saw her. "Good morning, I'm Amber, and will be doing everything I can to make your breakfast experience as positive as possible."

She had welcomed me with that endearing, albeit lengthy, line the first time I'd stepped inside the Dog. I couldn't have received a more pleasant welcome to Folly Beach.

I caught her eye, and she winked and tilted her head toward my favorite table. Charles had already commandeered the spot and had his nose in a book—not that surprising a pose. The smell of frying bacon whiffed through the air.

His gaze drifted over the top of the book. "Did you know Scarlett O'Hara was originally named Pansy? A friend made Maggie change it."

If it weren't for trivia, Charles wouldn't have much to say. He was reading *Gone With the Wind*, so I assumed Maggie was Margaret Mitchell.

Charles often read from the same etiquette book as Bob. "Didn't know that, Charles; thanks for sharing."

"Then I guess you didn't know this tome has sold more books worldwide than most any other book except something called the Bible." He turned back to the book and didn't wait for my answer.

I ignored his priceless information, put my hat on the corner of the table, and took the seat opposite him. Amber delicately placed a mug of steaming coffee in front of me before I had time to pull the chair back to the table. Her unencumbered arm grazed my shoulder and hesitated.

"Yuck," said Charles, barely taking his eyes from the page, "can't you see this is a public restaurant? Kids are here; stop making out … yuck."

Even Atlanta burning couldn't keep the silliness out of Charles. I tried another tack. "Les was killed with an arrow from a crossbow."

That worked. Amber had already giggled at the "making out" comment and left to fulfill her duties to the rapidly filling restaurant. Charles put a wrinkled, catsup-stained seven of spades in Maggie's book and set it in the chair next to him. His attention was no longer on the Yankees and Rebels.

"Crossbow like the Chinese invented in the fourth century BC?" he asked.

I quickly responded, hoping to avoid a history lesson. "I suspect it was a newer one; but, yeah, a real crossbow."

"I knew the arrow was too short for a regular bow, but thought it had broken off when poor Les bit the mud," said Charles. "You know, a crossbow arrow's called a bolt. It's usually around twenty inches long, where a regular arrow is longer, twenty-nine inches, give or take."

I didn't know that; didn't care. I wanted to know how he knew, but common sense stopped me from asking.

"Bob told me," I said.

"Let me guess; Louise heard it on the scanner and called Bob?"

Charles knew the answer, so I didn't respond. I make up for my lack of exercise by eating unhealthy foods. Amber's on a one-person crusade to break that habit. She brought Charles a breakfast burrito he ordered before I'd arrived and a bowl of oatmeal with bananas for me. I scraped the bananas off and covered the oatmeal with a layer of sugar. You can lead a hundred-eighty-pound, five-foot-ten, exercise-avoider to healthy food, but you can't make me eat it.

Being in a room full of people with Charles is like hanging out with an extrovert running for office. Breakfast was interrupted by Marc and Houston, two city council members who held court most every day in the Dog. They stopped to ask what he was reading. Then, a real estate agent whose office was across the street wanted to know if he would be interested in cleaning a condo she had for sale. The president of Preserve the Past, a group dedicated to saving the historic Morris Island Lighthouse from erosion and neglect, interrupted next. And finally, Wynn Stamper, one of Folly's most vocal antigrowth advocates, couldn't restrain his curiosity. His favorite saying was, "Folly must stay the same to grow." One day someone will tell me what that meant.

With the exception of Stamper, each had managed to bring the conversation around to what Charles had learned during his "investigation" at the scene of the murder. Stamper had begun to head down that trail when Charles told him that the Chinese army had more than fifty thousand crossbowmen in 209 BC.

Stamper scampered!

CHAPTER 6

Charles and I left the Dog after he shared his version of what happened with most of the regulars and a couple of vacationers who found the nerve to wander over.

"Time to check damage on the beach," said Charles as he got in the car.

That was Charles's excuse; my suspicion was that he wanted to case the Edge, the boardinghouse where Les Patterson had last hung his hat.

Folly Road became Center Street once it crossed the bridge to the island. Center Street dead-ended at the parking lot of Folly Beach's tallest—and most out-of-place—structure, the Holiday Inn. The nine-story hotel was not only the most conspicuous structure on the island, but for years its color—charitably called pink—had been proclaimed by no less than Mayor Amato as the "ugliest building on Folly Beach." And that was among mighty stiff competition. But pink was in the past. The Holiday Inn had closed during the winter for a complete renovation and exterior painting. It had reopened to rave reviews.

While I didn't quite rave about the remodel, I found comfort in knowing the local ownership was committed to improving the hotel. Besides, my main interest in the hotel was its coffee bar, intended for use by those who rented rooms. Fortunately, its local owners had a more liberal view of the service, and I had taken advantage of its "complimentary" coffee for the last three years. Charles and I filled our cups and then asked the clerk how the hotel had fared in the storm. Between yawns, she said only a handful of the sliding glass doors on the upper floors had failed to hold back the windswept rains and the pool area suffered only minor damage.

The thousand-foot-long, majestic Folly Pier jutted over the Atlantic to the left of the Holiday Inn. The pier was relatively new and constructed to withstand hurricane-strength winds and surfs that far exceeded Frank's best efforts. We walked halfway to the end of the pier, leaned against the wooden rail, and looked up and down the beach for damage. From our vantage, there was a large, modern, four-story condo complex to the left of the hotel. Several units had sliding glass doors covered with plywood, and patio furniture was strewn haphazardly in the neatly manicured grassy area between the building and the beach. The condo owners would be thrilled if that was the worst Frank had wrought. Looking to the right of the pier, the buildings were not as new, and a few of them were visibly damaged. Plywood shields had blown off some windows, small palmettos were uprooted in two yards, and dune fences were carried onto three patios that overlooked the beach. Still, the aftereffects were minor. The quirky island I had fallen in love with had survived with only a few bruises.

"Ready to check the Edge?" asked Charles. He was getting antsy; he tapped his cane on the pier and used his canvas Tilley to fan his face.

"Sure," I said, clearly the answer he wanted. Besides, I was hot and still had remnants of yesterday's supersized headache.

The boardinghouse was a block east of the pier and ranked as probably the strangest house among many strange residences on Folly Beach. I hadn't known anything about it but had captured it in my viewfinder from every legal perch I could find. It was large, long, and narrow and constructed from concrete block, stone, brick, and massive wooden beams. On two corners, the concrete blocks were neatly coated with cement and resembled stucco; an industrial-looking, concrete block wall faced the ocean. The superstructure was wood covered with a thin layer of cement. Bricks were haphazardly located in the front yard, and a stone wall protected the property from moody ocean tides.

"Margaret Klein's the owner," said Charles, sharing a fact I'd learned from Chief Newman a day earlier. We approached the house from the beach. "She converted the house into eight apartments years ago."

"Where'd it get its name?" I asked. We were walking about three feet from the water, and I sidestepped the methodical waves to keep my shoes dry.

"Don't know for certain." Mr. Trivia surprised and disappointed me. "Folly Beach is called 'The Edge of America,' so I figure she got it there. After all, it's on the edge of the edge."

"Designed by a drunken architect?" I asked, more serious than not.

"It's got character, Chris. Don't forget where you are—Character World."

Ms. Klein was in front of the house fussing with one of the potted cactuses that were randomly placed in large pots on the fence and in the yard. She had been about five feet two in her prime, but now was growing closer to the ground and dipped below five feet. She was oblivious to a single pontoon from a boat, pieces of erosion fencing, and a man's bathing suit, all of which had been deposited in her yard by Hurricane Frank.

"Permission to board?" asked Charles. We stood at the bottom of a steel ladder leaning against the stone wall in the front yard. The distinct smell of rotting fish was strong along the dune line.

Ms. Klein looked up from the cactus, took a swig from a large tumbler filled with a caramel-colored liquid, and smiled. "Sure, boys, come on up—unless you're pirates."

Charles returned her smile, allaying her fear that we were pirates, and we climbed the seven steps to yard-level. I looked around to make sure there weren't any planks she might have us walk.

"Ms. Klein," said Charles. "Know my friend, Chris Landrum?" He took a step back, and I offered my hand.

"No, Charles, we've never had the privilege of meeting," she said. She took the gardening glove off her right hand and shook mine. "But I know who he is."

She was either near deaf or thought we were. A couple of sunbathers a hundred feet away turned to see who was yelling.

She caught my puzzled look. "Louise from over at Island Realty is a good friend. We go back ... well, we go back. She's told me how you keep getting into trouble and how her favorite nephew, Bob, has to save you time after time." She took another drink. "She also said you're mighty sweet, except everywhere you go, someone ends up croaked."

Charles took off his hat and wiped his brow with the sleeve of his T-shirt. "Ms. Klein," he said, "think we could get in the shade?"

"I guess. You youngsters sure are getting wimpy. A little heat ain't going to kill you."

We followed as she unhurriedly walked around the house to the patch of yard shaded by the house and to a battered, vinyl-covered, decrepit card table. The hem on her faded, print dress touched the ground as she walked. Four folding chairs were leaning against the house.

"Just rustled these up from all over carnation," she said as she grabbed the chair closest to the table. Charles and I selected two of the three that had the best chance of holding us.

"So my friend Louise is right," she said and sighed heavily. She took a cigarette from the pocket in her billowy dress, took her time lighting it, and enjoyed another sip from the tumbler. "Poor Les gets himself skewered, and you appear. You ought to be wearing a long black robe and carrying a big-ass scythe."

I was ready to agree when Charles came to my defense. "Now, Ms. Klein, Chris and I just stopped by to see if you and your house were okay and to check on our friend, Cindy Ash. She's one of your tenants, isn't she?"

"Charles," she said, "you must be taking advanced lessons in bull poop." She laughed at her comment and held the tumbler up so the last drop could land on her tongue. "You know good and well that that cute police officer lives here. As nosy as you are, you know she's just fine—she's out helping our citizens recover from Frankie."

"Any damage to your house?" I asked.

"Nothing bad," she said. "Couple more cracks in the walls than I had before. The old buzzard's strong like that." She pointed to the second floor, where I could see fresh breaks in the stucco covering the wood-studded walls. The first floor was solid concrete, and I doubted anything could hurt it.

She looked into the empty tumbler; her shoulders sagged toward the table.

"My glass says it's time to take a nap," she hollered and then giggled.

I didn't think Charles and I were that funny, so I guessed that something else accounted for her mood—the former contents of her glass.

We told her we were glad everything was okay, and she told us to come back anytime. Before we were out of hearing range—which could have been almost a half mile—she said, "Boys, y'all find Lester's killer, would you?"

I responded with a benign, "We'll see."

Charles yelled, "You bet."

CHAPTER 7

The surf shop is another institution on Folly Beach. I never got a straight answer out of its owner, Jim "Dude" Sloan, but legend is that he has owned the shop since the late eighties. Dude and I had become friends once I learned to appreciate his off-center outlook and his stilted communication style. I giggled every time I remembered his response when I had asked him why he bought the shop. "Needed job; liked area; couldn't cook. No skills; saw ad in paper; went to bank. Idiot bank lent me money. Rest be history."

After he told me that, I decided not to ask why he didn't capitalize the first letters of the shop's name.

Dude's shop was the next stop on our "any damage?" tour. The aging, wooden structure was only a block from the pier but was elevated and had withstood several hurricanes over the years. Its exterior walls were protected by countless layers of paint plastered with surfboard-sized decals promoting surf products. I doubted it had suffered much.

Dude met us at the front door. He was a near exact replica of Arlo Guthrie, the folksinger. His flowing gray/white hair was pulled into a ponytail by a bright red, children's hair band; he wore a psychedelic, tie-dyed T-shirt with a huge yellow peace symbol on the front.

"Boss waves yesterday—catch any?" he said.

I assumed he meant the hurricane, but with Dude I was on shaky ground assuming anything.

"Nope," said Charles. "You?"

The two clerks had the handful of customers taken care of, so we followed Dude to the rear of the shop. There was one wide aisle, but most of its floor space was covered with surf gear—boards, wet suits, clothing, and stuff I had no idea of its function. In one of my weaker moments, Dude had introduced me to surfing. My main recollection was that I thanked God that I'd survived. My surfing career had begun and ended that day. To put it mildly, I was not a regular customer at the surf shop. Dude was a regular at the Dog, so we had our regular, irregular conversations there.

He ignored Charles's question, so I gathered that he wasn't surfing in Hurricane Frank.

"Hear my bud Les used for target practice?" asked Dude. He had grabbed a root beer from a mini-frig and nodded to the open door. Charles bypassed the bottle of peach schnapps and pulled out two Diet Pepsis and handed me one.

"Yeah," said Charles. "How well did you know him?"

"Few years," responded Dude. "He be fox surfer."

"Huh?" said Charles.

"Fox surfer," said Dude, "like fake—thought you knew it all."

"You mean faux?" asked Charles.

"Duh, yeah, fox. He bought surfer stuff two plus one years back. Only bought when under influence of moons aligning, or beer, not sure which—fox surfer."

Dude took two quick sips of root beer. He had spoken too many words and needed a break.

"Idea who shot him?" asked Charles.

"Nope. He be into flying saucers, ghosts, who killed JFK, weird crap. But who isn't?" he shrugged. "No reason to arrow him."

"He have any friends?" I asked.

"Likable guy—slacker on the surf—but likable. No friends I know of."

"Who killed JFK?" asked Charles.

I knew he couldn't let that one slip by.

"Les said it was someone not from South Carolina; some other planet, he shared. Les was a bit strange, truth be known."

Dude calling someone strange was scary. But his knowledge of other planets was not unusual. He was a voracious reader of *Astronomy* magazine, and Amber had often claimed he wasn't from earth and maybe not from our solar system.

Dude had shared all he knew about Les and assured us his shop hadn't suffered significant storm damage. Our task was completed.

Before we weaved through the surf shop crowd, Dude whispered to us, "You be finding out who offed Les, right?"

I told him it was a matter for the police and none of our business. Charles interrupted, "Yeah, Chris, it's your duty; he was wiped out on your street. You be dissed!"

Clearly, "to be or not to be" was not the question. "Dude," I asked, "have you been talking to Ms. Klein?"

"Who be she?" he asked.

CHAPTER 8

An unseasonable hot weather pattern had covered the area. I was on the porch trying to force the twisted screen frames back into their pre-Frank positions before it got too hot. No rain was forecast for the next few days, so I didn't have to borrow a ladder and tackle the bent roofing. It was Sunday morning, and the rush of shoppers at Bert's clogged the street. I caught the flashing blue lights of a Folly Beach police cruiser out of the corner of my eye and figured it was there to "politely" ask someone to move a vehicle blocking a drive—a fairly common occurrence during the summer.

Instead of heading toward Bert's, Officer Cindy Ash was walking toward me. She had her head down and seemed more intent on staring at the ground than at her destination. Cindy had joined the police force a year ago after moving from east Tennessee. She was in her mid-forties, short, full-figured, with curly dark hair. Not only was she the most attractive member of the force (from a male's perspective), she dated Larry. That was welcome news to all who knew him, and certainly brightened his outlook. She didn't seem any the worse for their budding relationship.

I leaned the screen against the house and walked out to meet her. She usually had a quick, wide smile; today her eyes were red, and tears streaked her minimal makeup.

"What's wrong?" I put my arm around her shoulder and herded her into the house. "Something wrong with Larry?"

She shook her head and didn't respond. I offered her coffee. She declined and flopped into an overstuffed chair in the living room. "Sorry for the tears. It's so … so unprofessional."

I sat opposite her in a smaller chair and waited.

"The chief's in the hospital," she said. Her tears began flowing freely. Her foot tapped the floor.

"What happened?" I asked and walked to the kitchen to get her coffee. She needed it.

"Heart, they think." She continued to stare at the floor. "He wasn't … wasn't breathing when our guys got to him. Spencer escorted the ambulance to Charleston … he'll call when he knows something."

I was stunned. Chief Brian Newman was in his mid-sixties and trim, exercised religiously, and had the physique of a fifty-year-old. Of everyone I knew, he would have been the last I'd guess with a heart problem. "Where?" I asked.

"He was helping a guy push his car out of some muck on the side of Tabby Drive—the hurricane had washed debris against the curb and trapped water behind it. Somehow the guy got stuck." Cindy finally looked up from the floor. "Thanks for the coffee. He's such a great boss, and person. I don't know what I'd do if … if he wasn't here."

"Don't get ahead of yourself; the EMTs know what they're doing." I didn't have a clue how the chief was, and the words caught in my throat.

"Fortunately, the man had a phone, and our guys were there in minutes." Her voice cracked. "But Chris, they said he was already turning blue. Spencer said it looked bad."

"What hospital?" I asked.

"Charleston Memorial, I guess."

"I'll go over and see if I can find out anything. Want to go?"

That was the first glimmer of hope in her since she had arrived. It didn't last long. "No, better not," she said. "I got off before I came here, but Spencer asked if I could hang around in case I was needed."

"Call if you hear from him," I said. "I promise I'll let you know as soon as I know anything."

"I'd better get back on the streets," she said and hurried to stand. She was nervous and trembling. She stumbled on the ottoman but caught her balance and slowly walked to the door.

The hospital was on the edge of Charleston and only about a dozen miles from the house. I called Larry before I was out of the Folly Beach city limits and told him what had happened and, butting in where no one asked, suggested he call Officer Ash to offer his sturdy, yet vertically challenged, shoulder. I also called Charles. He had known Chief Newman for many years and had great respect for him both as a person and as Folly Beach's chief law enforcement official. He agreed to look in on Larry and make sure he checked on Officer Ash.

I made good time to the hospital; being the Sabbath, traffic was light. Most days, I would have spent the leisurely drive admiring the marsh, with its chameleon-like grasses changing colors to match the season. Not today; my mind wandered to how unfair, and unpredictable, it was that heart problems had struck Brian Newman. It also made me worry about my health. Here I was, just turned sixty, slightly overweight, with high blood pressure—what was in store for me? If this could happen to someone in Brian's condition, were my days numbered?

I almost rear-ended a blue Chevrolet Malibu that was turning left in front of me. My concentration was shot. Instead of watching the road, I wondered who had said something about bad things coming in threes. I knew it wasn't one of Charles's presidents, but that's where my knowledge ended. Whoever said it was right. In three days, I had experienced a hurricane, stared at a body sporting a crossbow arrow, and now, a friend was near death, or worse.

At least, the three bad things were over.

Weren't they?

CHAPTER 9

A Folly-Beach-marked Crown Vic was parked at the emergency canopy, and an unmarked dark blue Crown Vic from the Charleston County Sheriff's department angled, nose-first, close behind. My dented, aging Lexus didn't have official status, so I parked in the visitor's lot.

Officer Spencer was standing in the emergency room lobby just inside the automatic sliding-glass door. He rushed to my side as soon as he saw me. Strangely, I thought it was a good sign that Newman was still in the emergency room.

I shook his hand and was surprised how clammy it was. "How is he?"

"No clue, Mr. Landrum." He stuttered through my last name. "They haven't told us anything. He didn't look good. They got him here quick. That's a good thing, isn't it?"

The two EMTs who transported the chief were seated across the room on institutional gray, waiting-room chairs. A young couple walked out of a treatment room carrying a screaming baby. A middle-aged man in bib-overalls sat by himself in another part of the room, his hand wrapped in a shirt. Blood seeped through the cloth. In the far corner of the room, I saw the unmarked car's driver. I barely recognized her; her head was bowed, and she wore tennis shoes, light green shorts, and a tan, short-sleeve Nike polo shirt.

I had several opportunities to talk with Detective Karen Lawson over the last three years—most in her official role and related to unfortunate circumstances. She was always polite, efficient, and dressed in a pantsuit, her chestnut brown hair pulled back out of her face. She had oozed professionalism.

She looked up from her stupor, saw me talking to Officer Spencer, did a double take, stood, and walked toward us. Her normal greeting was a handshake, a firm grip, and a professional smile. I was surprised when she gave me a tentative hug. She was only a couple of inches shorter than me and trim, and her normally beautiful smile gave way to a tearstained face. She was Chief Newman's daughter.

"Chris … oh, Chris," she mumbled, "thanks for coming." She paused. "I can't believe this. How … how?" She continued to cling.

"Detective," I said awkwardly. I had never used her first name. "I'm so sorry. Do you know anything?"

She sniffled, took a deep breath, and took a step back. "Call me Karen. No, they won't tell me … anything. All I know is what I guess Spencer told you. My phone number was in dad's wallet, so the hospital called me. I was off and don't live far from here. I got here a half hour ago."

A grossly overweight man in scrubs came out of a double door marked *No Admittance*. He looked like he should be the one with a heart attack, not the healthy, trim Brian Newman. He looked around the room, saw the three of us huddled together, and approached.

"You family of Mr. Newman?" he asked. His face gave nothing away.

Karen took a step toward him and introduced herself; Officer Spencer and I stayed close to hear.

"Ms. Lawson," he started, his voice low, but audible, "I'm Doctor Melkin. Your father's holding on."

"Thank God," she murmured.

"It's touch-and-go, though," Melkin continued. "To put it bluntly, he's suffered a major heart attack. If he didn't get here when he did, we wouldn't be having this conversation. He's out of surgery but will be in critical care for hours—no visitors." His chubby finger pointed to a door leading to another corridor. "You can go to the CCU waiting room if you want. Down that corridor, second door on the left." He looked at the large digital clock on the wall behind us and then toward the double doors he had come from. "Someone will keep you updated. I'm sorry." He turned and left. No time for questions; no further explanation. On the other hand, if he saved Brian Newman's life, all was forgiven.

"Officer Spencer," said Karen, "why don't you call the station and let them know." She turned to me, "Would you go with me to the waiting room?" I nodded. "I'm going to thank the EMTs. I'll be right there."

The two EMTs were paying attention but were keeping a respectful distance. I followed the doctor's directions and found the CCU waiting room. It was empty.

I knew word would get to her quickly, but I still called Cindy and gave her an update. I was upbeat, but the doctor's caution that it was "touch-and-go" kept me in check. She thanked me and said she would tell Larry and Charles.

The CCU waiting room was small, but the furniture was more comfortable and attractive than what was in the emergency room waiting area. A flat-screen television was on the wall opposite two comfortable couches. It was tuned to CNN, with the sound muted. Nicely framed poster art adorned two of the other walls, and the hospital's overly wordy Mission Statement was conspicuously displayed on the remaining wall. Several magazines were neatly stacked on an end table by one of the couches. The magazines were less than a year old—new by waiting room standards.

I was mindlessly watching a story about a mudslide in Mexico when Karen came in.

"Thanks for staying," she said. She forced a smile. "I couldn't stand to be alone now. I know how much dad admires you. It was ... was sweet of you to come."

I knew very little about Karen Lawson. I assumed she was married since she had a different last name than her dad, and was confused about her comment about being alone.

"Do you have any family here?" I asked.

She managed a slightly more sincere smile, "Just Joe Friday—he's a seven-year-old, ornery black cat. Didn't think a hospital would be a good place for him."

"*Just the facts, ma'am,*" I replied.

She giggled. "That's the one. Most people I tell the name to look at me and say it's a stupid name. They've never heard of *Dragnet!*"

"That doesn't surprise me," I said. "That show went off television about the time you were born, I suspect."

"In fact, yes. Same year, 1970. Dad loved that show. I think that's how he learned to talk like a cop—just the facts, flat voice, heaven help him if a smile left his lips."

"He was in the military then?"

"Actually, when I was born, he was in Special Operations Forces. We lived in California, but I didn't see him much. He was deployed all over the world—secret missions he never talked about. Late in his military career, he transferred into the military police. He loved being an MP."

"He loves police work?" I asked. Karen was more relaxed and stopped staring at the door. I wanted to avoid the reason we were there.

"He relishes his job," she said.

"How long's he been there?" I knew the answer but thought it would be good to keep her talking.

"Fourteen years," she said. "Took the job as chief as soon as he retired after putting in his thirty in the army. He was only fifty." She hesitated. "He loves it—especially the people. He won't tell you, but that's the best part for him. He prized his jobs more than mom thought he loved her—may have been true."

Treading on thin ice, I asked, "What happened?"

"Old story. Mom couldn't stand it when he was away; couldn't stand it when he was home talking about being away. I was too young to understand, but learned later that she had some problems … chemical imbalance. It clouded her views, to put it kindly. She left him when I was ten, took her maiden name, Lawson. She resented him so much she legally had my name changed, too."

Way to go, Chris, I thought. Dredge up terrible memories to keep her mind off her dad.

She helped me out of that one. "I hear you had some excitement on your street," she said.

I took a deep sigh. "Yeah. I thought the hurricane was bad enough. Are you working the case?" I wasn't ready to call it murder, especially a murder by crossbow.

"No, when the storm hit, some of us were detailed to the low-lying areas to help with the rescue efforts. We have a couple of senior citizen centers that shouldn't have been built where they were; water floods them during bad storms. We didn't lose anyone, but it got tense."

A nurse in surgical scrubs stuck her head in the door. Karen jumped to her feet and dropped the *People* magazine she had been flipping through. The nurse was looking for someone else. I saw relief in Karen's eyes. She sat back and continued, "Where was I … oh, yeah, Detective Burton and one of the new guys caught that one … now, with this, I'm glad."

"Burton wasn't one of the first detectives on the scene," I said.

"No, the younger guy's wife had a baby that night, and Burton replaced him."

"I don't think Burton likes me," I said. I had met Detective Brad Burton the first week I was on Folly Beach. He and Karen were investigating a murder I had stumbled across. Burton had looked at me like he knew I killed the man but he couldn't prove it. I ran across him again when someone was threatening Larry for reasons no one could figure out. I got stuck in the middle of that case as well.

Karen smiled. "Don't worry about it. Detective Burton doesn't like anyone—he doesn't discriminate. Everyone's guilty of everything. I think he's been around the block too many times."

"Whoever has the case, I wish them well," I said. "It's a little unsettling to have someone killed with a crossbow within sight of my house. I assume that's not an everyday occurrence."

"Not even on Folly," she said. Her smile continued. "Not even on Folly."

CHAPTER 10

The next three hours lasted just shy of a month. Karen paced and then sat with her head pitched forward; hands covered her face. We made small talk about the hospital furniture, the surprising lack of others in the room, and how lucky we were to escape more damage from Frank. I paced and offered to find something to eat or drink; she declined. I sat and watched the soundless, mind-numbing pictures on CNN; something about soldiers finding a mass grave in a country I'd never heard of.

Finally, the nurse who had peeked in hours earlier, found the right person this time. She told Karen that her dad's condition had not changed. He was being closely monitored, and she didn't expect any change for several hours. It wouldn't do anyone any good to wait, she said. Karen argued but eventually agreed. The nurse assured her she would call Karen's cell phone if there was any change.

I walked Karen to her car, and we exchanged phone numbers along the way.

"It meant a lot you being here," she said.

"Thanks," I said, "but you don't need to say anything. I really like your dad. I wanted to be here."

She looked me in the eye; her tears were dry. "I'll call when I hear something." She gave me another hug and held it for a minute. She pushed away and wiped new tears away before opening her car door.

"Say hi to Joe for me," I said before she closed the door.

She smiled.

Mission accomplished.

I was hungry, and hospital food—while nourishing, I'm sure—took bland to a new low. The temperature hadn't reached the sweltering September heat that had recently enveloped the Lowcountry. I overcame my aversion to exercise and decided to walk to Al's Bar and Gourmet Grill. A walk would feel good after being cooped-up in the small waiting room for hours, and it wasn't like I was walking to Topeka, Kansas. Al's was three blocks away.

The bar and grill shared a one-story building with a 1950s Laundromat. Charleston was chock-full of historic structures. Al's had aged enough for a historic designation—some might say prehistoric—but it was simply old. The equipment in the Laundromat was one step above beating clothes on rocks in a creek, and by bar standards, Al's had everything in Dodge City beat by a few years. The once-white paint on the concrete block building was peeling in dollar-bill-size fragments, exposing a cheap-mustard colored earlier life. Two overweight women were stuffing the ancient washers with sheets and blankets, while five kids, all under age three, scampered around chasing a red and white beach ball.

I couldn't see in Al's because the lower half of the large plate glass window was painted black. The flickering neon sign over the door let me know the bar was "OP N." The only noticeable illumination that greeted me as I pulled open the heavy steel front door was from a large Budweiser and two smaller Bud Light neon signs backlighting the bar. I hesitated enough for my eyes to partially adjust to the dim lighting. The aroma of frying French Fries, stale beer, and the bitter smell of cleaning liquids added to the ambiance. James Brown was wailing that he felt good from the jukebox in the back corner near the tiny restrooms and the restaurant's only booth. Six mismatched tables and a conglomeration of well-worn, equally mismatched chairs filled the center of the dark space. Six men occupied three tables.

"Well, if it isn't Chris," said a frail-looking man behind the bar. He appeared as worn as his chairs; his gray hair contrasted with his mocha colored skin and coffee-stained teeth. He was in his early seventies, but Al could easily be mistaken for ninety. "Where's Bubba Bob?"

The few times I had been in Al's, it was to meet my friend, Bob Howard, who swore Al made the best cheeseburgers in the contiguous forty-eight states, and, most likely, Alaska, Hawaii, and, for some reason, Bob always included Scotland.

"Don't know," I said. I walked over to the bar. "I was at the hospital, got hungry, and couldn't think of a better place to eat."

"Golly," said Al as he slowly wiped the already spotless bar with a striped bar towel. "Considering the cafeteria there, you made a wise decision. Who's at the hospital?"

I told him who, and then he interrupted, "Your booth awaitin'. I'll start a cheeseburger, pour a glass of Chardonnay, and bring it back to you. I want to hear all about the chief."

I felt honored that Bob's seat-of-choice was now my booth. The other six patrons stared as I confidently strolled to the back of the room. Other than the beer delivery man, Bob and I were the only Caucasians I had seen in Al's. Either Al considered Bob and me VIPs or he wanted to hide us in the back and the booth was as far as he could send us without taking up valuable restroom seating. I favored the VIP explanation.

Two tables of diners were leaving—unrelated to my arrival, I hoped—when Al slowly made his way to the booth. The other two customers were in deep conversation and looked like they were there to stay. Al set my food and wine on the table and sat himself on the cushioned bench seat opposite me.

"The music sounds different than when Bob's here," I said. The Supremes were sharing one of their Motown favorites from the jukebox.

Al laughed, his eyes shared in the twinkle of humor. "For some reason," he said, "George Jones and Clint Black don't get as much money on them when Bob's not around. My regulars ain't as tone-deaf as Bubba Bob."

Bob and Al had been friends for years and regularly traded barbs, but I knew Bob had tremendous admiration for the bar owner. Bob had told me with great admiration that Al was an American hero. He'd single-handedly saved a dozen fellow soldiers and civilians during the Korean War; and then after the war, he and his late wife adopted nine children after social services had all but given up on finding families for them. For some mysterious reason, Al liked Bob and had salted his jukebox with some of Bob's favorite country songs.

Al's breath was back to normal after his walk to the table, and he massaged his arthritic left knee. "So, what happened to your police chief?" Al had never been on Folly Beach but knew some of the happenings from Bob and me. He had even provided a decisive clue to solving a series of murders on Folly last year.

I shared what I knew and bemoaned not knowing more.

"Let me call Tanesa and see if she can find out anything," he offered.

Tanesa was one of Al's adopted kids and an emergency room doctor. I hadn't met her and didn't see any female doctors on duty earlier. I handed him my phone to save him the laborious walk to the bar. He said she wouldn't answer if she didn't recognize the number. "Don't worry," he said, his chin held high, "she'll answer her daddy's call—even if her hands are in the middle of somebody's gut."

Not quite the image I needed, but I appreciated Al's efforts. He slowly—very slowly—headed to the bar and braced himself on two chairs along the way. I ate some of the cooling, juicy, and extremely tasty cheeseburger and fries, sipped the cheap white wine, and then looked around the room. Garage-sale nature prints adorned two walls. The furniture was old but clean and sturdy. I was daydreaming about what it would be like to have nine kids when Al returned with another glass of wine and a beer for himself.

"Want the truth or sugarcoated?" he asked.

Sugarcoat, sugarcoat, please. "Truth."

"Your chief's barely hanging on," he said. "Tanesa wasn't in the OR with him, but the other doc told her they lost him a couple of times and was surprised he kept coming back. It sounds strange, but she said if he wasn't in such good health, he'd be dead."

"Prognosis?"

"Less than fifty-fifty. Sorry." Al took a sip of beer, "Sorry."

"I appreciate you checking," I said.

"That's what friends do," he said. I think he truly meant it.

One of the men from the other table stood and looked our way.

"Cash or charge?" asked Al over Fats Domino on the jukebox.

"Greenbacks," said the customer.

Al shut his eyes for a second and then said, "Eleven fifty. Leave it on the bar."

"Lazy old coot," said the elderly customer, who then laughed.

"Stiff me, and I'll poison your next meal," said Al.

During Al's threats, I debated if I should call Karen and tell about her dad. Would it help anything? Did she need to know? I was leaning toward not telling her when Al said, "Chris, Chris."

"Sorry," I said.

"I was asking," continued Al, "what's the deal on the body with the arrow in it?"

I was surprised, "How'd you hear about it?"

"Bubba B. called last night. He was cackling and said something like, 'Guess what my Folly friend's got himself into now?'"

"Why something I've got myself into?" I asked. Al and I were alone in the restaurant. Before he answered, Al hobbled to the jukebox, fiddled with something on the side of the machine, pushed some of the numbers, and returned to the table.

"Funny," said Al, "I asked Bob the same thing." Al hesitated and listened to the opening notes of "Wabash Cannonball" from the jukebox. "Bob said cause you always do."

Please be wrong, Bob.

"What's with the crossbow?" Al stared at me like I was an expert.

"No idea." The cheeseburger and fries were gone, and I started on the second glass of wine. "You have a guess?"

"When I was in basic, getting ready to head to Korea, I heard about soldiers training with crossbows. They were somewhere in Texas and not even Indians."

He had my attention. "Why?"

"Stealth combat, they said. They could sneak up on enemy camps and take out the sentries; in and out, no sounds. The enemy couldn't tell where the shots came from. They could be accurate from fifty yards or more, or so they said." He paused. "Never heard more about it."

"Makes sense, I guess."

"Yeah, Bob said it could be a hunter or someone who wanted to symbolically show that people were animals and could be hunted like animals." Al giggled, "Bob's too deep for me sometimes, so I just says 'could be.'"

"Deep and shallow are close kin when it comes to Bob," I said.

We both laughed. Even if Al's cheeseburgers weren't the best in the United States and Scotland, the way he served them garnished with wisdom and conversation made them great.

"Chris," the smile was gone from his face, "can I trust you with a secret?"

"Sure." I didn't know what to expect.

"Tell Bob, and your cheeseburgers will never taste the same again. Agree?"

"Okay, okay," I said.

"When I joined the army at the start of the Korean conflict, I'd never been around any country music, especially not at home." Al stared into his glass. Beer must be fascinating. "Then," he continued, "I was thrown in with a bunch of crackers—no offense, but that's what we called you white boys …."

"That was kind compared to what you were called, I suspect," I interjected. "No offense taken."

"Anyway, I started listening to Kitty Wells sing 'It Wasn't God Who Made Honky Tonk Angels,' Hank Snow, Lefty Frizzell, and other country singers. It wasn't bad—pretty good, truth be told. My favorite's Johnny Cash. If that white boy wasn't a Negro, he missed his calling."

"That's why you have so much country music on your jukebox?"

"Sort of. I had a couple of country songs on it, white man's blues, I call it." Al giggled. "Then Bob starts coming in and decided I needed more. He gave me fifty dollars and said to get some good music on the machine. That's why it's about half and half—white man blues, black man blues."

"Your secret's good with me," I said. "Besides, Bob wouldn't listen if I tried to tell him."

Al's giggle became a full-blown laugh. "You do know that man, don't you?"

The grinding sound of the steel door drew our attention away from Bob and "I Walk the Line" on the jukebox. Three men entered and walked directly to the table by the front window.

"Time to go to work," said Al. He rubbed his left knee and used the back of the chair to stand. "Come back anytime. Especially when you don't bring Bubba Bob." The twinkle in his aging eyes said he was teasing about Bob.

I finished the last of the wine and gave Al a few minutes to see what his customers wanted before I headed to the register. He took my money, leaned across the bar, and whispered, "It takes a damned scary fool to be out there shooting someone with an arrow. It ain't your job to catch him. Be careful."

Good advice, I thought. Would I take it?

CHAPTER 11

Summer traffic between Charleston and the beach moved at a snail's pace, a worn-out, lame snail. Compounding the already slow-moving line of cars, it was the middle of Labor Day weekend. I stopped at the Piggly Wiggly, the last chain-anything before reaching Folly Beach. Technically, the large grocery was in the Folly Beach city limits, but few on the island considered it a part of the "real" Folly Beach. According to Charles, it was an annexation ploy to bring more money to the city coffers. Charles was an expert on many things, but I took his comments with a grain of sea salt when it came to city planning and taxation. After all, he hadn't paid taxes since the invention of the personal computer.

The aisles were packed with vacationers stocking up on the necessities—toilet paper, beer, chips, beer, salsa, and more beer. I followed their lead and filled my cart with the normal health foods that occupied my cupboard: Doritos, Cheetos, Hershey Kisses, and Oreos. I skipped the beer aisle but did restock the wine supply. Between the beer and bakery section, I was stopped by Marc Salmon, a city council member I had a passing acquaintance with from the Dog. He and Houston, a fellow council member, met there most every morning.

"Heard anything about the chief?" he asked as he slowly moved the six-pack of Coors he held in his left hand behind his back.

"He's still in CCU," I said. I didn't see any reason to share the other information with someone who would broadcast the latest gruesome details to anyone who'd listen.

"Yeah," he responded, "that's what I heard. Pressure from the mayor must've got to him."

The chief had confided that he and the mayor had issues, but I figured they were the normal flare-ups that take place between elected officials and appointed employees. "What pressure, Marc?"

"No one thing." The council member pulled his cart to a wider spot in the aisle so other shoppers could get by and then leaned against the steel end cap. He was a talker. "The mayor's been on him hot-and-heavy about traffic; worse this summer than since the Civil War, says the mayor. Some of those young folks buying the McMansions are complaining about too much noise, drinking, and trash on the beach and drunks on the streets—walking, driving, riding bikes." He shook his head and rolled his eyes. "It's pure bunk. They think it should be like Kiawah or Hilton Head—ritzy, well-manicured, and dull. I've lived here all my life, and Folly Beach is … well, Folly Beach. Love it or leave it." He slapped his hand on the cart handle. He was on a roll. "On top of that, the mayor says that with the economic situation, the chief has to lay off three of his staff and park two patrol cars. My view is the mayor's trying to force him out."

The first notes of "My Way" flowed from Salmon's phone and interrupted his rant. He mumbled a few words into the mouthpiece, took a sheet of folded, lined notepaper from his pocket, and wrote mustard, oatmeal, and chocolate chips on his list. "Gotta go," he said after closing the flip phone. "Ms. B's waiting. Good talking to you."

More like talking *at me*, I thought, as he walked toward the fresh meat section. He was on the opposite side of the mayor on most issues and didn't always have his facts straight, but I was surprised to hear that about the mayor and the chief. The Lester Patterson's murder investigation was under the jurisdiction of the County Sheriff's Department, but I wondered if another murder on Folly Beach would put another nail, or arrow, in the chief's coffin.

I left the Pig, as we locals call it, and pulled off the right side of the road at a boat that hadn't floated for twenty years. *The Boat* was deposited between the marsh and its shimmering, green grasses and Folly Road by Hurricane Hugo, which ravaged this part of the country in 1989. No one had claimed the thirty-five-foot-long fishing boat, and in the quirky style of Folly Beach, it had become a landmark and community bulletin board. Cans of spray paint and a little creativity were all it took to leave messages on the ever-changing side of the water-challenged craft. It was not uncommon to have a new message each day. Larry had told me that spray paint was his best selling item. Instead of "I love you Aunt Susie" or "Congratulations Michael and Leigh Ann," today's message was a simple, "Hurricane Frank, was that your best shot?"

Folly, with the exception of Les, will live to see another day.

CHAPTER 12

The last time Charles had a steady job was nearly a quarter of a century ago. After he had seen the light, the light of the beach, and became fed up with the light from headlights he had installed on new Fords in Detroit, he surrendered his urge to work for a living. I had retired from a "real job" three years ago and opened the doors at Landrum Gallery whenever I wanted. So, today was Labor Day, and Charles and I couldn't have cared less. What we did care about was that the island was swarming with vacationers who spent months each year drooling over the chance to take the long Labor Day weekend and celebrate the traditional end of summer. I couldn't understand why the way to celebrate labor was to not labor, but whoever created the holiday hadn't asked me.

I met Charles at the Dog earlier than usual to beat the nonlaboring laborers. Amber greeted me with a subtle hug and a steaming mug of coffee. Charles had already staked out our table. He was leaning back in his chair and proudly displayed a red and gold Arizona State University Sun Devil long-sleeve T-shirt. His Tilley hat and handmade cane were sitting on a nearby chair.

"Any news on the chief?" he asked before I settled. He was worried and stared at me until I answered.

I took a deep breath, soaked in the welcoming smell of burritos, and shared that Al had called to say that his daughter reported the chief was still in critical condition. She said he only had a fifty-fifty chance. But he was alive.

"I don't understand," said Charles. "The chief is in great shape— trim, eats well, exercises."

Dude Sloan mysteriously appeared before I could respond. He nodded twice at the vacant chair. "Empty?"

"Casper the Ghost and two of his buddies sitting there," deadpanned Charles. "Want me to move them?"

"Appreciate it," said Dude.

He said it like he often had to shoo ghosts.

Charles made sweeping motions with his arms and proclaimed the seat vacant.

"Thanks," said Dude. "Chuckster, own a word-shirt factory?" He stared at the Sun Devil on Charles's shirt.

"Nope," replied Charles, alias (only to Dude) Chuckster.

"Number got?" said Dude.

"A gross, give or take," said Charles, with his head held high.

"Cool," said Dude, who looked at Charles with new admiration. He put his finger to his chin. "Cool and weird."

Dude sat and turned to me. "Chief ready to surf?"

I hadn't imagined I could be so relieved to talk about a heart attack. I repeated what Al had told me. Dude nervously ran his hand through his long, gray hair. "Bummer," he said. "Not that many moons old. Why him?"

"He's sixty-four," said Charles, who felt the need to quantify *not many moons*. "That's older than me, and even older than Chris here.

"Charles," I said in mock exasperation, "you're only two years younger than me; don't make it sound like a dozen."

Charles held his right hand in front of his face and stared at his palm. "I look a dozen years younger."

"Don't know what you see in that hand-mirror," said Dude, "but the view be warped. Me be around fewer Halloweens than both of you."

"How old would that be?" I asked Dude. Charles and I had speculated on Dude's age a couple of times. Charles had said he knew it was between forty-one and seventy-three.

"Fifty-seven people years," said Dude. I assumed he meant earth-people but didn't ask. He barely paused, "You passed the big seven forty-two, didn't you?"

Dude looked at me. I looked at Charles for a translation.

"If that means sixty, yes." Charles responded.

"Thought so; no secrets here." Dude turned to Charles and then took his Sharpie pen from the side pocket in his cargo shorts and wrote something on the copy of *Astronomy* magazine. He added some numbers and put the pen's cap in his mouth. "Chuckster," he said, "how many full moons you seen?"

Charles put his fork on the side of his plate, let out an exaggerated sigh, and said, "I'm fifty-eight. I don't know how may days, leap years, full or empty moons, and don't care. Fifty-eight be fifty-eight."

Charles couldn't stand being called Charlie, much less Chuckster, any more than the pope liked being called rabbi. He tried to hide his cringe, but it nearly vibrated the table. He held his tongue and took a deep breath. "Guys, as Abraham Lincoln once said, 'In the end, it's not the years in your life that count, it's the life in your years.'"

Dude slowly lowered his head onto the top of his hand that was near the top of the table. "My bud, Les, was only forty-three." Charles and I had to lean forward to hear what he said. "He'll never grow as historic as you two, or the chief. A shame."

"Sorry, Dude," said Charles, "I didn't know you were close."

Dude kept his head lowered, "Close—not too. I'm short on friends; I liked him." Dude raised his head and looked at Charles. "He not be perfect; sipped too much; sang at GB's bar; hung out with insanity. But we had good talks."

"Any idea who'd want him dead?" I asked.

Dude grinned, "Les would say Lee Harvey Oswald or John Wilkes Booth or some green man from the other side of Mars." He then leaned toward us like he was about to impart a deep, dark secret. "Don't think they be his problem. Know what I mean?"

Before we could clarify what he meant, Dude said he had to go. "Surfers a-waitin'!" He bounded from the chair and almost skipped to the door.

Charles watched him weave through the tables, nearly bumping into two kids headed to the restroom. "He be out of words," Charles speculated.

Dude almost ran headlong into Cindy Ash, who had pulled the door open as our strange friend exited. She stepped out of the line of fire and looked around the restaurant until her gaze paused on our table. She headed toward us; there was no doubt, we were her target.

She took the chair Dude had occupied, ignored the ghosts, sat, and nodded for us to lean closer. "There's been another crossbow shooting." She glanced around to make sure no one had heard her. I gasped. Charles whispered, "Who? When? Where …?"

"Arno Porchini …"

Charles inhaled, "My God. Arno's a friend … what …"

Cindy interrupted, "He's not dead. He's damn lucky."

"What happened?" I asked.

"Just after sunrise, Mr. Porchini was fishing off his small boat near the bridge. Said he didn't hear anything; the arrow slammed into his left arm and spun him around." She looked around the room. "He was lucky he didn't fall out and drown. Said next thing he knew, he was coming to on the bottom of the boat, blood all around, and his arm feeling on fire."

"Anybody around?" said Charles.

"Not a soul. Porchini said he was afraid to sit up, afraid the killer was waiting for his head to appear above the side. He thought the shot came from the road. He wasn't more than seventy feet from shore."

"And he never saw anybody or a car?" I asked.

"No," said Ash. "He has no idea how long he was out, and when he came to, he waited a long time before moving. He wrapped his arm with his T-shirt. If he hadn't, he would've bled out. Said all he could do was lie there shivering and looking at the arrow in his arm."

Charles waved for Amber to bring Cindy coffee. "Who found him?" he asked.

"Mr. Porchini heard traffic pick up and figured whoever did it was long gone—too much risk. He got the motor started, yanked it with his right arm, and powered his boat to shore at the road at the far side of the bridge over the river. Somehow he managed to climb the hill to the road. A truck driver saw the blood all over the T-shirt and then the arrow, dialed 911, and went to help."

Amber slipped the mug under Cindy's arm and left without a word.

Cindy took a sip and thanked Charles for getting it for her.

He waited for her to set the mug down. "They think he'll be okay?"

"Don't know," she said. "Officer Spencer and I got there about the same time. I think we got to him in time. He lost a lot of blood and was lucky to bring his boat directly to the road. He wouldn't have made it to the dock. It was gross—blood everywhere in the boat."

"Lucky," said Charles.

"You bet," she said. "Charles, you're his friend, so you know he lives at the Edge."

"The same place Lester Patterson lived?" I asked.

Charles nodded and looked at Cindy, "And where you live?"

"Yeah," she whispered. She took another sip of coffee. "He lives on the second floor over Mrs. Klein. We haven't said more than twenty words to each other. He's real quiet, not rude, just never says much."

"Do I know him, Charles?" I asked.

"No reason to," said Charles. "You may have seen him in Bert's, but he won't speak unless you talk first. He's about forty, sandy hair, little taller than us, muscular, not like us; overall, nothing special."

"How do you know him?" asked Cindy.

Charles leaned closer. The Dog was packed, and it was easier to hear what was said at the closest tables than the other side of ours. "Arno and I worked construction together. He's a carpenter, bright, appreciates my outstanding qualities—what's not to like about him?"

I didn't ask what qualities.

"He from here?" I asked.

"Don't think so," said Charles, "but I don't know anything else; been here off and on around three years. Like I said, he's pretty quiet, except on Tuesdays when he sings at the Country Jamboree at GB's Bar."

"Didn't Dude say Patterson sang there?" I asked.

Charles nodded again.

Cindy had her back to the room and kept turning her head to see who was coming and going. Her hands were shaking. I doubted she heard a word we had said.

"This is way too spooky," she said to both of us, or neither of us. She shook her head and focused on Charles. "I'm from east Tennessee. Been around hunters all my life; rifle and bow and arrow. I thought I'd seen it all but … but a crossbow? And both of them live in my building. Guys, there's only eight of us renting there and old Mrs. Klein."

Charles gently touched her arm. "Maybe you should stay with Larry for a while. I don't think he'd mind." He cocked his head in my direction. "Do you?"

She and Larry had been dating for nearly a year, so I didn't think his house would be a foreign land to her, but I'd kept my meddling to a minimum to counter Charles who had perfected the fine art of butting in. "Something to think about."

"How would it look if one of Folly's crime-stopping, criminal-catching police officers ran to her boyfriend's house at the first sign of trouble?" she asked.

I thought it beat an arrow through the heart, but shrugged.

We sat in silence for a few minutes, and then Cindy called the station to see if there was an update on Porchini. He was in stable condition, but they were going to keep him at the hospital overnight. That was the best news we had all morning. Amber was standing about ten feet from the table and dying to know what we were talking about but stayed away. I motioned her over and asked if she could get some oatmeal for Cindy and whispered that I'd fill her in later. That soothed her curiosity—temporarily.

The customers at a nearby table had headed to the beach and took much of the noise with them. It was easier to hear. I told Charles and Cindy what Al had said about the killer using a bow and arrow—in this case, a crossbow. It could be for stealth, could be a hunter, could be symbolic. What we did know for sure was that something terrible, terrible and deadly, was happening on our island, and it was hitting close to home.

Would there be more?

CHAPTER 13

Labor Day was a holiday and I was sort of retired, but I still wanted to open the Gallery. The island crawled with vacationers and long-weekenders, my bread and butter. If I didn't sell photos today, I should lock the doors for good—something I may need to do anyway.

Charles, my unofficial sales manager and staff optimist, joined me to welcome the crowds and, with some luck, wear out the cash register. It turned out to be a busy day, but the cash register was far from overused. Gaps in business exceeded the busy moments, so we had plenty of time to talk about the disastrous last few days. There were countless adventurers and risk-takers who led an event-filled existence. But to a slightly overweight, out-of-shape, retired desk jockey from Kentucky, one hurricane, one friend's heart attack, one murder, and one attempted murder in three days exceeded anything I had experienced in my sixty years (742 full moons in Dude-speak). Charles had led a more adventurous life, but after a few minutes of contemplative thought, agreed that this was at the top—or bottom, depending upon perspective—of his *this is the pits* list.

By late afternoon, we decided that some liquid libation and pizza would help us gain a better perspective on the events of the holiday weekend. A phone call to Larry turned our *couple of guys sharing a pizza and drinks* into a Labor Day party of three. Larry said he'd stop at Woody's Pizza and pick up the well-rounded meal, and Charles agreed to stop at Bert's for the liquid portion. Cindy had to work, and Amber's son, Jason, was running a fever and she needed to stay home. I promised to call later with what we had been talking about at the Dog.

The comforting aroma of the Woody, the restaurant's eighteen-inch specialty, beat Larry in the door. Both Larry and Charles were prompt, nearly to a fault, so Charles was only a few steps behind the hardware maven/pizza delivery person.

Charles wore a long-sleeve University of Toledo T-shirt and panted as he hurried up the steps. "Sorry I'm so late," he said as he gasped for air. "I couldn't get out of Bert's. Everyone wanted to talk about the crossbow killer. Why do people think I know all that stuff?"

He Frisbeed his hat across the room toward the chair, a well-practiced move. He missed—the usual result.

Larry returned from the kitchen table, where he had deposited our supper. "About time you got here." He made a stage gesture of looking at his watch. "Hmm. Seven, eight seconds late."

A prosperous day at Pewter Hardware extracted humor from our petite friend. I wished another day of abysmal sales at a specific local gallery could cheer me. I counted on Charles, Larry, Amber, and a few other left-of-quirky friends to liven my days.

"Better late than Lester," Charles replied.

That silenced Larry as Charles carried his assignment to the kitchen. He put the twelve-pack of Bud in the refrigerator and the two bottles of low-priced Chardonnay on the rack in the door. Brain surgery, nanotechnology, and cooking were three subjects I had never cluttered my brain with, so there was plenty of room in the refrigerator. It could have held another 153 bottles, with room to spare.

I couldn't accurately describe the smells from the pepperoni, sausage, meatball, and other ingredients from Woody's finest, but I was drawn to them more than a human should be. The three of us remembered that we hadn't had lunch, which was extra incentive to devour the doughy delight. All but two slices of the Woody were gone before any real conversation began.

Larry unsuccessfully held back a burp and followed it with a gulp of beer. "Charles, what did you tell the people at Bert's?"

"Huh?" said Charles. He had finished eating and leaned back in the chair contemplating the ceiling.

"You said they kept asking about the crossbow killer—is that what they're calling him?"

"I said that an hour ago. And yes, that's now his official moniker."

Larry pointed to the pizza remains. "We've been busy. So, what did you tell them?"

"The truth. I had no idea," said Charles.

Charles wasn't going to let the subject go, so I ventured where I knew he would tread next, "What do we know about Les Patterson and Arno Porchini?"

Charles decided he wasn't finished after all and had stuffed one more bite in his mouth, so Larry answered, "Not much. I know both by sight; they're in the store on a regular basis. Les worked in HVAC and Arno's in construction—a carpenter, I think." He paused, shrugged his shoulders. "That's it, I guess."

Uncharacteristically, Charles had waited for Larry to finish. "Yeah, we know that. I like Arno. He's quiet and knows what he's doing with a hammer and saw. When I help on the construction jobs, I'm an extra set of hands—'carry this,' 'carry that,' 'help hold the lumber,' —but he always treated me well. That's rare for a skilled tradesman. Les was fun to goad. When he started talking about flying saucers, I'd ask if he had met any of the occupants, or if they'd taken him for a ride, or other silly questions. He'd answer like I was a reporter for the *New York Times*—all serious and sincere. On weekends, his answers were slurred; think it had to do with his blood alcohol level." Charles took another sip. "He was a nice guy."

"They were both in construction," I said. "Did they work together?"

"Could have," said Charles. "I never saw Les on any jobs I worked, but I only helped out occasionally. I think most of his company's work was off-island."

Larry said, "No idea."

"What else did they have in common?" I asked.

"Both lived at the boardinghouse—their rooms were across from each other," said Charles. He looked toward the front of my house. From my porch I could see a corner of the Edge even though it was more than a block away.

"You know," said Larry. He looked at Charles and then back at me. "So does Cindy."

Charles and I nodded.

"She's working until three," said Larry. "I've asked her to stay with me tonight. Don't know if she will; said she'd think about it. She's scared but won't admit it."

Charles went to the refrigerator and got another beer for Larry. "I don't see how this could have anything to do with her," he said. "She'll be fine."

I hoped he was right but knew he had no solid reason to believe it. "They both sing at the Country Jamboree," I said as I searched for anything they had in common other than the boardinghouse.

"Yeah," said Charles. "They had to know each other. I don't suppose we know if they knew anyone with a crossbow."

That sent me for another glass of wine, and Larry for a change of subject. He started telling customer stories in the aftermath of Hurricane Frank. A handful of houses had portions of their roofs damaged, so he had a run on tarps. He only carried the blue plastic tarps, but one customer demanded a red one. Larry said he tried to explain that blue would keep the rain out as well as any other color, but the guy left, saying he would just have to go to Home Depot. Larry wished him well. One man asked if he carried alligator traps; he'd heard that the storm ran the gators out of the marsh into yards. Larry told him he had a pair of alligator shoes, but the man just stared at him. Larry finally told him that he didn't think there were alligator traps and recommended that if he saw an alligator in his back yard, he should call 911.

Charles had listened patiently—not his strength—but finally interrupted, "Did anyone ask if you sold crossbows?"

Larry's lack of response told me that our Labor Day party was over.

No sooner than Charles had time to walk home, he called, "Want to go to a bar tomorrow night?"

"Maybe, where?" I responded. I didn't want to commit until I knew what he had in mind.

"GB's—the Country Jamboree."

"Sure."

CHAPTER 14

Several years ago, a group of bluegrass music aficionados organized a weekly "get-together" on Folly Beach. Each Thursday, bluegrass musicians from Charleston and the surrounding area gathered at the Roadhouse Cafe for an evening of picking, strumming, singing, and all-around good times. The musical quality ranged from great to "good try," but the enthusiasm and camaraderie of the musicians, their families, and fans was always outstanding. The Bluegrass Society thrived.

There might not be a discernable difference between bluegrass and country music to the uninformed, but to country musicians and fans, the differences were huge. Not to be outdone, a smaller group of country pickers decided that they needed a similar forum and convinced Gregory Brile, the owner of a small, neighborhood bar just off Center Street, to give them a night and to switch his theme from contemporary rock to country. It wasn't hard to convince Brile to change; he was in the fast lane to bankruptcy. So, *Greg's: Home of Rowdy Rock* became *GB's*. A local wag had convinced him that if he used his initials as the name, the "ignorant vacationers" would think the bar was owned by Garth Brooks and would bring him more business than he could handle—all music (country music) to Greg's ears.

* * *

"I'll catch you at the end of your story;
I'll be there when life starts to fall.
I'll catch you at the end of your story;
and we'll be together through it all."

The sounds of the slow, sad tune greeted us as we walked though the door of GB's. The music came from a small, raised wooden bandstand at the far end of the building. Its lone occupant was a lanky singer, with a look out of the 1950s. He was at least six foot three and looked taller with his cream-colored Stetson riding high on his head. His spine curved toward the mike, and his rhinestone-studded jacket sparkled from the sole spotlight illuminating the stage. He strummed an old acoustic guitar with a four-inch-square piece of plywood covering what I assumed to be a hole on the front. The instrument had never visited a professional repair shop.

Despite the bar's name, Garth Brooks had never set foot in the building, but his song "Friends in Low Places" would be a perfect description of the patrons. I would describe GB's as beach-bar-bohemian. The walls were painted dark green; a beat-up dark wooden bar sat on the right side with a tiny kitchen behind it. The smell of stale beer and onions frying on the grill was almost as sad as the song.

The room was packed. There were a dozen tables—a combination of four-tops and barstool-height two-tops. Four stools at the bar were taken. Two tables were unoccupied, but purses were on them and three guitar cases leaned against the chairs. A twelve-by-twenty-foot dance floor made of laminate flooring squares was in front of the small stage. Four couples were swaying to the melodic sounds of pure country. Two women stood inside the door waiting for a table.

The song finished; the singer bowed and was greeted by enthusiastic applause.

Two men from the table closest to the door slipped a twenty under an empty beer bottle and walked past us and out the door. The two women rushed to the table before it could be cleaned. One stared at Charles like she was afraid he would arm wrestle her for the piece of valuable real estate. She outweighed Charles by about a ton—it would have been no contest. He smiled and tipped his Tilley to her; she quickly turned away.

"Thank you. Thank you. Appreciate it," mumbled the tall crooner into the mike. He paused and looked around the room. "I'd like to dedicate my last song to my friend Lester Patterson, who was brutally murdered just the other day, and my friend Arno Porchini, who barely escaped the heinous killer." He removed his Stetson and carefully set it on the floor beside his Budweiser. He began strumming "Amazing Grace."

The room turned silent as the words of the hymn echoed off the concrete walls. I didn't hear anything after "… that saved a wretch like me." What kept reverberating in my head was "… my friend Lester Patterson" and "… my friend Arno Porchini."

The haunting hymn ended, and the only sounds heard were a few amens from a table near the dance floor. The singer bowed from the waist, put his guitar in a beat-up, black case, picked up his beer and Stetson from the floor, left the stage, and headed to the restroom beside the stage.

A rotund, baby-faced man walked to the mike. He looked to be in his forties, but his stooped shoulders, his grease-slicked, muddy gray hair, and his sad face made him seem much older. "Thank you, Cal," he said as he looked toward the restroom. "Such a terrible tragedy has touched all of us in the GB's community. All our prayers are with Lester and to Arno for a speedy recovery. Yes, they are."

His head nodded; I assumed it was a moment of silence or a prayer, although he could have been falling asleep. He jerked his head up and gave a big smile, "And now back to the show. Let's have a great big GB's welcome for one of our favorite girl singers, Miss Heather Lee."

Before Ms. Lee tuned her guitar and reached the stage, Charles was on his way to the restroom.

Heather wore a wide-brimmed straw hat, a bright yellow sequined blouse, a floor-length Kelly green skirt, and an "aw-shucks" smile. I suspected she wore colorful cowboy boots, but her skirt was touching the floor and I couldn't tell. She was attractive, and freckles on her nose added to her wholesome look. She was in her forties and looked like she stepped out of a cheap cowboy movie from the 1930s.

She began a cover of Patsy Cline's, "Sweet Dreams," and I knew she'd never get a singing part in any movie unless silent pictures made a comeback. Her beauty ended with her looks. Fortunately for the customers, the increasing noise of clanking bottles, calls for a waitress, and sounds of people yelling to be heard over their neighbors, kept them from hearing the terrible warbling of Ms. Heather Lee.

Smoking was permitted in restaurants and bars, but most of them self-regulated and prohibited it. Thankfully, GB's was one of those, so

I could see Charles heading back to the table without having to look through a cloud of smoke. He had the Hank Williams Sr. look-alike in tow.

"Chris," said Charles, "I was telling Cal here how we were big country fans and asked him to join us for a drink."

I knew Charles was as big a country music fan as I was of opera—near zilch; his reasons for the invite were not quite pure.

"Howdy, I'm Country Cal," said the tall, not dark, stranger. He reached with his right hand while pulling out the chair beside me with his left. He quickly sat and raised his hand for the nearest waitress. "Where're you from, Chris?"

"Kentucky," I said. "Louisville."

Cal was still waving his hand in the air. "Jackson, Hazard, Ashland, Princeton, Pippa Passes ... played them all—Kentucky, I love it." With his hand still waving, he turned to Charles, "And you, my country music fan?"

"Detroit, originally," said Charles, "But been here most of my life."

"Romulus, Flat Rock, Windsor over-the-border ... been there, sang there. No offense, Charles, I prefer the South."

"Me, too," said Charles, without skipping a beat or taking offense. "And you're from ...?"

"Remember when Mac Davis sang that happiness was Lubbock, Texas, in his rearview mirror?" Cal finally got the waitress's attention and gave her his broad stage smile. I nodded yes; Charles shrugged. "He stole my hometown and my sentiments."

The lovely and untalented Heather Lee had finished her song, so I was able to hear without them having to shout. There was only one window in GB's, and most of the light in the room disappeared with the sunset. Apparently GB's had the same lighting consultant as Al, or a good beer salesman, since most of the illumination came from a Miller and a Budweiser neon sign over the bar.

After our hometowns were analyzed, Charles told me how he had run into Cal in the restroom and *quite by happenstance* they had started talking. And, what do you know, they knew some of the same folks—Arno Porchini, Lester Patterson, and one that surprised me, Cindy Ash.

"Fine job, fine job, Miss Heather," Chubby-slick-hair was back on the stage and wrestling the mike from Heather.

Cal leaned closer to Charles and me, gave a big belly laugh, and said, "Tuesday is open-mike night. Gregory'll let anybody sing who shows up with a guitar and a breath."

"So that's GB, Gregory, up there?" I interrupted.

"Yep," said Cal. "Not hard to figure out. He says the name of the bar about every other word." He looked toward the bar and then back to us, "Wasted words, if you ask me. If you can hear him, you're already throwing your cash away at GB's." He laughed again. "If you have even a glimmer of talent, Gregory'll let you sing two songs. If you've ever released a record, you get three."

The waitress quickly brought two beers and a glass of white wine. Hosting Country Cal got us VIP service.

"Guess Heather hasn't released a record yet," said Charles.

"Her only record's for grand theft auto," said Cal. "I hear she borrowed a car from an ex-boyfriend and forgot to tell him about it. The boyfriend was lucky." He paused and smiled. "The car didn't sink all the way in the river, so the police found it. Name isn't even Heather; it's Eileen Gordon Smith or maybe Jones—no, I'm sure it's Smith. Sweet gal, though."

I took a sip of the finest white wine three fifty could buy and looked at Cal. "Speaking of police, how do you know our friend Cindy?"

"We're roommates," he said and breezed past sip to gulp his beer.

"Oh," I said.

"Well, not really roommates; more like housemates. She lives under me at the Edge."

And to think, only four days ago I didn't even know the strange house on the beach had a name. "Lester Patterson lived there, and so does Arno Porchini, right?" said Charles.

"On my floor," he said. "Harley Something-or-other, too, but he ain't a singer. Course, neither is Heather, and she lives on the first floor." He laughed.

I glanced at Charles, and he gave a quick shake of his head. He was a bulldog when he wanted information, so I followed his lead and didn't pursue the list of residents.

"So, Country Cal," said Charles, "Your mother must've had a sense of humor to name her son Country." He faced Cal with his best straight face.

Cal burst into another stage laugh, something we were learning came with the territory. "Name's really Calvin Ballew. Born and reared with that name until my agent—God bless the son-of-a-warthog—told me that if I was going to be famous, the name had to go. The name went, and so did all my money—stolen by that son-of-a-warthog." He raised his hand to the waitress and waved two fingers at her. He didn't know what to raise for wine.

"You're big country fans," Cal continued, "so you must know my big hit."

I was a big country fan, had been for years, but had never heard of Country Cal, much less his "big hit." But Charles, who had never feared to tread where no man had two-stepped, said, "Sure, you were singing it when we came in."

I wish I'd been that quick. Cal had sung three songs—being a big recording star and all—and didn't know we heard only part of one of them, and more importantly, didn't know when we arrived. His "big hit" would have been on the playlist.

"Yep," said Cal. He had an ear-to-ear grin and tilted his head back. "'End of Your Story,' released spring, sixty-two; I was only eighteen— had the world by the tail of its coonskin cap. Went to number seventeen on the national charts; top five on some regional lists; number one in Lubbock. Yep, world by the tail."

"Other hits?" asked Charles.

"Nope, 'End' was it. The end of my story." Cal looked down at his drink. "You boys don't want to hear all of this. I'll stop bending your ears."

"Cal," said Charles. "I love to hear about country music; don't stop."

That was the same Charles who had described country music as "whiny, sad, pitiful, beer-guzzling, cheating, kick-your-dog, leave-your-wife, and watch-your-girlfriend-leave-you-for-the-Roto-Rooter-man kind of music." He wanted Cal talking so he wouldn't get suspicious about why we were interested in his house.

"Sixty-two was the best year of my life." Cal looked at the green wall at the far side of the bar. "Played the Grand Ole Opry. Roy Acuff introduced me. The Opry was in the Ryman then, not out by that monster hotel where it is now. Yep, met Patsy Cline, 'She's Got You' had gone to number one; George Jones called me his 'buddy.'" He smiled and then continued. "George took me across the alley to Tootsie's Orchid Lounge and introduced me to Miss Tootsie—nicest lady. I think she adopted all country-pickers and strays, even gave them a few beers and bucks when their hits weren't." He smiled.

Since Cal's best days of his life were nearly a half-century ago, I wondered how he got from the Ryman Auditorium to singing at the open-mike, country jamboree at GB's. I wasn't about to ask. That's why I had Charles.

Charles shrugged his shoulders at me and then nudged, "And then?"

"I was big stuff," continued Cal. "I went from a regular on the Opry, to a once-a-month appearance, to every night at Tootsie's and over at Ernest Tubb's Record Store across the street and sang a few times at his Midnight Jamboree. It was on the radio after the Opry's last performance of the night, you know."

I knew Charles didn't.

"That had to be exciting," said Charles.

"Yep, fans recognized me. Problem was, fans recognized me. They bought me beer." He held his Bud bottle in the air. "They shared some weed. They wouldn't let my hand stay empty—bottle, toke, bottle, night after night. God love fans … almost killed me."

The two women who were waiting on a table when we came in walked over. The less hefty of the two, not Charles's almost-arm-wrestling buddy, leaned over to Cal and whispered, "Great songs. Could you sign this for my friend?" As her top runneth over, she handed Cal a page from the *Folly Current*. He took it and found the page with the most white space and scribbled his name. She giggled and handed the paper to her friend, who was standing directly behind her. Cal was enjoying every second—the attention and the view.

"You haven't lost it," said Charles as the two headed back to their table.

"Fans like those gals were the beginning of my downfall," said Cal, who was still staring at the women. "Somewhere between the walk from the Opry to Tootsie's, and Ernest Tubb's, I lost my fame, self-respect, record contract, personal appearances, and my son-of-a-warthog agent. Lost all my money, too."

I was surprised that Cal was so candid with strangers. I was also thinking that Charles and I could be sitting here listening to the hard-luck story of the crossbow killer.

"We heard you say Lester and Arno were your friends," I said. I wanted to move the conversation forward about five decades. "Did you know them well?"

Cal shook his head and took another sip. "Nope, not really." He looked around to see if anyone was close enough to hear. Another singer was onstage telling about his *new hit* that would be released in "a couple of years."

Cal smiled, no stage laugh this time. "If I had a buffalo nickel for every time I've heard that, I'd be in one of those mansions in the hills near Nashville." He turned back to us. "Truth be known, I had little use for Patterson. We'd gotten into a couple of fistfights—well, more like shoves—over splitting tips from the jamboree. He wasn't much of a likable fellow; had a good voice, but wasn't as good as he thought." He paused a moment to listen to the two-years-from-now-hit. "Age ain't going to help that song."

"What about Porchini?" asked Charles. He was back on target after spending time with Cal in 1962.

"Quiet guy; hardly ever talked to him even though his room was across the hall from me," said Cal. "Works in construction, but I don't know doing what. Whatever he did, he was better at it than singing. Yep, quiet guy—hope he's okay."

I asked Cal if he wanted another round. He laughed and said no—said that's what got him in trouble to begin with. We ran out of conversation about the time another country wannabe was taking the stage and Gregory Brile was telling the audience that we should all come back Saturday night when Country Cal would be doing three sets.

Cal stood, waved at the customers, smiled, and then sat back down. He leaned closer to me; his beer breath preceded his words, and he said, "Yep, that's what a big hit will do for you. Ya'll are coming back Saturday, aren't you?"

"Wouldn't miss it," said Charles.

I stared at Charles and thought, *Wouldn't?*

CHAPTER 15

A westerly breeze had shoved some of the day's heat out of the area, so Charles and I leisurely walked along Center Street. Walking was far from my list of favorite activities, but we went slowly and enjoyed the sounds of soft-rock and beach music drifting from the outdoor bars along the main drag.

"Wouldn't miss it?" I said as we passed Woody's Pizza. I gave him a sideways glance and an arched brow.

"Nope," he said, and continued to stare straight ahead. "I figured Cal's our only lead to the crossbow killer. Looks to me like he's the killer or, who knows, maybe the next victim."

It had entered my mind, but wondered why Charles thought so. "Why?"

Charles abruptly stopped, tapped his cane three times on the sidewalk, and then looked around. "My coincidence barometer says he's got too much in common with Mr. Dead and Mr. Near-Dead."

Charles waited for a black lab to pull one of the city's residents across the street in front of us.

"You know ... Patterson, Porchini, and Cal, all country singers; all live at the Edge. My gut tells me Cal's not the killer. He seemed like a nice guy."

"Remember, Charles, Hitler had a mother and was probably a cute baby; bet he even had friends."

Charles lifted his hat and rubbed the sweat from his face on his T-shirt. "Hitler never lived at the Edge and sang country music."

Charles gave me a wink and headed toward his apartment. I continued the short walk home—sometimes words weren't necessary.

Cal's greatest hit remained in my head ... *"I'll catch you at the end of your story; And we'll be together through it all."*

*   *   *

I varied from my usual route to the complimentary coffee at the Holiday Inn and walked by the house that had garnered so much attention. The roar of chain saws filled the air as homeowners were getting an early start on the tree limbs rudely removed by Hurricane Frank. Two dark blue Crown Vics were conspicuously parked in a beach access area at the side of the boardinghouse. Only a blind burglar wouldn't recognize the *unmarked* vehicles as cop cars. My eyesight wasn't what it used to be, but I recognized the County Sheriff's Office detectives' modes of transportation. There were no flashing lights or marked patrol cars, or ambulances, or vans marked Coroner, so I assumed the detectives were looking for evidence or talking to the occupants of the increasingly-infamous house. I continued to the coffee bar.

Early morning was the best time to experience Folly Beach this time of year. The sun was raising its glowing face over the pier, so most of the residents of the near-full hotel were still in their rooms or sipping coffee on their balconies overlooking the Atlantic. A bored desk clerk was the only other person in the lobby. I took my coffee and walked the short distance to the pier. Several fishermen were doing what fishermen do—staring at the water as if they could will the fish to choose breakfast from their hook instead of the zillions of other morsels in the wide, deep ocean. I walked past three fishermen, exchanged good-morning nods, and then sat on one of the many fixed wooden seats that dotted the impressive structure.

Golden rays from the morning sun provided direct, low illumination on the houses and condos facing the beach. Off to the right, I could see the Edge. Two crew-cut-topped men in fish-out-of-water dark suits slowly walked around the small yard where Charles and I had talked— yelled—to Mrs. Klein. They were looking at the ground and using their feet to push rocks, bricks, and various remnants of Hurricane Frank. I wondered if they expected to find a fingerprint-laden crossbow under the rubble. I tried to connect the dots between country singers, residents of the boardinghouse, crossbows, and one and a half murders. I failed miserably and concluded that it was none of my business; after all, that's what the detectives in the backyard were earning my tax dollars to do.

My mind also drifted to a subject I had successfully avoided for decades—health. Brian's heart attack had scared me. Here was a healthy, active man, only a few years older than me, and now hanging on by a thread, if that.

I had been relatively healthy most of my life—a few minor surgeries here and there and cholesterol level above desired. But here I was, overweight (but shy of fat, I told myself), years of being averse to exercise, and beginning my seventh decade. Would I be strapped to a gurney in an ambulance, EMTs pressing on my chest; would I become a burden to ... to whom? Amber and I had dated for a while, but was I ready to make that permanent? Would she have me; could I change my years of a comfortable routine and adjust to having a twelve-year-old living under the same roof?

And then there's Landrum Gallery. Sure, it had been a good idea, but I thought I'd be able to break even. I could survive on my savings if the gallery didn't continue to be a drain. But it was a drain—a drain that sucked more money away each month. The current economy gave little hope that things would improve soon. I needed to have a serious talk with Charles about the future of the business. I dreaded that conversation.

I don't know how long I spent on the pier, but I forced my thoughts back to the beautiful, sunny day on Folly Beach. The detectives must have left sometime between my pondering health, death, marriage, and business.

I must savor the moment; I was healthy, had a roof over my home, had several fantastic friends, and, even if I kicked the bucket today, I wouldn't choose anywhere else in the world I'd rather be. Besides, I'm still in much better shape than Lester Patterson and Arno Porchini.

CHAPTER 16

Jason was spending the night with one of his classmates working on a class project, so Amber had a rare free evening. The Lost Dog Café was only open for breakfast and lunch, so it gave her time to be with Jason most afternoons after school. Since he'd reached the ripe old age of twelve, he continually said, "Mom, you don't have to babysit me." Like most young men that age, he was right—and wrong. He was away, so she didn't have to debate with herself over whether she could leave him alone, and we decided to go to Charleston for supper.

"Nice character dent," she said as I gallantly opened the passenger door for her outside her apartment. It was the first time she had seen the car since Frank remodeled the door panel.

"Thanks," I said. "Thought you'd like it."

She laughed. "Follyized it," she said. "It was sort of bland before—you're one of us now."

She spent most every day waiting tables on Folly Beach, so she preferred that we travelled off-island. Neither of us needed a white tablecloth under our plate to enjoy the food, so we went to the family-friendly Charleston Crab House, a few miles from the beach. We arrived early enough to get a table on the deck overlooking Wappoo Creek, one of the many waterways surrounding Charleston.

Amber knew that I preferred white wine in the summer and agreed, or pretended, it was her drink of choice. She had finished a hectic day at work and was in no hurry to eat. We ordered a bottle of wine, chips, and dip.

"Heard anything about the chief?" she asked. She leaned back in the blue, fan-backed, plastic chair and put her feet on the wooden rail between the deck and the creek. Her long hair, held back with a rubber band when she's at work, flowed over her shoulders and gently shimmered in the light breeze.

"Nothing more than what you know," I said.

She raised her chin, pushed the hair from her face, and was catching a few rays from the setting sun. A couple of boats meandered down the creek. A Doberman was barking at us from the stern of the larger vessel. Amber waved at the dog. She swore it grinned back.

The wine, chips, and dip had arrived. "I'm going to the hospital tomorrow and check on him. His daughter seems pretty torn up."

One of the many things I liked about Amber was that she didn't feel the need to fill silence with words. She could carry on a conversation with anyone, and could listen to the strangest, most boring, drawn-out stories without uttering a sound—a skill she had learned after many years as a waitress. And, with me, a person prone to silence, she could sit and silently appear to enjoy my company. We had finished the bottle of wine with hardly a word spoken; her head leaned on my shoulder. She was unwinding from work, and my mind was racing with thoughts of the chief, the murder, and my financial future.

"The chief only began talking about his daughter the last year or so," said Amber. "They weren't close when she was growing up. He was away most of the time in the military. He said the only reason she joined the police was because he had been an MP."

Amber had a way of getting people to open up, and she was one of the key unofficial information depositories on Folly Beach. For the second time, our waitress had politely asked us if we were ready to order. Amber giggled and said the clock was running on our table and we'd better order. Our table was prime real estate this time of day, so we agreed on fish and chips and the waitress left happy.

Amber watched her leave and then continued, "The chief is a little embarrassed that Karen—Detective Lawson—idolizes him so much."

"She could have worse idols," I said. "He's a fantastic person and has given me more breaks than he should have."

"If you'd stop meddling in police business, he wouldn't have to give you breaks." She laughed and then tapped me on the arm.

"I'm prone to be in the wrong place at the wrong time," I said. "It's the island's fault, you know. The only murders I ever knew about before I got here were from the media."

"Right," she said, "It's all our fault." Her smile faded, and some wrinkles—cute wrinkles, to be sure—began to appear on her brow.

"What's wrong?" I said.

"Nothing." She turned away, and I could see a tremor in her shoulders.

"Amber." I stopped and waited.

"I'm worried."

"About what?"

"You."

"Why?"

"I never met the Chris who lived in Kentucky, but I know the one who's here."

Our food arrived, but she ignored it.

"And ...," I said.

"And," she continued, "let me tell you what'll happen. Someone got himself killed just down the road from your house, and someone else nearly got himself murdered out by the bridge. Both of them made the mistake of living in the same boardinghouse—the house where Larry's girlfriend lives. See where I'm going with this?" She spread tartar sauce on her fish and took a dainty bite.

"No, go on."

"Okay," she said. "Now Folly Beach is swarming with detectives from the Sheriff's Department; cops are everywhere. The Dog was full of them today. They blend in about as well as President Obama would."

I giggled, but her stare screamed, *I'm not being funny.*

She continued, "I didn't hear everything they're saying, but it was clear that they don't know what's going on."

"What's that have to do with me?"

"Real soon you and Charles will sit down around an unhealthy pizza, and he'll say something like, 'We've got to figure out who the killer is,' and you'll say something like, 'That's what the police are for; it's none of our business.' And he'll say, 'Of course, it's our business; the killer was on your street, and Larry's girlfriend could be next.'"

"Amber ..."

"No, let me finish," she said. "You two will go back and forth about why and why not get involved, but the seed will have been planted and will start to grow. I've known Charles for much longer than you have. He won't leave it alone."

I put my arm around her waist and gave a gentle squeeze. "Thanks for worrying, but it's not going to happen. Besides, the police will have it wrapped up before Charles will make his case. They're good at what they do."

"Right," she said, and turned her attention to her food.

Amber was bushed, so I declined her offer for me to join her in her apartment—more accurately, the bedroom. After letting her out, I wished I wasn't so considerate.

I parked in front of my house. Before going in, I replayed Amber's imaginary conversation between Charles and me. Scary as it seemed, it was accurate. Even more frightening, Charles was right.

CHAPTER 17

Morning started on a high when I yanked Bob Howard out of a pleasant dream and invited him to lunch at Al's. It usually worked the other way around. He ranted, raved, said I'd ruined his beauty sleep, and then asked what time? I told him ruining his beauty sleep would be impossible, he should be awake at 6:30, and lunch was at 11:30. He slammed down the receiver. I smiled; he'd be there.

I arrived at Al's a few minutes before time and saw Bob's dark plum—don't call it purple—PT Cruiser in front.

I opened Al's heavy door and went from daylight to Budweiser-neon dark and to a cheerful greeting from the owner.

"Hi, Chris; Bubba Bob's awaiting." Al nodded in the direction of his only booth. Roger Miller's version of "When Two Worlds Collide" was playing on the color-blind jukebox. I glanced around the room and saw that the number of customers had just doubled.

"Well, you've damned well done it this time," said Bob before I reached the booth. His stomach pushed against the table; his arms were clasped behind his thinning gray hair. A half-eaten cheeseburger was on the plate, competing for space with a three-inch-high stack of fries. He looked down at his plate, grabbed a fry, and swiped it through a pile of ketchup on a coffee saucer next to the plate. A dollop of ketchup had already landed on his green Hawaiian shirt.

"Did what?" I knew asking was a mistake; he'd tell me anyway. I played along. I sat across from him—a challenge since he had pushed the table toward my seat so he could fit his ample body in the booth. I squeezed in; maybe I wasn't as heavy as I thought. Compared to the body on the other side of the table, I was emaciated.

"I hear you damn near started a race riot the other day. Just sashayed in here, pale white face a grinnin', no protection from your courageous friend Bob. Damn lucky you're still alive. Near riot I hear." He was getting louder.

"Don't believe a word that tub of lard jabbers," yelled Al from behind the bar. Roger Miller tried to mask Al's voice, but failed.

Bob's eyes never left the fries. "Mind your own business, you old fart," he shouted. "Where's my next beer?"

My eyes had finally become accustomed to the light, or more accurately, dark, and I saw the grin on Al's face as he headed to the table. He was carrying a beer for Bob, a glass of wine, and "the best cheeseburger in the United States." Al's arthritic seventy-plus-year-old legs slowed the trip considerably.

Al wasn't anxious to make the trip back and slowly pulled a chair from a nearby table. "Chris," he paused and caught his breath, and then said, "the intelligence and charm of the place increased more when you came in the other day than it ever has when your *friend Flubber* here arrives."

If I didn't know that Bob and Al had been friends for years, I'd be looking for a way out the door in one piece, or at least crawling under the table.

Al took a couple of deep breaths and put his elbows on the edge of the table. "Everybody getting back to normal after Frank?"

"Mostly," I said.

"Anybody crossbowed over there the last twenty-four hours?" asked Bob. "Damn dangerous place. People need to move out, sell their houses—they need a good Realtor."

That's Bob—always thinking of the welfare of others. Al and I ignored him—not easy, but wise.

"Any idea who's doing it?" asked Al.

"No," I said before Bob could answer. "Not that I know. But police are everywhere. Now the media's starting to swarm—a crossbow killer's big news."

Bob couldn't stay out of a conversation. "How's the chief?"

"Don't know," I said. "I'm going over when I leave here."

"Didn't think you came just to buy me a big lunch, five beers, dessert, and a meal to take to Betty."

Once again, I ignored him. From the jukebox, the Statler Brothers were telling us what happened to "The Class of '57."

That reminded me of a question I wanted to ask the country music expert in the room. I turned to Bob. "Ever hear of a country singer called Country Cal?"

"One-hit wonder, Country Cal, 'End of Your Story,' early sixties?"

Al grinned, "Not Motown."

"Nope," said Bob, who put his head back and started singing, using the term loosely, *"We changed homes, friends, and stories; you went your way as I did mine; I'll catch you at the end of your story...."*

"That's the one," I said quickly to head off another verse.

I told them about talking with Cal at the country jamboree. Bob said he didn't know much about Cal and then proceeded to tell us that Cal had drug and alcohol problems after his big, and only, hit and that he had spent years traveling around the South singing for tips. Bob was a virtual encyclopedia of country music.

Al perked up when I said that Cal lived in the same boardinghouse as the crossbow victims. Al raised his arms and gave the universal time-out signal. He slowly headed back to the bar for more drinks. Neither Bob nor I protested. When Al was gone, Bob pushed away from the table and slid several dollar bills into the jukebox. "Damn money pit," he said and pushed the table into my ribs. "Used to only be a nickel."

"Used to be Indians here," I said.

"Hmm," replied the articulate Realtor.

"Could this Cal guy be the killer?" asked Al. He put the drinks on the table and folded his tall body on the chair.

"Did you ask if he had a crossbow?" Bob interrupted.

I slapped the side of my head. "Sorry, Bob, I forgot to ask."

Bob shook his head. "And you and your idiot buddy, Charles, think you're detectives."

Charles and I weren't detectives any more than Bob was a spokesperson for Weight Watchers. A few times over the last three years, we had lucked into helping the police catch some killers—the key words being *lucked into.* We were poster children for being in the wrong place at the wrong time, and Bob knew it. He even helped catch one of the killers and will never let us forget it. In his humble opinion, he was the sole reason the bad guys were caught; he also knew he was the greatest Realtor in the free world.

"The police have it under control," I said, looking first at Bob and then to Al. I said it with more confidence than I felt.

We each took a sip of our beverage. Al had been quiet for a couple of minutes—not that difficult with Bob around, so Bob and I looked at him when he cleared his throat.

"Chris, you and your buddies have a way of stepping in the dog shit that most of us walk around. From what you've said, there're more piles of it on your island than ever." His hands were rubbing on the label on his beer bottle; he stared at it like he had never noticed the writing before. "I've thought about it a lot since you were in the other day. No normal person—not even a normal killer—goes around shooting people with a crossbow. You ..."

"Hell, Al, there hasn't been a normal person on Folly Beach for ninety-seven years," interrupted Bob.

Al didn't skip a beat. "You need to be careful. You're going to get involved—you always do. This time you'd better look places you wouldn't normally look. This is a strange one." Al looked up from the bottle. His dark, piercing eyes met mine. "Don't assume anything."

Bob put both elbows on the table and shifted his gaze between Al and me. "Before Al gets all teary and starts hinting for a group hug, I'm out of here. Gotta sell some overpriced condos and make money for my honey."

Bob had been married for more years than most of the population had been alive. Betty was a saint. She was sweet and kind, and had a fantastic attitude and smile. None of it had rubbed off on her husband.

Bob pushed himself up from the booth and was out the door before hugging could commence. As usual, he stuck me with the check. Al laughed.

Don't assume anything, I thought.

CHAPTER 18

I walked to the hospital rather than fight hospital-parking-lot-musical-chairs. Sadly, I had learned where the various departments were at the massive building. I ignored the information desk and went directly to the CCU waiting room. Most of the chairs in the room were full. The television was still tuned to CNN, volume still muted.

Karen Lawson was sitting in the corner under the television and flipping through a dog-eared copy of *Coastal Living*. She was going to or coming from work. Her chestnut brown hair was tied neatly back, and she was wearing a dark blue pantsuit. Her black flats were professional but comfortable enough to chase down a fugitive. She had the unmistakable aura of law enforcement around her.

The chair beside her was vacant; no one wanted to sit next to a cop. I was already seated before she looked up from the magazine.

"I'm glad you're here," she said, her bored gaze at the magazine turning to a kind smile. "The doc came out about an hour ago and said Dad's improving." She reached over and gave me a hug. Her arms loosened and tightened again; she was squeezing hard. I was embarrassed, but it felt good.

She let go and leaned back toward her chair. "Sorry," she whispered. "I'm so happy." She looked around the room and seemed surprised it was full, and then turned back to me. "The doc said he'd send someone out when I can go in."

We talked about the weather and hospital parking until a young lady stepped into the room; she couldn't have been out of her teens and had a smile on her face. "Karen Lawson?"

Karen stood and leaned down and grabbed my arm. "Come with me."

"That's okay," I said, "go ahead. I'll wait."

"Please come," she said and pulled my arm.

I wasn't ready for a wrestling match with a detective in a room of witnesses. I surrendered and stood.

Karen gave a glancing look at the nurse. "We're together," she said in her decisive, don't-challenge-me, voice. She took my elbow as we followed the intimidated young lady.

The room was about five times larger than a standard hospital room and was divided by cubicle curtains. I had never been a fan of hospitals and would only visit under threat of harm. My phobia intensified as I'd grown older. I could literally feel my heartbeat as I walked in. The walls closed in. If it wasn't for Karen's grip on my arm, I would have bolted. Handcuffs may be needed.

The sound of alien medical equipment assaulted my ears—beeps in regular cadence, compressors huffed and puffed, a sound similar to a digital alarm clock vibrated in one of the cubicles. Moans came from another area.

The nurse weaved her way though the portable equipment in the center of the room and led us to the farthest cubicle. The curtain was drawn on one side, and a handful of tubes were attached to the prone body in the bed. To my untrained eye, the graphs on the digital monitor behind the bed appeared to show a regular heartbeat. The unwilling resident didn't look anything like the strong, agile, healthy Chief Brian Newman. I caught myself backpedaling. It was terrible.

Karen hesitated and then cautiously moved to the side of the bed. I stopped a few feet from the foot of the bed. The unmistakable smell of hospital filled my nostrils. The nurse whispered that we must keep the visit to no more than five minutes. I had no argument with that and nodded.

Karen gently reached for her dad's left hand. Tears gathered as she leaned to give him a kiss on the forehead. His dry, scaling lips formed a weak smile. I couldn't hear what they were saying. After a few minutes, she looked up and gestured for me to come closer. She put her arm around my waist and pulled me toward the bed. Brian had an oxygen tube in his nose and was sedated. He looked past Karen and saw me.

"Thanks for … for coming," he mumbled. He blinked a few times; his focus wasn't clear. "Karen … Karen told me you've been here … I …"

He was struggling, and I knew we shouldn't drain him more. "Just wanted to see how you were. After all, you're my only police chief," I said to keep the conversation light and not horn in on Karen's time with her dad.

The nurse had moved to the foot of the bed and tapped her watch. Karen was whispering to Brian, and I put my arm around her and said we needed to go. On our way out, the nurse told us he was still in critical condition and didn't need more visitors today. Karen told her she would be back tomorrow.

I had to get out of the hospital and urged Karen to the door.

"Going on duty?" I asked as we exited the horrible building.

"No," she said, "I got off and came here." She was looking around for her car.

"Want to get a drink?" I asked. *Where did that come from?*

She smiled. "Thought you'd never ask."

My car was still at Al's, so I suggested we walk there. She said she'd never heard of it. That wasn't a surprise, I told her.

"Lordy, lordy," boomed the voice from behind the bar as we walked from light to dark. "First you're here with Bubba, bombastic, blubbery Bob; and now with a gorgeous, white, lady cop. There goes the neighborhood!" Al walked around the bar to greet his new visitor. "I must have died and gone to the Promised Land."

I laughed, and was glad that Karen did, too. I introduced the two.

"Ms. Karen," said Al, "I've heard a lot about your daddy; hope he's doing better."

Karen shared the update and then asked Al how he knew she was with the police.

"See these gray hairs?" he asked as he rubbed the top of his head. "See this old broken-down, ancient, brown body?"

She nodded but didn't say anything. Al was on a roll. "Know how many gorgeous, young, white ladies have graced that door since I opened this place just after the Civil War?"

Karen smiled and shook her head no.

"One," he answered his own question. "Know how many of those ladies had a bulge in her jacket covering a gun?"

"My guess is you're looking at all of them," I said.

"Accurate," said Al. "Would you like me to escort you to Bubba's booth?"

Karen looked at me and shrugged.

"Thanks, Al," I said. "I can find the way."

"Then what can I get you?"

"Wine for me," I said. "Karen?"

"Beer, any kind," she said.

"Good," said Al, "since that's all the choices you have."

I took my customary seat at the booth, and Karen easily slid into Bob's space. I pushed the table toward her so she could reach it. I explained that she was in Bob's favorite spot, and she said no wonder the seat's smushed. She was able to laugh. I began giving her the *Reader's Digest* version of Al's Bar and Gourmet Grill and some background on Al and his incredible life. She knew her dad would like Al and would bring him over when he was able.

"I don't suspect that Al's menu is very heart-healthy," I said. It was a pleasure to see Karen with much of the weight lifted off her.

"The wine will be good for him," she said.

Al arrived with the drinks and asked if we wanted any food. I was still full but said I'd share fries with Karen if she wanted some.

She looked at me and then turned to Al. "Fries, sure; but I want one of your world-famous cheeseburgers that I've heard so much about."

Al beamed. "Coming right up."

Two of the tables had filled since I was in earlier. Two men were sitting at one, and three at the other. The jukebox played vintage James Brown, so I knew Bob's choices would not be heard for a while. The three men at the nearest table kept turning to look at us.

I leaned closer to the table and whispered, "I don't think they can keep their eyes of the beautiful lady at this table."

Karen smiled. "It's the gun, Chris. It's the gun."

I nodded. That wasn't what I was looking at, but let it pass.

"Dad didn't look good, did he?" She turned serious.

"I wouldn't expect him to, considering what he's been through. He's strong and healthy." I cringed at the irony of my comment and continued, "It takes time."

Karen was silent for a moment. "Dad had two brothers," she finally said. "One was killed in Vietnam. He was a dentist but enlisted during the heat of the war. Killed his third day there."

"That's terrible."

"I think that's the reason Dad spent so much time in the military … he never said it, though. The other brother is an attorney in Seattle, Washington. He and Dad haven't talked for years. Don't know what happened between them; it must have been bad."

Al returned with our food. He had piled a double helping of fries on the plate. The burger smelled so good I almost ordered one. I made the wise choice for once and passed. Karen asked for another beer. I followed Al back to the bar. He gave me an appreciative nod.

When I got back to the table, Karen told me that each of her dad's brothers had three children, but she had never met them. The wife of the brother who was killed had moved to Colorado and remarried. Karen was an only child. I didn't ask about her mother.

Karen attacked the cheeseburger like a pit bull. From what I had learned from our dealings over the years, that was the way she attacked her cases. It was interesting seeing the other side of the highly-skilled detective. I was enjoying it.

She wiped her mouth with a paper napkin. "This morning I was talking to one of the detectives who's working the crossbow case." She set the napkin down and looked at me. "I shouldn't tell you this, but it's no big secret." She paused. "They have zero leads. The crossbow bolts are common and could be bought at most sporting goods stores. None of the local stores remembered selling any recently. They could have come from anywhere."

"Anything in common with the victims?" I asked.

The two guys left who had been staring at our table.

"Nothing you don't know," she said. "They both lived at the same place; both worked construction; and, strange as it may seem, both sang country music. But according to Arno Porchini, he didn't really know Lester Patterson; they didn't talk much at the boardinghouse, didn't work construction jobs together, and other than seeing each other at that country bar, didn't talk."

"Any unsolved cases involving a crossbow?"

"Good question," she said. "Maybe you should be a detective." She smiled. "No. We checked the databases and contacted the FBI. There have been a few incidents over the years where hunters were killed by arrows—none near here. And they were accidental, or so the records show. None with a crossbow."

"Sounds like the police are at square one," I said. "Scary."

She nodded. "Be careful."

I said I would. She finished her cheeseburger and second beer and said she should go home and get some rest. Regardless of what the nurse had said, she planned to go back to the hospital later.

We stopped to say bye to Al.

"Young lady," he said, "you are always welcome here. You can come by yourself. Bring your friend Chris here. Just don't drag Bubba Bob along." Al laughed at his own joke and waved as we left.

I offered Karen a ride the short distance to her car at the hospital and was surprised when she accepted.

"Nice dent," she said.

"Thanks to Hurricane Frank," I said.

"It adds character," she said and got in.

I had planned to have the unsightly wrinkle fixed, but was reconsidering. My friends constantly are telling me I need to become more of a character; this could be a start.

I edged close to her Crown Vic, and she leaned over and gave me another long, tight hug, and whispered, "Thank you."

On the twenty-minute ride back to Folly Beach, I kept picturing the beautiful, smiling face of Detective Karen Lawson. And then the equally attractive smiling face of Amber Lewis.

I nearly rear-ended a Dodge pickup when the cold, stark, frightening mental image of a crossbow wiped out the visions of both ladies.

CHAPTER 19

Friday nights during the summer had an emotional edge other evenings didn't share. Many of the *weekers*—Charles's made-up (but appropriate) name for the vacationers who came for a week—left on Saturday for the long, sad, depressing drive home, where they are met with jobs, overgrown lawns, houses needing cleaning, and the arrival of credit card bills that they used to pay for the trip.

Tonight was no exception. Larry, along with Cindy, his significant other, Charles who had no significant other, and I met on the concrete patio at Rita's. Amber was at home with Jason, who still wasn't feeling well. Cindy had arrived before the rest of us and, with her charming smile and reminder to the owner that she was a cop, secured the prime outdoor table at one of the newest and best restaurants on the island. The view from the table closest to the stucco-covered walls in the corner overlooked Center Street, and the Holiday Inn wasn't especially scenic, but it was about the busiest corner on Folly Beach and allowed us to check on the foot and vehicle traffic. The Friday evening activity was nearly as good as cable television and much cheaper. The other tables were already full with date-night couples, groups of college students, and two couples and their preschool-aged children in varying stages of bemoaning tomorrow morning's long drive home.

Cindy had an east Tennessee, droll sense of humor and could make fun of almost anyone while still maintaining a smile and calm voice. She was telling us how "excited" she was to have been on duty New Year's Eve, when she was called to break up a disturbance up the street at Woody's annual meatball drop.

"You have those in Tennessee, don't you?" asked Charles, without the smile.

"Sure," she said. Her sweet voice spewed calories into the air. "But we leave the meat in the cow; drop the whole thing. On Independence Day, we usually launch a donkey. Haven't seen that around here yet." She grinned. "We tried not to be political, but the elephant was too heavy for the catapult."

I hoped that she was kidding, and asked, "What was the disturbance about?"

A black Chrysler 300 with tinted windows gunned its engine and didn't slow as it turned on East Ashley from Center Street directly in front of us; it interrupted before Cindy could answer. Cindy looked up from her Reuben Burger. Her face went from saccharine to her most effective police stare. If she was on duty, she would have run down the street and yanked the side mirror off the car before it reached the next block. She took a deep breath and turned back to Larry. "Not my problem—tonight." She took a sip of beer. "Now where was I … Oh, yeah, it wasn't much of a disturbance." She held up her beer. "Two good ole boys had too many of these and were fighting about how much the meatball weighed." She stopped, took another sip, and giggled. "One said thirty-seven pounds; the other was sure it was thirty-five."

Charles interrupted, "How much was it?" He was always a stickler for detail; I suspect he wanted to add this speck of trivia to his collection.

"The official meatball-weigher said it was only nine pounds. Didn't impress me; our cow drop is measured in tons."

"Well," said Charles, "did you shoot the guys or throw them in prison for life?"

She looked at Charles like he was an idiot. "It was New Year's Eve, and I walked them around the building and told them the meatball was thirty-six pounds—they were both right." She laughed. "They hugged and said, 'See, I told you so.' Heck, they may be engaged to each other by now."

Larry had taken all the silence he could stomach. "Makes my life selling nuts and bolts boring. I live my life of adventure through Cindy." He scooted his green-framed metal chair so it touched Cindy's, and he put his hand on her arm.

"I think you've had enough adventure for several lifetimes," said Charles.

We knew he referred to Larry's former occupation as a cat burglar. If it hadn't been for an eight-year "time-out" he had spent with the Georgia Department of Corrections, Cindy might have met him under drastically different circumstances. Larry had gone the straight-and-narrow many years before we met, and he was one of the most honest, thoughtful, and kind people I knew.

Charles wasn't interested in Larry's nuts and bolts. He fidgeted with his napkin and took a deep breath. "Ah, the smell of hamburgers." He spread out his arms and raised his cane and pointed it at Cindy. A cherry-red owl stared at Cindy from Charles's white, long-sleeve Temple University T-shirt. "Now that we're having so much fun, Cindy, have you caught the killer yet?"

She sat erect in the bar-height chair, looking both ways to see if anyone other than present company could hear. "Don't get me on that topic." A strand of cheese from her three-cheese burger drooped out the side of her mouth. "The blankity-blank Sheriff's Department is running roughshod over us. They're treating the local officers like gofers—'go get this,' 'go get that,' 'any coffee here,' 'hey hon, go for some sandwiches.'" The temperature was in the eighties, but Cindy shivered like she had stepped out of an igloo. I had never seen her this agitated—I wasn't sure we could get her off the topic if we tried. To be honest, none of us, with the possible exception of Larry, wanted to.

"They're the experts on this, and on that; we are the dumbest gaggle of goof-offs they've ever seen," she ranted. "It was never this way when we worked with Detective Lawson. She respected our opinions. We live here, they don't; we know our citizens—warts and all, they don't. I wish she'd caught this one."

There was always tension between the Sheriff's Department and the Folly Beach Department of Public Safety. Folly didn't have any detectives, so if a case got rough, the outsiders had to be called. Even with that, I was surprised to see Cindy so irritated; it was unlike her.

None of us spoke. Cindy abruptly pushed her chair back and stood. "I'll be back," she said. "Get me another beer." She turned and stomped off the patio and around the back of the building.

Charles watched her walk away. "Think she's going to find that Chrysler?"

Larry stared at Charles and didn't comment.

I turned to Larry. "What's wrong?"

In a voice I could barely hear, he said, "She's scared." He stared at the giant Holiday Inn logo looking out over Center Street like it was keeping watch on its children. He shook his head.

"I know," said Charles. "She has reason to be."

"Charles," said Larry, "she'll never say it—trying to be cop-like and all—but she knew both victims and lived only a few feet from them. She's just been here a little over a year and doesn't know that many people outside this table. She doesn't know who to trust, doesn't know what's going on. And the Sheriff's folks are treating her like marsh scum."

"Why don't you see if she'll move in with you?" I asked. "You know you want her to."

"I've tried to ..."

Cindy bounded back. "Well, where's the beer?"

Larry pulled her chair out and grabbed her hand as she sat. "You okay?" he asked.

"Yeah, needed some air." She forced a smile and looked around for someone to get her drink.

I didn't want her to get back on the Sheriff's Office versus the Folly Beach police, so after the second round arrived, I asked, "Any word on the chief?"

"Oh, mule manure," she said as she snapped her fingers. "I almost forgot." She leaned close to the table and looked to see if anyone was listening. She waved for us to come closer. "This is in confidence. Okay?" We nodded and moved closer. She looked around again and then continued, "It'll be announced tomorrow. Mayor Amato has appointed an acting director of public safety."

"Do we know him?" asked Charles.

"No, and you don't want to," she said. Her voice hardened. "I only heard his name yesterday. Name's Clarence King, and he's a member of my *favorite* police department."

From the derisive way she spitted out *favorite*, I asked, "The County Sheriff's Department?"

She nodded and then shook her head side to side.

"Know anything about him?" asked Larry.

"Not personally," she replied, "one of the guys called a dispatcher buddy." She paused and took a bite of pizza and then looked around again. The patio was packed, but no one had the slightest interest in what we were saying. To me, that was a little depressing, but the older I got, the more people seemed to ignore me—especially those under forty.

"And …?" asked Charles, who never wanted gaps in rumor sharing.

"In a nutshell," continued Cindy, "he's near retirement. When the mayor asked for candidates, someone in the Sheriff's Department thought this would be a good way for them to get rid of King the last months before he quit. He has a reputation as a hard-ass. They say he has a horrible temper, numerous citizen complaints, and even some charges brought by fellow officers. The rumor is he was involved in an unexplained shooting a few years back."

"Sounds like a gem," said Charles. "When's he start?"

"We get to meet him in the morning," said Cindy. Once again, she shook her head.

Charles stood, stretched his arms over his head, and then returned to his seat. "Sounds like the perfect person to bring the two departments together."

Larry leaned over and gave Cindy a quick kiss on the cheek. She smiled. "Tomorrow's not here yet—drink up," she said, and held her glass in the air and toasted the heavens.

CHAPTER 20

A night of watching traffic—foot and vehicular—on Center Street, listening to stories about a New Year's Eve meatball drop, and dissing the County Sheriff's Department and the soon-to-be acting chief of the Folly Beach Department of Public Safety, had ended around midnight. Little was achieved, but we had convinced Cindy to spend the night with the local hardware store owner. Larry was thrilled, and Cindy had rolled her eyes and said that she'd spent the night in worse places. Charles had asked her to list them. She declined.

I spent the morning pretending I was a roofer. I borrowed the neighbor's ladder and attacked the bent tin roof corners with hammer, roofing nails, and caulk. The entire time I thanked the Lord for not directing me to a career in roofing.

Charles and I met at the gallery at noon. I may have missed a couple of customers, but was close to conceding that a couple of sales wouldn't save the business. Charles was more optimistic, but that was Charles. Besides, he wasn't writing the checks for rent, utilities, insurance, taxes, and countless other expenses. We sat in the back office, waited for the doorbell to ring, and twiddled our thumbs.

"What time are we going to GB's?" he asked as he got us a couple of soft drinks.

I looked up from the table. "You don't like country music."

"What makes you think I don't like that screechy, nasal-sounding, cheating, drinking, kick-the-dog, wreck-the-pickup, sell-the-kid-to-pay-for-beer, momma's-gone-to-prison music?"

"Guess I was wrong." I had heard his less-than-stellar opinion of country music several times—the latest, only four nights earlier.

"Well," he continued, "I've heard worse. Besides, we told Cal we'd be there."

"We?" I said.

Cal had told us his first set would begin at nine, so Charles met me in front of the fire station across the street from GB's a little before then. The sun was gone, but GB's Saturday night crowd hadn't yet arrived. We took the table near the back door, as far as possible from the oversized speakers that dominated the space on each side of the small stage. The bar was half-full—from GB's perspective, half-empty.

The same waitress from Tuesday was quick to our table. Charles ordered his normal Bud Light, and I had to choose from the extensive wine selection: white, red, or pink. Being the wine connoisseur, I quickly ordered white. I was tempted by the welcoming smell of frying onion rings, but resisted—momentarily. The wrinkle in her brow told me we'd better order some food or our welcome would soon end. Charles told her we'd order when she brought our drinks.

The amplified sound of hand-taps on the classic, baseball-sized, silver microphone got our attention. "Testing, testing," hissed Gregory— GB—into the mike. He looked around the half-whatever room and smiled. "Welcome to GB's. I appreciate ya'll coming out tonight. You'll be glad you did."

I looked over at Charles, who nodded agreement. He was already leaning back in the wooden chair; his Belmont College, long-sleeve T-shirt with a red and blue bear snarled at the stage. The waitress returned before GB could tell us why we'd be glad. I ordered fries and onion rings; her smile reappeared.

Apparently, GB had introduced Country Cal because the next sound I heard was the first few notes of "End of Your Story" from his road-weary guitar. He stopped playing, took a stage bow, and broke into a version of Hank Williams Sr.'s "Hey, Good Lookin'."

I knew Cal must have sung the song a zillion times, but he looked like he was debuting it tonight. His right foot tapped to the beat, he smiled from ear to ear, and Charles and I were the only two people in the bar paying attention. As soon as he finished the Williams' classic, Cal broke into another Hank Sr. hit, "My Bucket's Got a Hole in It."

Charles took a sip and looked over at me. "You've got to be kidding. That's really a song?"

I smiled. "Clearly, you failed to experience the full cultural aspects of America's music up in Detroit."

"How could I have lived this long without hearing that ditty?" he asked. Charles was making fun of Cal's playlist, while at the same time his fingers tapped on the table to the beat.

"Thank you, thank you," said Cal. "Now, boys and girls, I'm going to slow it down so you can get a-gropin' up here on the dance floor."

"Want to dance?" asked Charles. He leaned on his cane like he was going to stand.

I laughed. "Don't you dare get up," I said.

Cal was already into the second verse of "Take These Chains from My Heart" before Charles resettled and attacked the fries that had finally arrived. He was teasing about dancing, I prayed. A few couples were beginning to pay attention to the entertainment, and two were on the dance floor—not necessarily groping, but their bodies were moving closely together.

Charles's mouth was full, but it didn't stop him from talking; very little did. "Think Cal's the killer?"

"Not a clue," I said, using a phrase I was using more and more lately.

"Mighty big coincidence: him living in the same building and singing at the same place as Arno and Les." Charles turned to the stage and stared. "Could be."

"Want to ask him?" I queried. Charles's approach to life and difficult questions had begun to rub off on me.

"Let's see how many beers he has." Charles smiled, but I could tell he was considering my question. Then, in a segue that should be considered a case study in a college logic class, he said, "How're we going to get Cindy to move in with Larry? Like full-time."

In the background, I heard Cal skip several musical decades and sing a solo version of the Oak Ridge Boys' megahit, "Elvira." A strange choice for a solo act, but I'd never had a hit so who was I to question his playlist. "Charles, I know you need to be king of the world and control everything, but I'm counting on Larry and Cindy to figure that out."

"They're being a little slow about it. I haven't been to a wedding for years and have that good sport coat that's only been to funerals lately."

Charles and I have spent our entire lives on opposite ends of most everything, but he had a way of finding humor in the most unlikely places. And since I met him three years ago, we have been in situations most people only dream about—nightmares.

"Good point," I said. "We need to get them hitched right away. Next time you see Larry, tell him he needs to change his entire life so you can wear your sport coat."

"Good suggestion; I'll do that. I can always count on you for good advice."

Before the strange drifted to absurd and further, Cal finished his first set. He slung his guitar over his shoulder, smiled at the fans who were finally filling all the tables, and headed our way.

My college degree was in psychology, but I couldn't tell if he had the gait of a deranged crossbow killer or a new friend—or both.

CHAPTER 21

"Hey, Kentucky," said Cal. He looked at me and then turned to Charles, "Michigan." He raised his right hand to get the attention of the waitress. "You said you'd be here; thanks for coming."

Charles moved his cane and Tilley from the next chair and waved for Cal to sit.

"Be right there," he said. Cal turned to a nearby table occupied by three women. Two were giggling, and the other one leaned on the table to push herself into a standing position. She lunged at the singer and wrapped her ample arms around his waist. She must have weighed as much as my Lexus, dent and all; I feared for Cal's life. She was a foot shorter than Cal, but her bouffant hairdo made up the difference. He caught his breath and thanked her for the hug. She offered to buy him a drink. He said that he'd like to but was meeting friends. He nodded toward our table.

Charles leaned toward me. "You heard that, didn't you?" he asked.

"Don't get too excited about our 'new friend,'" I said. "He figures we're safer than being pythoned to death."

Cal's beer arrived at the same time he did. "Well," he said, "what'd you think about the set?"

Charles looked at the empty stage and then at Cal. "Old Hank'd be might angry with you; yes, he would."

Cal looked surprised—a sign that he didn't know Charles very well. He said, "Huh. Why?"

Grin lines appeared around Charles's mouth. "Because you're singing his songs better than he ever thought about—he'd be might angry. I'd never heard 'My Bucket's Got a Hole in It' sung better."

Finally, the truth, I thought.

"Being compared to the 'hillbilly Shakespeare' is quite a compliment," said Cal. His grin was as large as his Stetson. "Thanks, Michigan."

Before Charles could spout off more country knowledge than I knew he had, Cal had turned to the exit and the person standing in the doorway. "Look who's here," he said as he stood and headed to the door.

Arno Porchini squinted as he looked around the room. His left arm was in a sling; he looked like he had been hit by a train rather than an arrow. His sandy hair was heading all directions, his shirt was half–buttoned, and one of his mud-covered work boots was untied. He was in his forties but looked older.

I couldn't hear what Cal whispered, but he was shepherding him to our table. Arno grimaced with each step. We were in the darkest corner of the already dark room, so Arno nearly stumbled over the table before he saw who we were.

He managed a pain-infused smile. "Hi, Charles," he said, "good to see you."

I was glad he called my friend by his name. Charles, who couldn't stand to even be called Charlie, had to be on the border of violence by the Michigan proclamation.

"How're you feeling?" asked Charles.

I moved my Tilley from the other chair and pulled it out for Arno. Cal had leaned his guitar against the chair and moved it from Arno's path.

He slowly lowered his body in the chair. "Like spoiled manure," he said.

Charles nodded like he heard that all the time.

"Pills are keeping me going." Arno turned to me and stuck out his right hand. "Hi, I'm Arno."

I introduced myself, expressed condolences for his injury, and asked if he wanted a beer.

"Better not. Pills and alcohol don't mix," he said as he looked around the room.

"Amen to that," said Cal.

Arno then turned to me. "I've heard of you. Some sort of detective?"

"Not really," I laughed. "Charles and I've helped the police a few times."

"Then you'd better help them find who done this," he said and grimaced as he tried to lift his wounded wing. He then shook his head. "Cops are running all over the place; I don't think they know what they're doing."

"They'll figure it out," I said.

Arno shrugged, or half-shrugged—his left shoulder didn't move. "Cal, that's a nice guitar." His attention was now focused on the instrument leaning against the wall. "Rosewood back and sides, mahogany neck?"

Cal slowly nodded. "Sure is, John Cash had one just like it; it's a Martin."

"Who knocked a hole in it?" asked Arno as he pointed to the amateur patch job.

Cal picked up the guitar and rubbed his hand on the plywood patch. "Some old drunk in Cumberland Gap, Tennessee."

"Who fixed it?" said Charles.

"Same guy," he said. "Next day. He worked in a lumberyard. It was nice of him to try to make good, so I didn't say anything. Never had a chance to get it fixed right."

"Doesn't hurt the sound," I said. I like music, but I'm tone-deaf and wouldn't know if it affected it or not.

Arno took the instrument from Cal. "I'll fix it up good; let me know when. I'm not very good at avoiding arrows, but am a better-than-fair carpenter."

"Thanks," said Cal. "I'll take you up on it. I sure know where to find you."

Both laughed, and Cal looked at his life-beaten Timex. "Gotta go entertain my fans." He gingerly took his Martin from Arno and walked his lanky frame to the stage.

Arno seemed content with our company—or was in too much pain to move. Charles walked to the bar and bought him a Coke.

"Thanks," said Arno, "it's time to take a pill." He slowly reached into his unbuttoned shirt pocket and pulled out a prescription bottle.

"How well did you know Les Patterson?" asked Charles.

Arno popped two pills and took a swig of soft drink. "Hardly at all. We saw each other in here on Tuesdays, of course. We lived in the same building; talked some but not about anything—never really knew much about him." He hesitated and took another drink. "He worked HVAC, but not on my jobs. Seemed like a nice guy sober. After dark or on weekends, he wasn't worth seal spit."

Gregory appeared behind Arno and put his hand on his good shoulder. Arno jerked his head before turning around and seeing who it was.

"Geez, Gregory, you nearly scared the piss out of me."

"Sorry," said the bar's owner. "I just wanted to check on you. You had us scared."

"No problem," said Arno, "I'm still jumpy. Terrible about Les, though."

Arno and Gregory commiserated, while Cal began his set with the first few notes of his hit, his only hit, "End of Your Story," before going up-tempo with George Jones's blockbuster, "The Race Is On."

"Good to see you back," said Gregory, who then turned to speak to another table of patrons.

Charles was on a mission and wasn't going to be distracted by Gregory or Cal's singing.

"How well do you know Cal?" asked Charles.

"Not much more than I did Les," he replied. He kept watching Cal but was talking to Charles. "Funny, isn't it? Les, Cal, and me living at the same place and singing in here. There was no love lost between Cal and Les. I heard they even got in a couple of fights over Tuesday tip-splitting—maybe more to it, but I never heard what."

"Who started it?" I asked.

"Think it was Les. Cal's a nice guy, they say; doesn't mess with anyone. Just does what he loves—sing. He was big once, you know."

The veins in Arno's neck throbbed less; the pills were working.

"Did you see anything or anybody before you were hit?" I asked. I knew he had told the police he hadn't.

His drug-glazed eyes stared at me. "Wish to hell I did," he said. "I've pondered it a thousand times. I remember hearing a few cars, trucks, a motorcycle, but that wasn't unusual, so I didn't look that way. One could've stopped, and I wouldn't have paid attention. All I remember was a burning pain in the arm and blood squirting everywhere. It felt like I was being branded." He looked down at the sling and in a much lower voice said, "I knew I was gone. Damn, I was scared."

The crowd noise had picked up. GB's was finally filled to overflow, and Cal had turned up the mike to hold everyone's attention.

Arno began to shudder and rested his good arm on the table. "I thought I could make it out tonight," he said. "I think I need to get home. Good meeting you, Chris; see ya, Charles."

"Want me to walk you home?" asked Charles as Arno stood. His legs wobbled.

"Thanks," said Arno, "I can make it just fine; need some fresh air. Again, thanks."

He walked by the bar and spent a couple of minutes talking to a couple of people, waved to Gregory, and then headed out the door.

"Who wouldn't be scared?" asked Charles.

Who wouldn't be was right, I thought.

CHAPTER 22

Sunday morning was my favorite time. Citizens seemed more courteous; they dressed less sloppily; their dogs didn't bark as loud. The pounding on my front door made me think this wasn't going to be one of those Sundays. When I saw Charles, I knew I was right.

He was gasping for breath and leaning on his cane. His hat was askance, and he had on a long-sleeve T-shirt with Southeastern Baptist Theological Seminary on the breast pocket. "There's been another murder," he said and then brushed past me and into the kitchen. "Got any juice?"

I pointed at the refrigerator. "Who, when, where, how?"

"Stop sounding like a reporter," he said, grabbed a small container of orange juice, and made himself at home. "Give me a sec."

I had peacefully been sipping coffee when he stomped on my morning. I refilled the cup and waited.

"I was heading to the Dog for breakfast and rumors," he began. "There were a gazillion police cars in front of the Methodist Church, two fire trucks, two television vans, and yellow crime scene tape twisted around two trees and an old Chevy Corvair." He took a sip of juice and then continued, "Something was amiss."

No wonder he thinks he's a detective, I thought.

"I rushed to the tape and spotted Officer Spencer. I yelled, and he came over. I asked if Officer Ash was there. You know what my first thought was, don't you?"

"Is she okay?" I asked.

"Yeah," he said. "Spencer said she was behind the church, looking for clues. I asked him clues about what. He said there'd been another murder. Female; heard her name was Pat Rowland, but he didn't know for sure; cause of death ..."

"Crossbow arrow," I finished his sentence.

"Bolt, not arrow ... but yep. Shot in the back." He pushed his empty glass to the center of the table and stood. "Ready to go to the Dog?"

I didn't know I was going to the Dog but knew why Charles wanted to. What better place to get all the information, and then some?

*　　*　　*

"About time you got here," greeted us instead of Amber's more pleasant, typical welcome. "I've held your table, but couldn't much longer." Customers were already standing in the door, and both outdoor patios were full. Dogs were tied to the fence outside, and several were at their masters' feet, panting and patiently waiting for scraps.

"Thanks," I said and gave her a peck on the cheek. She blushed. "How'd you know I'd be here?"

"Simple—anytime there's murder and mayhem, your radar comes on, and you come running. Voila, here you are."

Soaking in nasty stares from the people waiting at the door, we took our seats, and Amber went for coffee. The smells of bacon frying arrived before the smell of steaming hot coffee. I felt at home.

"What've you heard?" I asked as she set the mugs in front of us.

"Not much," she said, and then proceeded to tell us more than I'd bet the police had discovered. "Her name's Pat Rowland—around fifty, rail-thin, attractive in a tomboy sort of way. Short cropped hair; northern accent; jogged most mornings at sunrise; wore those shiny jogging shorts, red, and usually a black T-shirt ..."

"Logos?" asked Charles.

I ignored him and thought Amber would be dangerous if she found out anything about the victim.

She gave Charles a sideways look, rubbed her chin, and then said, "Oh, yeah, I almost forgot, she lived at the Edge."

My chin dropped; the coffee mug was staring up at me; I could see my startled reflection in the dark liquid. A dog barked on the patio and jarred me to attention. "I don't suppose you know if she sang at the jamboree?" I asked, afraid of the answer.

"Don't know," said Amber. "I do know I'd better get back to work, or you'll have to hire me at your gallery."

"She didn't," said Charles. He was looking at Amber as she weaved her way among the tables.

"Didn't what?" I asked.

"Didn't sing at the jamboree. Cal told me all the singers the other night; she wasn't one. But ..." He nodded his head and looked at my coffee.

I was finally waking up, and so was my lack of patience. "But what?"

"But she was at GB's last night."

"Sure?"

"Think so—shiny red shorts, black graphic-T. She was sitting at the end of the bar. She kept looking at our table. I knew she must have been staring at the handsome young man with the stunning cane. That stick's a chick-catcher, you know?"

I didn't. "And ...?" I pushed.

"I finally figured out she was looking at Cal. She was there when we left. I gave her a chance to whistle me over, but she didn't notice my charm. I think she was arguing with GB, so that's another reason she missed my obvious appeal."

I vaguely remembered something about her, but couldn't recall what. I had also missed Charles's "obvious appeal." Before Charles continued in his fantasy world, I saw Dude headed toward the table. He was decked out in his tie-dyed, peace-symbol-adorned, T-shirt and carried *Astronomy* magazine.

He looked at the chair beside Charles. "Taken?" he asked.

"Nope," said Charles.

"We be in bow season?" asked Dude. He threw his magazine in the other vacant chair.

"Know anything about the lady?" I asked. I got Amber's attention, and she went for Dude's coffee.

"She be dead."

Charles was shaking his head. "Anything we don't already know?"

"Tough question," said Dude. "Don't know what you know."

"Had you met her?"

"Sort of."

"And ...?" asked Charles. My lack of patience was contagious.

"Heard her sharing words with that washout I have working in the store," he said. "Scrawny chick be asking if we sold sports bras. Washout told her she didn't need one. I stepped in before she told him he'd need a splint for broken nose." Dude sipped his coffee from the colorful ceramic mug Amber had slipped under his left arm. He then laughed. "She told washout where he could go—a lot hotter than Folly Beach, you bet—and she zipped out. Don't think she be doing more undergarment shopping at surf shop."

I had known Dude a year before I knew he could string together more than ten words before he would self-destruct. Now I know he can; he just doesn't very often.

None of us had ordered, but Amber brought Charles a plate of pancakes, a breakfast burrito to Dude, and for me, a bowl of god-awful granola with a pile of fruit on the side. I pushed it aside and asked for what Charles had. She said something that sounded like, "You're phenomenal," but it may have been, "You're impossible."

What happened to the customer always being right? Although I had begun to notice that my everyday attire of faded golf shirts and khaki shorts was shrinking and getting tighter.

Dude meticulously cut his burrito into tiny chunks and took a bite. "Feared I was headed for the hoosegow yesterday," he said between bites.

"Interplanetary police catch you?" asked Charles.

We had often teased about Dude coming from another planet, but had never said it to his face. *Couldn't say that again*, I thought.

If he understood what Charles meant, he ignored it. "Nope, local fuzz, blue LSD lights and all, pulled me over by the bridge at sunrise."

"LED lights," interrupted Charles, the stickler for detail.

"Lights on top of car—LSD, LST, LED … whatever," said Dude, who then turned to me. "Me tried to figure where to stash my stash until I realized I didn't have one." He nodded, "Deep breath—whew."

"What did you do wrong?" I asked. He finally had my attention.

"Nada. The Sheriff's goon squad asked if I saw anything strange the morning Arno was shot. Said they be checking all cars that zipped by around the time he be skewered. Told them asking me if I'd seen strange was like asking a shark if it seen dangerous fish."

Dude's regular table was on the other side of the restaurant and was being cleared.

"Other galaxies awaiting me," he said, waved his magazine in the air, and was gone as quickly as he had arrived.

"Chris, I've been thinking," said Charles.

My pancakes had arrived, along with a huff from Amber. She tried to encourage me to eat healthy; but overcoming six decades of bad habits, coupled with my lack of desire to present her with a challenge, I predicted she wouldn't win.

I was ready for a peaceful meal but knew once Charles began *thinking*, my digestion suffered. "I can hardly wait," I said.

"It's simple. We've got to find out who's killing these folks. It's cosmic, fate, planets aligning, the will of God, you name it ..."

I interrupted. "Foolish and dangerous."

"No, not those," he said. "For being so smart, you often miss important stuff. Let me explain. Les was killed on your doorstep—almost; Pat was near my apartment."

"And Arno was out by the bridge—nowhere near us."

"My cosmic theory's not perfect. But if you'll stop interrupting, I'll make it near perfectly clear."

I nodded and ran my fingers across my lips, officially zipping them for the duration of the explanation.

He continued, "Killing people in our backyard is a sign to get involved—plain as day. Now, who is one of our best friends? Larry. Right? Don't answer, just nod."

I did.

"Good, now who's his girlfriend? Cindy. Right?"

Another nod.

"Cindy lives at the Edge. Right?"

He continued without waiting for a nod.

"And so did Lester Patterson, Arno Porchini, and Pat Rowland, and even our new friend Country Cal."

Who might be the killer, I thought, but kept my mouth zipped.

"Chris, if anything happened to Cindy, I'd never forgive myself. And then there's Cal and Arno, both residents of you know where. This is scary. We've got to do something."

"I agree ..."

"I told you to keep quiet ..." He hesitated and then dropped his fork, "You agree?"

CHAPTER 23

Charles and I opened the gallery, but as had been typical lately, we had way too much time to talk. Customers were as scarce as winning lottery tickets. After Charles recuperated from me agreeing with him, we rehashed what we knew—the connection to the boardinghouse, the tie to GB's; and what we didn't know—motive, why a crossbow, and why we thought we had the audacity to uncover the murderer when the island was crawling with cops.

What were we missing?

"Call Larry and see when Cindy gets off," suggested Charles. "We can see what she knows about Rowland."

Cindy had to work until 7:00 p.m., but she would get lunch at 1:00; Larry planned to meet her at the Dog. I invited Charles and me. Larry was hesitant, but when I said I'd buy, he saw the wisdom of the offer. I asked Larry if we could meet at Blu, the restaurant at the Holiday Inn, instead of the Dog. There would be fewer prying eyes and ears, and those who were there would, most likely, be vacationers who couldn't care less.

Charles and I arrived a little before Cindy's lunchtime. The recently renovated restaurant was less than a third full. Most vacationers staying in the hotel were soaking in sun on the beach, touring historic Charleston, or exploring the plantations and other scenic venues in the area. They certainly weren't in the restaurant or the Landrum Gallery.

The rest of our party wasn't there yet, so we took the last empty table by the windows that overlooked the Atlantic Ocean and the majestic Folly pier. Charles asked if we were ready to hit the hard stuff or stick with soft drinks. The afternoon wasn't that old, so I said to go with the carbonated beverages. Larry walked through the door at exactly the designated time. He only had an hour since Brandon was manning the store and he was still busier than usual—a fiscal benefit of Hurricane Frank. I was happy for him, but felt a tinge of resentment. Cindy arrived during my mini-pity party. She did the typical police gaze around the room before heading to our table. The other customers watched as she crossed the room. I think they hoped to witness a drug bust—an objective look at Charles wouldn't make that farfetched.

Cindy pulled up a chair, and the others in the room went back to their mundane conversations or contemplating the choice between fries or fruit.

"Any word on the chief?" Charles asked before she settled.

"Nothing." She sounded frustrated. "Think that's bad?"

"It doesn't mean anything," I said. "I'm sure someone will let us know if there's any change."

"Get plenty of sleep last night?" asked my subtle friend Charles.

Larry turned three-days-in-the-sun red. Cindy laughed. And Charles smiled.

"Yep," she said.

"Anything on the murders?" I asked.

Cindy waited while drink orders were taken. "Not much," she said. She took a small, dog-eared notebook out of her uniform pocket and flipped through a few pages. "You already know her name was Pat Rowland, don't you?"

I nodded for all of us.

"She was around fifty," said Cindy, "an avid runner; some witnesses told me she ran every morning and most nights. I saw her running way out at the state park early some mornings. No ID. Some of our other folks are going through her room."

"Did you know her?" I asked.

"Not really. We lived on the same floor and said hello when we ran into each other. She asked how I liked it on Folly. I said fine … that was about it."

"Did she work?" asked Larry.

"If she did, she didn't say." Cindy's drink arrived, and we watched her take a gulp. She didn't notice. "Funny thing, though." Cindy paused and took a smaller sip. "She only lived there a month, but told Mrs.

Klein that she had been on Folly Beach for six. She said she spent the first five months staying here."

Charles pointed his cane at the ceiling. "Here?"

"Yeah."

"That'd be expensive," said Larry.

"Very," I said. "I don't know if they have extended-stay rates, but the rooms are more than a couple hundred bucks a night in the summer."

"Gulp," said Charles. For a second, I thought Dude was channeling through him.

"Does that make sense to anybody?" I asked as I looked from Charles to Larry to Cindy.

All head movement was horizontal.

Before one of us had a revelation about why someone would stay in a two-hundred-dollar-a-night hotel for five months and then move into a rundown boardinghouse, Folly Beach's acting director of public safety entered the room and focused a laser look at our table.

"Oh, oh," said Charles, catching him out of the corner of his eye.

Before the acting chief was within ten feet of the table, he growled, "Officer, what are you doing here?" He spat out *officer* like it was an overweight, four-letter word.

Cindy had grown up in a male-dominated home and community in Tennessee and had little fear of anything, but stood and came close to saluting. "Sir, I'm having lunch with friends."

He gave a dismissive glance at us and turned his attention to Cindy. "That's Chief King, officer. Got it?"

"Yes sir … sir, Chief King."

Cindy bent her knees to sit and then straightened back up. Chief King, although in his sixties, was a foot taller than Cindy and loomed over her and the rest of us. He ignored her and turned to Larry.

"You're from the hardware store, aren't you?"

Larry, unfortunately, had spent several years under the control of law enforcement officials and knew to kowtow to their whims. "Yes, Chief King."

"And you are?" he asked as he turned to Charles and me. I felt like I was being pulled over for speeding and getting ready to be strip-searched. We gave our names and remembered to throw in Chief King.

"Hmm. I've heard of you," he said. He leaned over and was inches from our faces, coffee breath and all. "Let me say this once and only once. If I hear of you meddling in police business, you will find your ample asses behind bars quicker than I can say *throw away the key.*" His teeth were clenched, but he still managed to add, "Is that clear?" His hands were balled into fists. An inch-long scar over his left eye pulsated as he spoke.

He stood to his full height and turned to Cindy. "Officer Ash, you've got a job to do. It isn't in here. Questions?"

"No, Chief King, I was …"

He turned and lumbered from the room; he sucked the good moods out as he left. The four tables of diners closest to us had stopped their conversations and were watching the drama unfold. Cindy stood for a minute and faced the ocean, her back to everyone. She regained her composure and turned and said, "Gentlemen, I need to get to work." She followed the chief out.

I said a silent prayer for a speedy recovery for Chief Newman.

"I'm glad you suggested we come here and not to the Dog where people would notice us," said Larry, oozing sarcasm.

Charles whispered to me, "At least our ample asses are behind us. His is on his shoulder."

Larry left to help Brandon.

Charles said he was going home and read a good book. I suggested he choose the Good Book. I went to my cottage and was tempted to climb into bed and pull the covers over my head. Instead, I sat at my computer and lost myself editing photos of the marsh. A late summer shower pelted the tin roof. The amateur repairs seemed to be working.

Did we really want to try to find a killer?

CHAPTER 24

I drifted in and out of sleep. The intense rain reminded me of Hurricane Frank, which had swept through a week earlier. Frank was a minor hurricane, but since it was my first, I didn't see anything minor about it. Minor surgery is only minor if it's happening to someone else. I shuddered at the thought of experiencing another hurricane.

Thoughts of Frank faded, and I pictured Brian Newman in a hospital bed. Would he live; would I get the chance to tell him how much I've enjoyed our time together; why was he there instead of me? Then I saw the image of Lester Patterson's lifeless body—arrow sticking in his chest, blood puddle in the mud—and only a few steps from my front yard. Pat Rowland was in the same room with me two days ago at GB's while I sat at the table talking to Arno Porchini, another target of the brutal killer. And they all lived in the same boardinghouse with Cindy. Would she be next? Was Cal a killer or potential victim? What was going on? I forced myself out of bed to check the locks on the doors. They were secure—why didn't I feel the same?

There was no way I was going back to sleep. The sun was still a couple of hours from appearing over the Atlantic, but I needed to get out of the house.

I took a shower, grabbed my Nikon and the one piece of camera equipment I hated, a tripod. It was heavy, awkward, nearly impossible to carry comfortably, but critical for low-light photos. Two hours before sunrise qualified.

Walking was not my favorite activity—truth be known, not in the top ten—but when I had my camera, it was tolerable. I walked the short distance to the Holiday Inn and was greeted by the front-desk clerk,

Diane. She was in her mid-twenties and had worked the overnight shift ever since I'd been on Folly Beach. All I knew about her was that she had a crush on Officer Spencer and had the figure of a bowling pin. What she lacked in statuesque beauty, she made up for in personality and a warm, wide smile accentuated by an overbite. That was a welcome sight to any hotel guest arriving after a long, hard drive.

I got my *complimentary* coffee and walked around the corner to the desk.

"Did you know Pat Rowland?" I asked.

"Sure," said Diane. Her hands moved away from the computer keyboard, and she leaned on the counter. "I think I saw her more than anyone here. She jogged every night around midnight. Sometimes she ran about this time in the morning, but not every day." She hesitated and then shook her head. "Many guests ignore us at the desk—like we're potted plants. Ms. Rowland spoke every time I saw her. She seemed real sweet."

I leaned closer even though the lobby was empty. "She stayed here quite a while, didn't she?"

"More than five months—five months and three days, to be exact. I looked it up for the police—some cranky old geezer from the Sheriff's Department."

I smiled and avoided asking at what age one became a geezer. "Sorry it wasn't Officer Spencer. Any idea what she was doing here?"

Diane blushed. "Umm ... no, she never talked about it. I've asked a couple of the other folks. They didn't think she worked. She had the *Do Not Disturb* sign on her door a lot. They didn't see her around the pool or at the beach. No idea what she did."

"Why'd she move?"

"You've caught me on a *no-idea* morning." Diane laughed. "She jogged the night before she left; didn't say anything other than, 'How are you?' She seemed the same. I wasn't here when she checked out."

I leaned even closer to Diane. "Do me a favor, would you? Check around. If you learn anything else about her, give me a call." I wrote down my cell number on the small Holiday Inn notepad on the counter.

"Sure," said Diane. She tore off the sheet, neatly folded it, and then put it beside the keyboard.

I started to walk away, but Diane stopped me. "Mr. Landrum … Chris … she seemed real sweet … real sweet."

I left the hotel with my camera strap slung over my right shoulder, the bulky tripod in my left hand and the coffee cup in my right. The hotel had an automatic door, so I didn't have a balance challenge this early in the day.

I walked past a couple of early morning fishermen on the pier and climbed the steps to the elevated deck on the Atlantic end. The day was already heating up, but the breeze off the ocean made it tolerable; the rain had moved out to sea. The upper deck was empty, so I had my pick of spots to set the tripod. I had often taken photos from this vantage point looking directly back toward the shore. I was never able to get any gallery-quality images, but I enjoyed the view. Looking through the viewfinder, to the left the view of town was blocked by the Holiday Inn; a few of the room lights indicated early risers. The hotel's parking lot was next, and then a four-story condo complex, the Charleston Oceanfront Villas, stared at me. Directly in front of me was the pier's gift shop and restaurant, and to the right were four smaller condo buildings. Past these condos was the location that I hadn't paid much attention to before; just another house—although a weird-looking one—but now the center of more attention than any one building should receive, the Edge.

I stared at the eclectically-constructed boardinghouse like I expected a neon light to come on giving the name of the killer. Unfortunately, the only illumination near the house was from a small streetlight that provided underwhelming illumination to the beach access path and small sand-covered parking area. I didn't know all the residents, but was certain there were two empty rooms this morning. Pat Rowland and Lester Patterson had checked out. Arno Porchini was still a resident, but barely.

I looked over the side of the pier into the darkness of the Atlantic Ocean and smiled. I remembered that there were twenty-one species of shark in the area, another bit of trivia gleaned from my fount of trivia, Charles. When I turned back to the boardinghouse, I wondered how many species of killer were here—surely a crossbow killer would qualify as one, one more dangerous than the creatures swimming below. My smile faded.

CHAPTER 25

"Good morning, Chris."

I recognized the voice but was surprised to see Detective Karen Lawson behind me. I had dropped the camera at the house and decided to drive rather than walk to the Dog. My moaning, bemoaning, and pondering the fate of my small part of the world delayed my arrival, so I couldn't be choosy when I got there. Trucks of construction workers, the two city council members, a handful of dog-walkers, and three tables of early-bird vacationers beat me. I was seated on the front patio facing the building.

"Morning, detective; join me?" I assumed she was on duty since she was in her dark pantsuit. My first thought was that something had happened to her dad.

She nodded and smiled. It was a good sign. She patted a large collie that was patiently waiting for scraps at the next table. Karen then pulled out the chair opposite me at the small table.

"I was going over to the station to update the crew on their chief, but wanted to let you know first. I knew there was about a seventy-five-percent chance you'd be here."

"Thanks. How is he?"

Amber opened the door to the patio and saw the detective. The patio was not usually Amber's station, but she had finagled her way to being the outside waitress when she had seen I couldn't find a seat inside. She was carrying two plates for another table and quickly deposited them. Her shoulders were pulled back, and she glanced—more accurately, stared—at Detective Lawson, then turned and headed inside.

Karen pretended not to notice, but she had seen Amber's less-than-hospitable look.

"Oh, yeah, dad ..." She smiled. "The docs say he should make it. They even had him up and walking a few steps last night."

"Great."

She reached across the small table and grabbed my hand. "I was so scared. Thanks for being there when he—we—needed you."

I was touched by her sentiments. She looked down and saw that she was still gripping my hand and pulled hers back. Tears were rolling down her cheeks—tears of happiness, I felt.

Amber came through the door. She carried an empty, orange ceramic mug in her right hand and a coffee carafe in her left. She stopped at the table and slapped the mug on the table in front of Karen.

"How's your dad, Detective?" she asked. She had a smile on her face, but it was her work-required look and not on the plus side of sincere.

Karen wiped her cheeks and then told her what she had shared with me. Amber filled her mug and sloshed coffee on the table. She didn't refresh my half-empty mug. Karen told Amber that she didn't want anything to eat and had to go. Amber asked her how much longer the chief would be in the hospital. She said a few more days, at least, and that he was extremely lucky to have pulled through. His excellent health was the difference. That still sounded funny, but I knew what she meant. She said that she should be going, but took another sip. She smiled.

"How are you getting along with your *acting* chief?"

I didn't know about their working relationship so chose the safe route. "Well, he has a much different approach than Chief Newman."

Her smile morphed into a laugh. "Then I suspect you've had a run-in with Chief King. My colleagues are pondering nominating the sheriff for sainthood for cleaning up our department in one brilliant move—donating his biggest pain in the ass to the Folly Beach Department of Public Safety."

I explained how the acting chief had threatened three of Folly's most "upstanding, law-abiding" citizens—Charles, Larry, and yours truly—with incarceration for simply doing their civic duty.

"*Upstanding, law-abiding*, hmm," she said between giggles. She then looked around the patio, leaned forward, and continued. Her smile was gone. "You didn't hear it from me; but Clarence King isn't just a bad apple, he's rotten to the worm."

"Why?" I asked. The dog and its owner were leaving the next table. Karen leaned over to pet it on its way out—the dog, not the owner.

She turned back to me. "I know of three sexual harassment charges against him; one of them's from me. He's heavy-handed and has been known to practice a few basic no-no's when interrogating suspects; he would have been the perfect cop in the 1930s. I'd go on, but you get the picture."

"Loud, clear, and in color," I said.

Amber was heading back to the table. "Anything else, Detective?" she said but was looking at me the entire time.

"No, thanks," said Karen. She began to stand. "I need to be going. I came over to tell the guys at the station about their boss."

"I'm glad he's doing better," said Amber. Her smile was slightly less strained. "We miss the chief around here."

We were all more than a little awkward with our byes. I stood, and Karen shook my hand and thanked me once again for being there for her dad. She nodded to Amber, who returned the nod.

I returned to my seat and asked Amber if I could get more coffee. She said, "Of course."

An interesting morning, I thought.

CHAPTER 26

I watched Detective Lawson back her unmarked Crown Vic out of the Dog's small parking area a couple of minutes before I saw Charles pedal his near-antique Schwinn bike up the street and into a narrow gap between two minivans. He swerved to miss a preschooler getting out of one of the vans. He gave the little girl a look like the-nerve-of-you-stepping-in-my-way, but quickly realized that he was the aggressor and lowered his head. I don't know if her fear was from the steel and rubber bicycle bearing down on her, or the strange-looking, shaggy man wearing a U.S. Marines long-sleeve black T-shirt and carrying a potentially deadly cane. Her mother scooted her out of Charles's way. He tipped his Tilley and apologized for his careless driving. The world was back to normal.

Charles saw me, walked around twenty or so customers milling around the front door waiting for a table, and made a beeline for the seat Karen Lawson had vacated. Her coffee mug was still on the table. He threw his hat on the third chair at the table and leaned his cane against the dog bone-shaped wooden railing.

"I see you have my coffee ready," he said as he plopped down in the chair.

I raised my eyebrows and said, "No, and if you'd been five minutes earlier, the holder of that mug would have arrested you for assaulting a toddler and reckless biking."

I reviewed the last half hour before Amber made her way back toward our table. Charles saw her coming.

"Morning, Amber," he said. He then stood and put his hand on the back of the chair. "Mind if I have a seat? Chris said I wasn't improving the appearance of your patio as was the previous occupant."

She grinned and nodded for him to be seated.

Thanks, Charles. I kicked him under the table.

She looked at the troublemaker and said with a demure smile affixed on her face, "You're a vast improvement, and *always* welcome on my patio."

He turned to me and cocked his head to the right. "See."

Amber took this opportunity to head inside to get Charles a fresh mug and breakfast.

"Other than trying to ruin my day," I said, "what brings you here?"

"Sorry," he said with about as much sincerity as a funeral home director saying "sorry for your loss" to a family paying for his livelihood. "The trouble with me is that I like to talk too much."

"You can say that again," I said.

"Oh, I didn't say it," he said. "That was President William Howard Taft." He paused, hopefully not waiting for applause. "Did you know she-crab soup was invented over in Charleston for Taft when he visited in 1909?"

I didn't know it, didn't care, and didn't care what President Taft had to say about anything, but that never stopped my friend.

"Let's try again," I said. "What brings you here?"

One of the drawbacks of the front patio was that some of the tables were close to the front door and those waiting patiently, and some not so patiently, for a table. The experienced patio diners had learned to sit facing the opposite direction. It didn't decrease the number of stares from those waiting and trying to goad the current occupants to leave, but at least we couldn't see the visual daggers. Charles and I were now experienced diners and faced away from the starving masses.

"Simple," he said. "I rode by the gallery and you weren't there, and then I headed to your house; your car wasn't there." He paused and looked toward the ceiling fan. "So I stopped at Bert's to ask if they knew where you were—they didn't; not even Mari Jon, and she knows everything."

"How many more stops before I get the answer?" I asked.

"Two; be patient."

Amy, one of the other waitresses, brought us refills on the coffee and said that Amber was stuck inside and asked me to apologize to Charles—only Charles—for not being here to *meet his needs*. He thanked her loud enough for everyone on the patio to hear.

He turned to me and said, "And then I rode by the boardinghouse to see if you were playing detective without your partner, or if there was fresh crime-scene tape."

I didn't comment, which I knew irritated him.

"And then I said, heck with him, and was riding home when I saw you sitting here waiting to buy me breakfast."

And he thought William Taft talked too much. "Next time," I said, "just tell me you were riding by and saw me."

"No fun," he said and leaned back in the chair.

The table beside us was occupied by two middle-aged men and a dog the size of a Smart car. The dog had apparently come from the beach, and the smell of its wet hair overwhelmed the appetizing smell of a large plate of pancakes Amy had delivered to their table.

Charles leaned toward me and said, "Ah, ain't the smells of the beach grand?"

He was teasing, but it was true.

He sat back again. "Why weren't you at the gallery?"

"You know Mondays are slow," I said.

"Probably because the door's locked."

We had had this conversation numerous times over the last year. To be honest, I was getting tired of debating it. "You know what I mean," I said. My hand was balled up, and the words came out stronger than I had intended.

My reaction surprised him. "Sorry," he said, "I didn't mean anything. You know how I jabber."

I felt bad. Charles was my best friend and would do anything for me. I didn't need to take my frustrations about the failing gallery out on him.

"Don't be sorry," I said. "I just can't continue losing money and don't know what to do."

"What would *we* do if you closed it?"

If I had a good answer, I would have shut the doors long ago. I shrugged.

Charles had lost interest in the trials and tribulations of a small-town gallery owner and was looking toward the street. He stood at the railing near his propped-up cane and waved. I turned to see what he had become so interested in.

Arno Porchini was crossing the street to the Dog. He looked worse than the last time I had seen him. His sling matched the color of the sandy berm beside the parking lot. Charles left the patio and met Arno before he could get to the others waiting for a table. The next thing I knew, Charles moved his hat off the vacant chair so Arno could sit without moving into the next table's comfort zone.

Arno's chest heaved, and he struggled to catch his breath. Charles called Amy over and asked for water and a second glass of ice.

"Thanks for the seat," he said to Charles. "I thought I was doing better and decided to walk. Stupid me. My arm's killing me."

"At least you're still with us," said Charles. It was intended to cheer our guest.

Arno grimaced and said, "I guess."

I asked if he needed to go back to the doctor or the hospital. He cursed and said the doctors told him it would hurt for a while and not to come back unless it got infected.

"Big help! Right?" he said. His anger was slightly muted by the pain. "They didn't tell me how a one-armed carpenter was supposed to make a living that *little while*."

"It doesn't help, I know," said Charles, "but you're lucky to be alive."

Amy returned with the water and extra ice. Arno downed the water in one gulp.

"Want something to eat?" asked Charles. "We're buying."

"Well," said Arno, "if you put it that way, sure. Thanks."

Amy took his order and promised a refill on the water.

"How well'd you know Pat?" asked Charles as soon as Amy was out of earshot.

"Not well; not well at all," he said. He gingerly moved his arm on the table trying to get it comfortable. "She hadn't been there long. Moved in a few weeks ago, I think." Amy returned with a pitcher of water and left it on the table. "Nice kid," said Arno. He watched Amy walk away.

"Did you and Pat talk?" asked Charles.

Arno laughed. Then his laughter turned to a grimace. "Oh, that hurt," he said. He hesitated until the pain subsided. "You two must really think you are detectives—all these questions." A smile returned to his face. "Found the killer yet?"

I was afraid what Charles might say, so I jumped in. "We're only worried about our friend Cindy Ash. The last thing we are is detectives." *Successful shopkeepers* would have ranked lower, but I didn't say it.

Charles took any unanswered question as an attack on his being. "So, did you and Pat talk?" he repeated.

"She'd heard me sing at the jamboree and asked me how long I'd been singing, where I was from, how I liked the boardinghouse— normal stuff like that. I never saw her that much."

"Where are you from?" said Charles.

"Good question," said Arno. He had popped some pills after he sat down. They were working their magic. His face was less taut, and he wasn't paying as much attention to his arm. "Nowhere for long. I was born in Maryland, near DC. After I left home, I bummed around the country and picked up carpentry skills as I went; don't think there's a state east of Missouri that I didn't live in."

"Ever married?" asked Charles. I sat back and wondered how long it would be before Arno used his good arm and punched my nosy buddy.

Instead of resorting to violence, Arno laughed. Yes, the pills worked. "Yeah, once," he replied. "Met her in Dayton, Ohio, got married, stayed happy three years—yeah, three years." He looked at his good hand and extended three fingers. "I thought we were happy." He paused and stared at a dog barking at its owner—begging for burrito bites, I surmised. "I came home from work building a house out by the river, and she was gone."

"Too bad," added Charles.

Arno shook his head, a sad, distant look peering out of his eyes, "Yeah," said Arno, "all she took was the checkbook, the goldfish, and my heart."

Sounds like a fine country song, I thought.

CHAPTER 27

"Think Cindy should move in with Larry?"

Jason was spending the night with his buddy Sam Perkins. Sam's father had taken the boys to Charleston after school to the latest Disney movie if the two promised to do homework together. His father worked at the Piggly Wiggly, and Monday was the one day he could count on being off.

Amber and I were sitting on the deck at the Charleston Crab House, our off-island restaurant-of-choice. She had been uncharacteristically quiet on the way over. Other than ordering, she had little to say, so I was pleased when she asked about Cindy.

I sipped my Chardonnay and then hesitated. "It's scary what's happening at the boardinghouse," I said. "She can take care of herself, but I don't see how she could stop a nut with a crossbow."

"Why would she be a target?" asked Amber.

"Why was Lester, why Arno, why Pat? I have no idea; until the police find a motive, she's not safe."

"Who else lives there?"

"Don't know for sure," I said. *Good question.* "I know Country Cal. He lived across from Arno. Les lived on the same floor, and I don't know if anyone else does." I paused and wondered if I had heard of any other guys. It seemed someone had mentioned someone with a strange name, but it didn't come to me.

"Who else?"

"Of course, Pat Rowland did, but only a month. One of the other singers at the jamboree, Heather Lee, is there, too. Mrs. Klein's the owner. She's in her eighties, and I can see her using a cross-stitch but not a crossbow. That's all I know about; there could be more."

Amber couldn't sit still. She played with her knife, took the napkin out of her lap a couple of times, and kept looking around the patio.

"I guess when I asked about Cindy, I wasn't thinking as much about her living at that boardinghouse, but if she and Larry cared enough about each other to move in together." She watched her knife twist in her hands and didn't look up.

With everything going on with a hurricane and a killer on the loose, I hadn't thought about it. "Don't know. They've been hanging around a lot lately, and Larry seems happier than I've ever seen him. Maybe so."

"They don't have much in common," she added and then giggled.

That was the first positive sign I had seen all evening.

She stopped giggling, looked back down at the knife, and slowly raised her eyes to mine.

"Don't guess we do either," she whispered.

The ball was in my court—hit it, swing and miss, or simply get out of the way.

"I think *stuff in common* isn't all it's cracked up to be. Larry and Cindy seem happy. What could Bob have in common with his charming wife, Betty?"

"Good example," she said and smiled. "What about us?"

How long could I stay in the game without hitting the ball? Where was she going with the questions? Where did I want her to go?

"No, we don't have much in common," I said. "But we have fun together. I love your sense of humor. I don't have to tell you I think you're beautiful. We get along well. I enjoy your company."

I realized how lame those reasons were. I could have said the same things about a pet Siamese cat. My floundering was interrupted when the waitress arrived with the food. I still didn't know where Amber was going with her questions; I didn't know where I would go with my answers.

She took a bite, then another sip of wine, and then stared at the creek in front of us. "Sorry I was so short with you and Detective Lawson this morning," she said. "I was surprised to see her with you." She continued to stare at the water and didn't speak for the longest time.

"To be honest, I was annoyed with my reaction when I saw her. I was … was jealous, I think."

She had set the knife down, and her hand was trembling. I reached across the table and took her shaking hand. "Jealous. Why?"

She finally made eye contact. Her head was tilted slightly, and her hair covered one eye. "I saw how she looked at you. I don't know. Something hit me; I can't explain it."

"She came over to update me on her dad. She knew we had become friends, and she wanted to let me know." I hesitated. "That's all."

Amber shook her head from side to side. "I've studied men and women for years—how they flirt, get angry, get bored, on and on. The Dog's a lab for seeing it all. Ms. Lawson has her eyes on you."

"I could be her father. I'm what, twenty-something years older? She just wanted to let me know."

"Men are idiots. You can't see what's in front of you. Why you don't run into walls is beyond me." She finally smiled. "Trust me; you're more than on that lady's radar."

She took a bite and then licked the tartar sauce off her finger. She looked down at her hands and started extending each finger, one at a time. I watched the exercise but didn't ask what she was doing.

She looked up, nodded her head, and then said, "Unless my birth certificate's wrong, I'm not that much older than your detective friend."

I tried to steer the conversation in a safer direction—even asked about her favorite topic, Jason. All to no avail. The return trip wasn't filled with any more conversation than the ride over. I held Amber's hand the entire way, but it didn't feel comfortable. I pulled in front of her apartment, and she said that she was exhausted and had to be at work early.

My day wasn't going to start before the crack of dawn, so I parked in front of the pier and walked halfway to the end. With a move lacking in grace, I plopped down on one of the benches.

What a day. Arno Porchini was on the road to recovery, the chief was going to live; an attractive detective from Charleston had her eyes on me, an even-more-attractive waitress from Folly Beach was angry with me over something I didn't understand; and I was politely reminded that I was an old geezer.

For the first time in years, I thought about my ex-wife. We had been married for twenty years, but our split was as amicable as any could be. She had decided that she needed more excitement in her life than a staid, stable, level-headed—boring—executive could provide. I could have argued, but, truth be told, she was right. When she packed the car and left for California, we both breathed a sigh of relief. I nearly laughed out loud and wondered what she would think now of her boring, crime-fighting, risk-taking ex. For a moment, I wondered what might have become of her. We hadn't had any contact for years. I hoped she was okay and found what she was looking for.

I sat for an hour and reflected on everything and nothing and then decided to head home—a home that didn't even have a goldfish for someone to take. Now I had to figure out how to get back to the car without a walker or running into a wall.

CHAPTER 28

All I felt after my evening of reflection was indigestion. The past wasn't a place I enjoyed visiting. I thought about Larry and Cindy as I stretched my aging arms and prepared for the day. An early-morning trip to Pewter Hardware should bring me back to reality.

Other than two construction workers who methodically fished through a nail bin, Brandon and Larry were the only people in the store. The smell of fresh coffee led me behind the counter to the Mr. Coffee that Larry had running full blast. He kept a handful of "borrowed" Krispy Kreme logo mugs under the counter for special visitors. Others who asked got coffee in a poster child for nonbiodegradability, a white Styrofoam cup.

"Morning, Brandon," I said. I'd finally reached the vaulted status of special and grabbed one of the ceramic mugs. "Is the tyrant working you to death?"

Brandon was standing by the register, his hands flipping through invoices. His starched, light brown Pewter Hardware shirt contrasted with the T-shirt he had under it. A glow-in-the-dark, large heart decal could faintly be seen through his thin uniform shirt.

"Nah," he replied as he looked up from the invoices. He put a hand on the pile to mark his place and then nodded toward the rear door. "He's been mighty antsy, though." Brandon looked toward the door to see if Larry was coming. "He's worried about Cindy. These killings have a lot of people worried."

Larry came back in and interrupted Brandon. He was carrying a large plastic trash container that was nearly as tall as he was. One of the construction workers hollered for him to come to the nail bin.

Brandon looked at Larry but whispered to me, "Don't tell him I said anything. He thinks if anyone knew, he'd be seen as weak."

I assured him Larry wouldn't hear it from me.

Larry and the construction workers headed to the counter. Pewter Hardware was more the dimensions of an oversize two-car garage rather than one of the big-box "home-improvement centers" off-island; I moved to the front door so Larry, Brandon, and the two customers could conduct business.

Out the window I saw Charles peddling in the direction of Larry's condo—not necessarily an unusual sight since Charles had become an unofficial patrol person on Folly Beach. Instead of writing tickets, he accumulated the latest rumors and had his finger on the pulse—however slow it may be—of the community.

I had to move again so the laborers, carrying small, brown paper bags of nails, could leave. Larry and I exchanged greetings, and he asked what had brought me in. I asked if I couldn't just come to visit a friend. He said I could, but didn't. I smiled and said that needed to change. Brandon feigned deafness and continued to look through the invoices.

The door opened. The hinges squeaked like they had ever since I had been on the island. I asked Larry once why the owner of a hardware store couldn't spray some squeak-remover stuff on the hinges. He said that the squeak was cheaper than buying a bell to announce the arrival of customers.

"Well, look who's here," said Charles as he entered the store and pointed his cane at me. "Morning, Brandon, Larry, Customer Chris. What brings you to the best hardware store on the island?"

"I could ask you the same thing," I said to the disheveled man standing in front of me. He wore a long-sleeve UCLA T-shirt; he leaned against his cane and put his canvas Tilley hat on the counter on top of the invoices that Brandon was trying to sort. That Charles-like move got a nasty look and "*Thanks*, Charles" from Brandon.

Charles didn't respond. I finally gave in and said, "I came to see Larry. Your turn."

"I was in the neighborhood and saw your car," he said. "I figured you and Larry were powwowing, so I rode by his apartment to see if it was under police surveillance—see if any female police persons ..."

"Okay," I interrupted. "I got it." I was curious if Cindy had spent the night at Larry's but wasn't going to ask. Larry would tell when he was ready.

Brandon looked up from the papers. "Officer Ash went on duty about an hour ago. She …"

"Brandon," Larry interrupted. "Why don't you go out back and move the wooden crates? We'll need somewhere to put the lumber this afternoon." He gave his full-time employee the evil eye. "I'll take care of customers and the paperwork."

Larry wasn't ready to tell, but his response to Brandon told us all we needed—wanted—to know.

I shared what I had learned yesterday about Chief Newman. Larry let out a deep sigh. The first week Larry moved to Folly Beach, he had gone to the chief and told him about his criminal past and that he knew that he would be a suspect in any crime committed on the island and not to hesitate to question him. That candid confession put Larry in good stead with the chief and led to a friendship that had grown over the years.

I neglected to tell Charles and Larry about Amber's thoughts about the chief's daughter. Nothing good could come from that revelation.

The squeaky front door drew our attention. Officer Cindy Ash, attired in full police regalia, smiled and walked to the counter. We exchanged pleasantries, and Charles asked if she had a pleasant evening. "Yep" didn't come close to the answer he wanted, but it would have to do.

"Glad I caught all of you," she said. She looked around the store and seemed satisfied that we were the only ones there. "The report on Pat Rowland's prints came to the station this morning."

"And …?" interrupted Charles.

She rolled her eyes at Charles and then looked at me. "And," she continued, "she was a private eye from Lexington, Kentucky—your neck of the woods, Chris."

"Hmm," said Charles. He grabbed his cane from the counter and pointed it at me. "You know her? Holding out on us?"

I pushed the cane out of my face. "You must know more about what presidents have said than you do about geography. We're talking about eighty miles between my hometown and Lexington."

"Does that mean no?" he asked.

"Do you know everyone on Pawleys Island?" I asked Charles. "It's about as far from here as Louisville is from Lexington."

He put his forefinger and thumb on his chin and looked at the ceiling. "Well, not everyone."

Larry had stayed out of the conversation until now. "Anyone, Charles?"

"Don't reckon," he said and pivoted toward Cindy. "This isn't about me; what else did you learn?"

"Unfortunately, little," she said. "She had a successful PI business—worked a lot with horse-farm owners, rich coal people, and even some Arab sheiks, whatever they are."

Larry gave Cindy his full attention—something he was doing more and more lately. "So why's a PI spending six months here?"

"Good question," said Cindy as she leaned against the counter and eyed the Mr. Coffee. "As soon as the Sheriff's Department found out who she was, they had someone in Lexington go by her office. She didn't have a secretary, but someone in the office suite next to hers told them she was taking an extended vacation. Someone came every few days and checked her messages and got the mail. Funny thing is she didn't give her real address when she stayed at the Holiday Inn; wrote down she was from Maryland and paid cash."

"Makes sense about the vacation, though," said Charles. "I started my vacation twenty-four years ago."

I looked at my perspective-challenged friend. "What successful anything did you leave?"

"There you go," he said, "talking about me again. We're trying to figure out the murders here. Focus."

Larry finally saw Cindy eying the coffeepot and grabbed one of the mugs for her. She must be one of the "special visitors." "Did they learn anything else?"

"Not really," said Cindy. She took the mug, gave Larry a more than a thanks-for-the-coffee look, and took a sip. "They'll get whatever legal papers they need and go in her office and search her house."

"Cindy, you said you didn't know her well, but did she give you any hint why she was here?" I asked.

She set the mug on the counter and smiled. "No, she didn't say much—girl stuff mainly ..."

"Like who're you sweet on?" interrupted Charles as he turned his gaze to Larry.

Cindy lowered her head; her face turned the color of the pink sales receipts stacked on the table. "No," she said, "more like where's the best place to get a haircut or buy makeup."

"Oh," said Charles, clearly uninterested in those topics although he could benefit from the haircut answer.

Cindy walked to the door and looked out. She put her hand on the door handle, and then mumbled something and came back to the counter.

"What's wrong?" asked Larry.

"Nothing," she said, a little too quickly. "Just keeping an eye out for our new king, Chief King. I'm on duty and on his list."

"What list?" I asked.

"You're not a fan of profanity, so I'll leave it as his poop list."

I wanted to laugh, but was impressed by her concern for my sensitive ears. "Why?"

She looked at Charles, and then at Larry, and finally returned her gaze to me. "Guilt by association. Our new king, Chief King has it in for you guys; says you're troublemakers and *his* island would be better off without you *slugs*."

We weren't going anywhere, but since Cindy needed her job, she had to get back on patrol. She reluctantly left, and Charles, Larry, and I got back to slug-talk.

His island, I thought. If he spent more time trying to catch the crossbow killer, there'd be a lot less meddling.

CHAPTER 29

The hardware store business began to bustle, so Charles and I headed to the gallery. Our customers must have been in the hardware store. We moved to the back room and hashed and rehashed everything we knew about the victims. All three were gainfully employed, although Pat claimed to be on an extended vacation; two had some tie to the country music jamboree; and most significantly, to us anyway, all lived at the rapidly-becoming-infamous boardinghouse.

Finding other similarities was more difficult. We knew that none were originally from the area. Arno was from somewhere in Maryland; Pat from Kentucky; and Les we weren't sure about but knew it wasn't South Carolina. Two were male; one female. All three knew each other slightly and didn't appear to have any history together. And all three had recent encounters with a crossbow arrow, or bolt, as Charles had clarified irritatingly often.

Regardless of how many times we analyzed what they had in common, the question "So what?" followed. After one more "So what?" Charles remembered he had a delivery to make for Dude. Along with working off-the-books for a couple of contractors, Charles made on-island deliveries for the surf shop. The money from these "tax-free" jobs allowed him to remain in his vaulted—unpaid—position as sales manager at Landrum Gallery.

He left, and I opened the business checkbook. Everything was written in black ink, but it screamed red. I listened to the doorbell not ring. I shook my head in disgust and disappointment. A bag of Cheetos kept me from falling deeper into depression—thank you, Frito-Lay.

Sometime in midafternoon, the phone—and not the bell over the front door—jarred me from my misery.

"Chris," said Charles. I could hear his labored breathing in his voice. "You'd better get over here."

"It'd help if I knew where you were. What's wrong?"

"Surf shop," he said, and the phone went dead.

If nothing else, he had my curiosity wide awake. I locked the gallery without fear of turning customers away, and briskly walked three blocks to the surf shop. By the time I reached the shop and huffed and puffed up the steps to the elevated store, I sternly told myself that I needed to lose weight. The air-conditioning slapped me in the face as I entered; it felt good. Most of Dude's sales force could have come to town for a tattoo convention. The twenty-something clerk with slicked-back hair and a sleeveless T-shirt advertising Xtrak, whatever that was, pointed toward the back. He didn't speak, and from other contacts I'd had with him, that was a blessing. His arm was covered with red and black ink; I wasn't sure, but thought the entire Gettysburg Address may have been imbedded.

Dude and Charles were standing in a corner in what could generously be called the office.

Dude saw me. "Me be amped, Chrisster," he said.

"Me be confused," I responded.

He looked at me like he couldn't understand why. Charles, who often served as a translator between Dude and me, stepped in.

"Dude's excited and a little upset," he said. "He'll explain."

That wasn't exactly what I needed to hear, but turned to Dude.

Dude's arms were crossed like he was cold. He leaned against the wall and then leaned toward me. "Travis be gone," he said and stared at me.

I shrugged, and Charles interrupted. "More, Dude."

"The Travster, be regular, youngin', under thirty, not big on surfin', he be goat boater, he be gone," said Dude, all in one breath—all meaningless. His eyes darted toward the front of the store, and then back to us, and then back to the front.

"Dude," said Charles, who was carefully watching the distracted shop owner, "let's take a walk. The store's in good hands."

"Hands," he said, still looking toward the front, "not good, but hands; let's go."

We walked out the backdoor and down the steps to the sand-covered lot. I wasn't anxious for a walk in the late-summer heat, but appreciated Charles's ploy to get Dude away from distractions.

As we walked away from the shop, I turned to Charles and whispered, "Goat boater?"

He smiled and looked at Dude, who was already a few steps in front of us. "Dude's insulting kayakers and wave skiers."

Maybe Kentuckians do need more education.

The walking, talking translator and president quotester yelled for Dude to slow down. He slowed but kept walking until he found one of the few large trees near the center of town. He walked around the tree like a dog staking out its turf and then sat and leaned against the trunk. Charles and I followed suit.

Charles spoke first. "Dude, see if I have this right. One of your regular customers, Travis Something-or-other …"

"Don't think that be his last name …" interrupted Dude.

"What is it?" I asked.

"Green," said Dude.

"Travis Green?" asked Charles.

Dude nodded.

"Okay," continued Charles, "Travis Green is in his twenties and is a regular in the shop."

Dude continued to nod.

"He's not much of a surfer but is a kayaker. Right?"

Another nod.

"And you know he's gone because he comes in every Tuesday morning before noon—has for two years—and hangs for a half hour or so."

Dude added a smile to his nod. That was a compound sentence for him.

I was getting a little impatient with the speed of Charles's translation, but my impatience came to an abrupt end with Charles's next comment.

"Travis lives at the Edge?"

Dude's smile was gone, but the nod spoke loudly.

CHAPTER 30

The roar of vehicles on Center Street, a block from where we were seated, was drowned out by the bass vibrations of "music" coming from the open windows of cars and monster trucks. The prime vacation season had ended, but there was still no shortage of visitors to the island. Squeals of preschool kids going to and from the beach were interspersed with yells of parents telling them to slow down, speed up, stop, or go.

Sweat rolled down my breastbone and my faded, red golf shirt was soaked, but I didn't want to interrupt Dude and suggest we go somewhere air-conditioned.

"Dude," I began, "what else do you know about Travis? Couldn't he have simply missed a day at the shop?"

"He be gone, Chrisster," he repeated. "He be regular as Pluto appearing. Real stable. My sun god, he owns a Volvo." He opened his arms. "How predictable that be?"

I wasn't sure about the logic, but Dude had no doubt.

"Dude," said Charles, "you might want to add that other snippet of information you told me."

"Not sure," said Dude. He was pulling on a thread on his shorts and didn't look up.

"Dude," said Charles.

His fascination with the thread abated, and he made semi-eye contact with me. "No biggie," he said, "when the Travster not show, I strolled." He stopped and went back to the thread.

"Dude!" said Charles, louder this time.

Dude slowly looked up again. "Dudester not big detective like you and Chuckster," he said. "Also, not—how they say it—constrained by search laws that inhibit the fuzz. So, visited Travis's pad." Dude turned to the tree trunk that had been his backrest, made a fist, and tapped the trunk four times as he said, "Knock, knock, knock, knock."

"And ...?" prompted Charles.

"Well," said Dude, "didn't want to make too much sound; didn't want to disturb Mrs. Klein, so turned the knob, and, big whoops, door flew open." He held both arms in the air and repeated, "Whoops!"

Charles lifted his cane, which had been resting beside him, and pointed it at Dude. "And ..."

"Heard the casa be haunted," said Dude. "Figured ghosts inviting me in. Had to go."

Dude paused. He wanted to choose his next inarticulate words wisely. My mind raced. I imagined Dude finding a dead body, a crossbow arrow protruding from the carcass; or a crossbow sitting on the table waiting for Travis to use it on his next victim; or Chief King hauling Dude to jail. Dude's response fell far short of anticlimactic.

"Didn't see the ghost. Didn't see the Travster. Didn't see a picture of the Dudester on the bedside table ..."

Charles interrupted before Dude shared a few thousand other things he didn't see. "What'd you find?"

"Smelly clothes on floor, some in closet; old TV, eighteen-incher; rotting, old orange life jacket; broken watch on table, three thirty-five o'clock; bottle of aspirin and safety razor on three-legged table near the door; and, oh yeah, road map of Colorado. That's all my nondetecting eyes viewed."

Dude didn't say much—at least not much that I could understand—but I knew he didn't miss much, so I wasn't surprised with how much he remembered. "From what you saw, Dude, did it look like he had left on his own?"

"Couldn't tell; don't rightly know how much he owned, so don't know what was gone."

"No blood or crossbow or crossbow bolt or dead body?" asked Charles.

"Didn't notice that," he said.

Dude remembered seeing a road map of Colorado and a razor; I suspect he would have noticed Travis stuffed in the closet with a crossbow bolt protruding from his chest.

"Guys," I said, "we need to tell the police."

"Tell them what?" asked Charles.

I started to reply, but Charles stopped me and started counting off on his fingers. "Should we tell them they need to call out the cavalry because one of Dude's customers forgot to come in today?" Finger two. "Maybe we could tell them that Dude broke into someone's apartment."

Dude yanked his right arm in the air like he wanted to ask a question in class. "Whoa," he said, "the ghost invited me; didn't break anything."

Charles ignored him and held up finger number three. "I got it. We could tell them Travis Green had the nerve to have a map of Colorado in his room, so he must be the killer—or dead."

I wasn't to be deterred. "Then how're we going to feel if Travis is the killer and he strikes again—what if Cindy's his next victim? What if he could be in danger, and we sat here under a tree and did nothing? What if this information could help them catch the maniac? This could help them solve it?"

Charles had finally closed his hand and stopped counting. He looked at Dude and then to his left in the direction of the Atlantic and the Edge. "Chris," he said, "as the late, not so great, president Richard Nixon once said, 'Solutions are not the answer.'"

If Nixon had really said that, he must have gotten the quote from Dude. I was clueless about what it meant but continued my argument. Finally, Charles—and even Dude, I think—agreed to tell our story to someone from the Charleston County Sheriff's Department and not risk an encounter with, as Cindy had put it, *king, Chief King*. Before we lost our nerve, or Dude disappeared back to his planet of origin, I called the Sheriff's Department from my cell phone. They agreed to have someone meet us at Landrum Gallery within the hour.

A young patrol officer strutted into the gallery forty-five minutes later. He introduced himself, and I promptly forgot his name. From what he said, I knew he wasn't well-informed about the crossbow investigation and didn't know much about the island. His hands trembled as he took notes. If this wasn't his first month on the job, it wouldn't be far off. I wasn't happy with his inexperience, but understood why our call was low on their list. Why would anyone take seriously a washed-up surfer, an unemployed whatever Charles was, and an outsider?

He listened to our story—a story that conveniently omitted Dude's invitation by a ghost to check out Travis's room. We had to repeat everything twice—not so the rookie could make sure we were consistent, but so he could get it all written down. He thanked us for being "concerned citizens" and said someone would get back with us. After he left, we remained in the gallery and agreed that that would never happen.

Dude summed it up best when he called the officer a frube—or as Charles translated, a surfer who doesn't catch a wave the whole time he's in the water.

CHAPTER 31

A hefty wind blew in from the ocean and rattled the tin roof. The unsettling noise startled me from my nap; it brought back feelings of Hurricane Frank sweeping over the house.

It had been hours since Charles, Dude, and I told our story—most of our story—to the "proper officials" and I headed home for a nap. Once I realized I wasn't going to blow away, the next sound I heard was my stomach pleading for nourishment. My cupboard was bare—its normal state—so I decided the short walk to Bert's would be my best bet to quench my hunger. A pizza warming bin was near the door. The smell of the warm, enticing pizza made my supper selection simple. I grabbed two slices of pepperoni and cheese and then walked to the cooler for a six-pack of soft drinks. From the crowd in Bert's, I knew I wasn't the only needy person on Folly Beach. But most of the customers were focused on the beer cooler and chip rack. I felt like a zookeeper studying the eating habits of my charges when I heard Cindy's pleasant voice behind me. She was wearing hot-pink shorts, a florescent lime-green sleeveless top, and pink Crocs—a drastic departure from her police garb.

"That's a healthy supper you have there." She pointed at the pizza and drinks.

She carried an identical box that had a distinct smell similar to mine. She hadn't made a drink selection yet.

"You're welcome to join me for supper," I said. There wouldn't be any pressure for me to fix food.

I was pleased when she said, "Sure. Now I don't have to buy anything to drink." She laughed.

I smiled and said, "Aren't you afraid the king will see you with me?"

She looked around the store. It was full, but no one paid attention to us. "You don't live that far from here; I'll make a run for it. You can go ahead of me and signal when the coast is clear."

"I'll get home and grab my flashlight. One flash for all clear; two will mean a king spotting."

"Hey, I'm a cop. We live on the edge." She paused and giggled, "I even live at the Edge. I'll take the chance. Now go ahead and do what men do, throw your dirty clothes under the bed and pick up the empty beer cans off the floor." She turned and headed to the rear of the store.

She was half right. There weren't any beer cans.

Cindy knocked and then opened the door before I could get to it. She stepped in and looked back outside before closing the door.

"I made it," she said. "Didn't see a single king." She was breathing heavily, and I suspected she actually did run.

During our heart-unhealthy meal, Cindy shared stories about how some of the officers had hidden some of the acting chief's papers so he couldn't find things when he needed them. Two of the guys actually let the air out of the tires on his unmarked car. And one officer, whom she refused to name, had made an anonymous call to the State Police sex crimes division to report strange activities between the acting chief of the Folly Beach Department of Public Safety and underage bathing beauties.

I told her I was shocked, but didn't try too hard to mask a smile. The police department was a close-knit community, and any outsider, especially one that was universally despised, would have a difficult time fitting in. Cindy had experienced some herself, but because of her can-do attitude and quickly learning how to play the game, her hazing was brief. Plus, she was a great cop.

She had already shared things that if word got out, could cost her, as well as her fellow officers, their jobs, so I felt comfortable telling her about Travis Green and Dude's invite by the ghost. Besides, Travis was Cindy's neighbor. She said she didn't know him much at all. He was younger and kept to himself. She occasionally heard some loud rock music coming from his room, but it wasn't on late and he was always polite. She said he drove an old Volvo, something I already knew, and worked somewhere off-island. She didn't know where, but saw his car leaving early most mornings. She thought he was off Tuesdays, which was consistent with Dude's story. She didn't remember seeing him the last few days, and his car wasn't in its usual spot.

She finished her pizza and asked if I had chips—and, while I was up, if I had beer. Fortunately, I met both of her culinary needs.

When I returned with post-meal appetizers and drinks, she said that she might see if Dude's ghost would invite her into Travis's room. I agreed that was a good idea.

"Cindy," I asked as I poured myself a drink a little more potent than Diet Pepsi. "Who else lives there? I know about Pat, Lester, Arno, Cal, Mrs. Klein, now Travis Green, and you. Anyone else?"

She had a mouth full of chips, so I waited. A few crunches later, she said, "Two more. Heather Lee and Harley McLowry."

I already knew about Heather. "She's the singer?"

"If that's what you call her. She lives behind me—one thin wall behind me. I hear her day and night doing what she calls 'singing.'" Cindy rolled her eyes, looked at the ceiling, formed a circle with her lips, and howled. "Heather calls it singing; back home we call it slaughterin' the hogs. A half-dead hog carries a tune better—a lot better."

Cindy had done what Charles, Larry, and Dude had failed to do. I laughed so hard, pizza came out my nose. After having listened to Heather, I readily agreed with Cindy.

"What do you know about her?" I asked.

"More than most of the residents," she said and then sipped her beer. "She's in her forties. With the voice God gave her, she wisely chose massage therapy to make a living. She works freelance at several spas in the area, including Millie's over here. One look at her hands tells you she uses them for her income." Cindy paused and fiddled with the chip bag. "Everything else is gut reaction. I think she's bipolar or running from something. Cops don't like to take their work home, so I don't press the issue."

"Think she could be involved in the killings?"

"Doubt it. She's a little nutty but seems harmless. She told me she's psychic. Funny what you said about the ghost though; she told me she knows the house is haunted. I figure if it is, her singing would scare any self-respecting spook away."

It was easy to see why Larry liked Cindy. She's funny, has a who-cares attitude, but is well-grounded.

She leaned back in her chair, totally comfortable with herself, and relaxed. "So, what's with you and Detective Lawson?"

That curve almost beaned me. "Nothing. Why?"

"Come on," she said. "Not only is she a fine detective—someone I could emulate—but she's an attractive woman—an attractive woman who has her eyes on you."

Has Cindy been talking to Amber? "She just appreciates that I've visited her dad in the hospital. Nothing more."

"Hmm. Then I wonder why she couldn't stop talking about you when she came to the station to tell us about the chief—how nice looking and sensitive you are and how kind of you to keep checking on them, how …"

"Tell me about Harley McLowry." I said. I'd heard enough about women's intuition.

Cindy laughed. "Coward," she said. "Okay. You know how some people start looking like their dogs? Harley told me once that his dad named him after his motorcycle. He couldn't have come up with a better name. Harley's low, wide, and loud—a Harley."

"Other than his outstanding body, know anything about him?"

"He's a plumber, but I think he's out of work more than plying his trade. He also brags about being an avid hunter."

"Bow and arrow, by any chance?"

Cindy smiled, "Yep."

"And …?" I asked. I was beginning to sound like Charles.

"And the all-knowing detectives from the Sheriff's Department say Harley had a 'decent' alibi for Lester's killing. Of course, in the spirit of openness, they wouldn't tell me what it was. Spirit of openness, huh."

"Oh," I said. "I thought that was too easy."

"Yeah, sorry," she said and looked at her pink Swatch. "I'm on first shift and need to get going. Thanks for the supper and company. To be honest, the less time I spend in my room, the better."

"I bet Larry'd do something about that," I said as I walked her to the door and noted to myself that Cindy added more pink to my house than everything in it combined.

"Yep," she said as she waved good-bye, looked both ways, and then made a run for it.

CHAPTER 32

Before Charles had a chance to settle in his favorite chair, I said we were heading to the boardinghouse. I gave him a capsule summary of supper with Cindy and the remaining cast of characters—Harley and Heather. A cool front had swept through the area, so it was in the low seventies. Charles talked me into walking.

"Hey, Harley, how ya doin'?" asked Charles. His right hand was out to shake the hand of the short, five-five or so, chunky man who was leaving the side door of the Edge as we walked across the sand-covered parking lot. The lot was also a walkway to the beach and a major thoroughfare for surfers and families headed for a day of fun.

"Umm ... fine as frog's hair," said the clearly confused gentleman. "How about you, pard?" He slowly raised his pudgy right hand and shook Charles's outstretched mitt. He was so loud that three surfers heading to the waves stopped to see what was going on. They quickly figured out it was nothing worth stopping for and continued their journey.

"Doing good, Harley. Doing good," said Charles like he was speaking to a long-lost cousin. "Meet my friend, Chris."

I didn't recall ever seeing Harley, and from what Charles had said earlier, I didn't think he knew him either. We shook hands, and I dropped Charles's name into the conversation twice on the good chance Harley had no idea who he was talking to.

I was relieved when Charles took the lead. "We're good friends with Cindy Ash and were going to see if she's in." Charles looked at the house.

"Oh, the cop," said—more accurately, yelled—Harley. The look on his face went from "who are you?" to irritation. Perhaps encounters with law enforcement had clouded his opinion of Cindy.

Harley lit a cigarette, tilted his head and blew smoke in the air, and then walked over to a shiny, black Harley-Davidson sitting beside a hand-painted, red, white, and green Volkswagen Bug. The Harley was the length of the German paint palette.

"Nice hog," said Charles as he followed Harley. "What year?"

That got a smile. "99 Road King Classic."

The bike was neatly pinstriped in red; the chrome sparkled. The parking area was sand- and occasionally dust-covered, so Harley must clean the bike often.

"Got it up in Jersey last year. Only seven thousand miles," said Harley. He was proud of his mode of transportation and was talking about something in his comfort zone.

"Stage two fuel injection?" asked Charles.

"Yep," said Harley, who was lovingly staring at the hog. "Got full manual pump for air shocks, too."

I was tempted to run to the surf shop to get Dude to translate for me.

"Wow," said Charles, who was rubbing his hand over the chrome-tipped front fender.

Harley took one last puff and flicked the cigarette butt into the parking lot far away from his prized possession. "Gotta go," he bellowed. "Got a part-time job. Have to pay for this baby."

Charles stepped back as Harley mounted his *baby*. "Know if Mrs. Klein's in?" Charles asked. "Got a question for her."

Harley leaned toward Charles. "Know about her imbibing?" he asked. He tried to lower his voice, but anyone within twenty feet would have heard.

"Tell us," said Charles.

"She's okay before 5:30; otherwise, she's 'under the weather,'" he began. "Between December 3 and March 20, the old lady drinks eggnog and Maker's Mark sprinkled with Hershey's cocoa."

I bit my tongue not to ask about the dates. Besides, Harley, Charles, and I were such good friends now, he might tell us anyway.

Harley seemed to forget about being in a hurry. He took out another cigarette and, to my chagrin, blew smoke in my face. He didn't do it on purpose; we were simply sharing a private conversation.

He continued, "She drinks Maker's the rest of the year without the eggnog and that good-for-bones stuff—what's it called?"

"Calcium," guessed Charles.

Harley aimed his fat index finger at Charles. "That's it. She drinks the bourbon on the rocks." He hesitated and then smiled, "More like, drinks it on the gravel. The ice is so small." He laughed at his joke. So did Charles; I smiled.

"She should be okay now; long way to 5:30," said Harley. He waved us away from the bike and started the engine. The pulsating roar of the motorcycle drowned out his final comment—no small accomplishment—and he slowly drove out of the lot. A cloud of dust followed.

"I didn't think you knew Harley," I said as the bike turned right on Arctic Avenue and out of our sight, but not quite out of ear range.

"Do now," he said.

"How'd you know it was him?"

"Well, the guy was alive, so I figured it wasn't Lester or Pat; knew it wasn't Cal, Arno, Cindy, or Mrs. Klein. You said Travis was MIA. He wasn't Heather. Besides, he looked like that hog that was sitting there." Charles pointed his cane to where the 99 Road King Classic had been parked.

I thought it would have saved a whole herd of words if he had simply said he recognized him from Bert's. But that wouldn't have been Charles. I didn't want to know how he knew so much about motorcycles; actually, I did want to know but didn't think I had enough time left in my life for the answer.

Harley had the look of a crossbow killer to me. I wondered how foolproof his alibi was.

CHAPTER 33

"Hello, boys. Good to see you again." Margaret Klein came to the paint-peeling apartment door dressed in a multicolored, faded lightweight robe, open-toed purple house slippers, and a hairnet covering her thinning white hair. "Come in."

I followed Charles into the tiny apartment. It felt like I'd stepped into a Charles Dickens novel. The main living area was small and felt even smaller because of the clutter and dark, wood-paneled walls. An old Victorian-style couch blocked most of the far wall; two dark-stained, wood rocking chairs with puke green cushions sat to the left in front of an exit door. There was one small window beside the blocked door, but it was covered with deep burgundy drapes. The sounds of a quiz show bellowed from the Kenmore console television.

"You're not bringing me another dead tenant, are you?" she asked as she pointed for us to sit in the rocking chairs. "My friend, Louise, was right about you, you know." She sat on the couch nearest the rockers and shook her head. "Now, poor Arno has a hole in his arm from the crazy archer; and dear, sweet Pat, oh so sweet, Pat is gone." She stopped and looked at the television. "Oh, I'm being rude. Can you hear it okay? Let me turn it up."

I would've been amazed if the volume knob turned further clockwise. A vase on the small table beside my chair vibrated from the sound waves. "No, it's fine, Mrs. Klein. Actually, we don't need to see the show; maybe we could turn it off."

"Well, okay—I guess."

Charles reached over and turned the set off before she changed her mind. All three of us stared at the television as the picture went from a quiz show to a white screen closing into a solitary, bright white dot in the middle of the picture tube. The vase stopped vibrating.

I wasn't certain what we had hoped to learn from Mrs. Klein, but I was surprised how kindly she had described Pat. I asked if she knew her well.

"Hardly at all," came her answer, interesting considering how *so sweet* she was. "She just moved in last month. Make it a point not to ask much about my tenants. That was my late husband's wish."

"Why's that?" asked Charles.

"Mind if I smoke?" she asked.

We did, but she didn't care. A crystal ashtray the size of a cake pan was sitting beside her on the overstuffed couch. It had about three packs worth of butts in it—a deadly house fire waiting to happen. She already had a cigarette in her left hand and a Zippo lighter in the other.

"My dear husband, Joseph, worked for the Ringling Bros. and Barnum & Bailey Circus from '36 to '41. He was their finance guy." She took a puff and continued, "The Ringling Brothers, seven of them in all, started the circus back in 1884 in Wisconsin—Baraboo, Wisconsin, I believe. They ran the only clean circus around. The others shortchanged customers and had gambling on the lot—nasty stuff. Well, moving on, the brothers merged with the Barnum & Bailey Circus in 1919."

"I've seen that circus a few times," said Charles.

I looked at him; I had a hard time picturing Charles at a circus—in one, maybe, but not attending.

"Not like when dear Joseph was with it," she said and shook her head, moving the cloud of smoke around above her. "Back in the day, there was only one big traveling RB circus; nothing like those three piddling units jumping around the country today. Did I tell you, the most famous clown of all, Emmett Kelly, joined the circus the same year Joseph left?"

"That's interesting," said Charles. I suspected he actually meant it.

"Being the money man with the traveling troupe, dear Joseph saw the writing on the wall. About that time, talkies were sweeping the movie world, and everyone wanted to go see the big-screen stars; the appeal of the circus was waning. So guess what?" Fortunately, Mrs. Klein didn't pause for us to guess. "Dear Joseph took the money he had made with the circus, borrowed more, and opened a chain of movie theaters." She smiled. "My dear Joseph made a boatload of money and invested it wisely enough for us to have plenty forever."

Charles leaned forward, tapped his cane on the floor, and said, "'Every *crowd* has a silver lining,' according to the circus founder, Phineas Taylor Barnum."

Mrs. Klein laughed and slapped her knee. "That's old P. T. for sure."

Mrs. Klein had shouted out an interesting story, and Charles continued to amaze me with his range of useless trivia, but nothing had been mentioned about a crossbow, nor had Mrs. Klein shed any light on why her boardinghouse was the target of a crazed killer. Why were we here?

"We ran into Harley in the parking lot," Charles said. "He's a character."

Mrs. Klein lit another cigarette and took a long draw before responding. "Old Harley has a bad habit of smoking, but he's still okay. Got one hell of a hog, too. See it?"

"Sure did," said Charles.

"Yeah," said Mrs. Klein. She set her cigarette on the overfull ashtray and focused on the black screen on the television. "It reminds me of those little motorcycles the clowns rode in the circus. I told you my husband, dear Joseph, worked for the circus, didn't I?"

We nodded. I didn't figure she could hear me without me screaming anyway.

"Now tell me again," she said, turning her attention from the screen to us, "why are you here? I don't rent rooms to homo couples—not that I have anything against the gay persuasion; don't rent to any couples."

"Cindy Ash is a good friend of ours," said Charles. "We're worried about her with the murders and all."

"I remember now," she said, "you are the boys who follow around murderers. Terrible, terrible."

"We also know Country Cal and Arno Porchini. Both live here, don't they?" asked Charles.

She turned back to the television. "After dear Joseph made all his money, he said he was tired of living in Middle America and wanted to be at the ocean. He had been to Charleston with the circus and remembered Folly Beach. Never thought to ask him why before he passed back in '84. Before starting the movie houses, he traveled the country by rail, living in circus cars. After he made some money, we traveled the world. He decided he wanted to build a house that was unlike any other. Said he wanted the circus look but plenty of space—something he never had with Ringling." She spread her arms out and looked all around the room. "This was his dream."

"He succeeded; it's unique," said Charles. He almost made it sound like a compliment.

She turned her attention back to us. "I think Travis Green killed those people." She looked at me and then back at Charles.

I finally asked why she thought that. She asked me what I said and I repeated it, at a decibel level just below a foghorn.

She nodded. "Well, he's always late with his rent, the police keep asking about him, and you know he's disappeared. He did it."

With our list of zero good suspects, we were in no position to argue—although I wouldn't have included late rent as a motive.

With that minor bit of detecting out of the way, Mrs. Klein seemed to shrink back into the blank television. "My husband, dear Joseph, owned some movie houses, you know. He had this house built for us; loved every second in it until he passed. He had an unhappy streak in him, you know. Every time he was around the ocean, he would look at the houses and say that only rich people got to enjoy living with the ocean in their backyard."

"I've often said that," commented Charles.

I'd never heard Charles say anything remotely sounding like that, but I don't always listen when he's rambling off on some obscure topic.

"Joseph made me promise that once he'd passed, that I'd turn his dream house into a boardinghouse, so poor people would have the view he adored. He didn't think I'd do it, so he had the lawyers plop it in his will. He even had an architect draw up the design to get the most rooms in it; gave me a storage room and two with private storage cubes for the renters; put in individual bathrooms for the units on this floor; the folks on the second floor have to share a bath. They squeezed a lot of stuff in here. He even joked about secret passages, like some of the circus cars had; I never saw any and think he was pulling my leg."

"That was admirable," I said.

"The lawyers said I had to do it, but didn't say when," she said with a grin. "I spent another decade rattling around this old place by myself before converting it. I hated it at first when I had to go from this big house to these tiny rooms and rent to people I didn't know. But, God rest his soul, my dear Joseph knew what he was doing. Lately, I don't need much room, and I do enjoy talking to the youngsters living here." She shook her head. "It's a shame Travis is a killer. And now I have three rooms to rent." She stared at Charles and then at his cane. "But I'm sorry. Even if you're a cripple, I won't rent to a couple, gay persuasion or not."

Charles looked at me and shrugged. "I appreciate your position, Mrs. Klein. I guess we need to be going."

"Thanks for visiting," she said. "Good luck finding somewhere to live."

Before she closed the door, she said, "Come back some day after 5:30—I'll share a jigger of Maker's with you."

We said we would and headed out.

As soon as we reached the sand-covered parking lot, Charles turned to me, put his hat on, and said, "Did you know dear Joseph worked for the circus?"

I slapped him with my Tilley.

CHAPTER 34

A cool front had lowered the temperature, but it was still in the eighties. The walkway to the beach was packed with surfers leaving the waves and college students from Charleston heading to the beach with their coolers; whiffs of suntan lotion trailed many of them. A couple of coeds carried orange boom boxes blaring the latest hits. I assumed they were the latest hits; they sounded like Cindy's hogs being slaughtered. Thankfully, my hearing wasn't what it used to be; but it was still better than Mrs. Klein's.

We had crossed Arctic Avenue and began walking up Center Street to the gallery. Coming toward us was the unmistakable wide-brimmed straw hat, with Heather Lee enjoying its shade. Instead of her bright yellow sequined blouse from the jamboree, she was wrapped in an off-white outfit that looked like a cross between medical scrubs and a karate keikogi.

As usual, Charles took the lead. "Hey, Heather," he said, "Great job on 'Sweet Dreams' the other night. Ole Patsy never did it any better."

Heather, who didn't know us from the president of Peru, didn't need a formal introduction after Charles's comment. She beamed and took a demure curtsy. "Why, thank you, kind sir."

"Coming from work?" he asked.

She was looking at my friend; her brow was wrinkled. She couldn't place Charles but knew she must know him from somewhere. "Just got off work from Milli's. I can give massages for only so long in one shift. I'm strong, but it takes a toll on my hands and arms. Heading to the beach to do some divining."

"Witch-hazel or metal rod?" asked Charles.

"I prefer willow," she said.

First Harley, now Heather. Dude, come help me translate.

"Since you're heading to the beach," continued Charles, "I'm guessing you're not looking for water."

Heather laughed like that was the funniest thing she'd heard all day. "I started divining in front of my boardinghouse for coins in the sand. Even found a man's ring last week." She paused, looked around her, and whispered, "My house is haunted … umm, and I've followed the ghost out the side door and to the beach. He's always making creaky noises in the house, but I think his psychic core is in the sand near the dunes." She looked at Charles and over at me. "The ghosts are moving on, getting out while the getting's good."

"It sounds like there's more than ghosts in the house," said Charles. "Are you scared of the killer? I'd be if I lived there."

"Not really," she said. "I'm protected by crystals in the room. And there's a cop living behind me. I'm protected. Besides, the killer's gone."

"Gone?" I asked.

"He moved the other day. Name's Travis, Travis Green." Her freckles moved closer together as she wrinkled her nose. "I told the Sheriff's Department Gestapo about him. They said they'd get him—not to worry."

"Why do you think it's him?" I asked.

"Easy," she said. "He lived across from me. His door hit mine when they opened at the same time. He called me a nutcase and said my singing gave him a headache. He did it." She snapped her fingers. "Oh, I almost forgot, I saw a demonic apparition leaving his room Monday at three in the morning."

"Yeah," said Charles, as close to speechless as I've seen him.

Heather looked at the sky and then back to Charles. "Got to go; burning daylight; ghost's psychic core is waiting."

"Think the ghosts are moving because of the killings?" asked Charles.

"Maybe … maybe not," she said and pushed the brim of her hat off her forehead. "Probably some other reason; after all, they're already dead, aren't they?"

Hard to argue with that, I thought.

She looked at her watch and said, "Ya'll come to the jamboree Tuesday. I'll sing a special song for you."

Heather skipped off toward her haunted home.

We continued our walk to the gallery. "There you go," said Charles as he looked over his shoulder toward the beach. "Case closed. A brilliant detective and cute as a button to boot."

I had unlocked the gallery door when Charles said, "Whoa. We need to go back."

"Where ... why?"

"Mrs. Klein's. Didn't she say there were private storage cubes for each of the renters?"

"Yeah, so?"

"So, after hearing her opinion of cops, think she might have forgotten to tell them about the cubes? She only told us when she shared how her dear husband deprived her of her spacious home on the beach and turned it into a pen for the indigent."

It didn't matter what I thought; Charles had already started the steamy walk back. I followed at a slower pace. He stopped before crossing Arctic near the Edge. "I'll go in alone," he said. "I can find out what we need, and I won't be tempted to fill out an application for us to move in."

Why didn't he say that before I trekked all the way back? I told him I'd wait at the Holiday Inn. He said, "Good plan, or you could go out on the beach and help Heather divine for the ghost's core."

I was lucky enough to find a seat in air-conditioned comfort in a spot overlooking the outdoor pool. It was near the end of the season, and the pool was nearly empty. The only children were preschool age and didn't seem to have a care in the world. I briefly wondered what their world would be like when they grew up.

CHAPTER 35

Charles stood over me, shaking my chair. I didn't know how long I'd been asleep. There was a large cardboard box on the floor beside him, a Bonterra Vineyards logo plastered on the side. If the box was to be believed, it had held eight bottles of Mendocino County Cabernet Sauvignon made with organically grown grapes. Charles grinned as he pulled the vacant chair near me and plopped down. He was a dedicated beer drinker, so I detected that his smile wasn't because he had hijacked a case of wine—organically grown or not.

"First, the bad news," he began. His smile was still intact. "Mrs. Klein still won't rent to us."

I couldn't tell if I was relieved or wanted to grab his cane and smack him across his thick skull. Instead of doing either, I waited for the good news. And wait, I had to do. He told me two stories that Mrs. Klein had shared about her late, dear Joseph, who air-conditioned all his theaters to bring in customers year-round and invented his own "secret formula" popcorn salt. I was beginning to worry that Charles was going to go off on a tangent about what president attended a movie at one of dear Joseph's movie houses. Heather's ghost must have been smiling down—or up—on me; Charles got around to the wine box.

He leaned closer, looked around the hotel to make sure no one was eavesdropping, and then, in a much lower voice, continued, "Now the good news."

Thank God.

"Mrs. Klein told me that the week before Pat Rowland was killed, she had knocked on the landlord's door and asked if she could come in." Charles continued to look around. "Mrs. Klein was surprised since this was really the first time Pat had talked to her since moving in; or, as Mrs. Klein put it, 'the first time she *remembered* Pat talking to her.'"

"Before 5:30," I said.

"Must have been," said Charles. "Anyway, Pat asked Mrs. Klein if she had somewhere she could store this." Charles nodded toward the box on the floor. "Mrs. Klein told her, sure, each room has one storage bin, and she could put it there. Mrs. Klein said that Pat didn't seem interested until she told her that the bin had a lock and only she and Pat would have the combination. That appeased Pat.

"Did Mrs. Klein tell the police about the box?" I asked. "I assume they asked her about Pat's room and other stuff she may have had."

"I asked her." He smiled. "She told me the 'terrible, blankity-blank, pissant new chief of police King' pushed his way into her apartment and demanded that she open 'poor Pat's door,' and that she 'damned well better do it now!'" Charles giggled. "And I won't tell you what she said instead of blankity-blank—I hadn't heard one of them myself; circus lingo, maybe."

"She didn't tell him about it?" I asked.

"She said he told her to open Pat's door, and that's exactly what she did. She said he had interrupted her cocktail hour. She also said that two other holier-than-thou detectives from the Sheriff's Department also demanded that she let them into Pat's room." Charles paused and cocked his head in the direction of the boardinghouse. "Don't think Mrs. Klein's a big contributor to the police benevolent fund."

I looked at the box, then at the kids playing in the pool, and then back to Charles. "Instead of giving a box of possible evidence to the police, Mrs. Klein just gave it to a disheveled, allegedly gay, tenant-reject carrying a cane."

"Of course not," he said in mock exasperation. "I told her how great a detective my friend was, and if I was straight, she'd be at the top of my A-list to come a courtin'. She walked over to her refrigerator, took out a tin recipe box, took out a coffee-stained note card, looked at the card, and said, 'Down the hall, third door on the right, door's unlocked, last box on the right, 17 right, 7 left, 4 right.'"

During my nap, I had become a great detective, and Charles had turned gay!

We brilliantly decided that the public area of the Folly Beach Holiday Inn wasn't the best location to start rooting through a box owned by the late Pat Rowland and secured by means that could easily be construed as ill-achieved. Charles carried the box and I followed as we walked up Center Street to the gallery. My imagination was in high gear. I could almost see everybody we passed looking at the box like it contained a knot of vipers. Maybe it did.

CHAPTER 36

Pat Rowland may have been a fantastic detective; she may have done superb work for wealthy horse-farm owners and Arab sheiks; but her organizational skills were one step below sucky. After ten minutes of wading through the pile of papers from the Bonterra box, I wished it still contained the original bottles of cabernet. Unless the papers were organized by fiber content or type font, we couldn't find any semblance of order. Most of the items were receipts from gas stations, motels, a few restaurants, and a couple of clothing stores.

We sat at the rickety table in the office at Landrum Gallery. My preference was to take the box to the house, but Charles reminded me that we had a gallery to run and he didn't want to deprive anxious shoppers the chance to buy photographs to adorn their walls. I said, "Whatever."

Charles shuffled a handful of gasoline receipts. "I thought I was disorganized. This crapola makes me look like the guy who taught Dewey how to organize his decimal system," he said.

"You are disorganized," I said, "but you're right about this."

The front bell gave me a welcome break from piecing together Pat's puzzle. A vacationer from Dayton had returned from an earlier visit and bought a framed photo of Folly's iconic Morris Island Lighthouse. I rang up the purchase, thanked the customer, and grudgingly realized that Charles had been right about giving customers a chance to spend their money.

I returned to the office to listen to my sales manager say he told me so and to see his effort to organize Pat's papers. Six stacks were in front of him.

"Most of the receipts came from five cities plus Lexington," he said and nodded to the pile closest to me. "Those are from Myrtle Beach; those from Savannah; that small group from Columbia; those from Atlanta; and this one from Charleston and Folly." He pointed to each group as he said the name of the city.

He still had about an inch-high pile in front of him. "And those?" I asked as I joined into the pointing game.

"Still working on it," he said and handed me a book from the top of the stack. "You figure this out; I'll wade through these." He looked back at the remaining items.

The book was the size of a standard hardcover novel but half as thick. The faux-leather cover was blank, as were most of the pages. It reminded me of a small sketchbook found in art supply stores. My guess was that Pat used it as a ledger and time sheet to bill clients. About half the pages had names, dates, and a column of times, with hours written to be billed. At the bottom of each page, she had written dollar amounts with a date beside each—some were noted as paid with cash, but most listed a check number. The gurus in the accounting department at my former employer would have gone into cardiac arrest if I turned in records like these; but if it worked for Pat, who was I to argue.

Pat wasn't around to explain her system, so I made assumptions. The last six pages began with the name Stewart Barlow. The name was underlined three times. Her organizational skills were lacking, but her penmanship was excellent. Of course, compared to mine, the writing of a dyslexic chimp would be excellent. The script was tiny but legible. The pages were unlined, but the writing was meticulous. Beside Barlow's name was two addresses in Lexington; one was on Main Street, so I guessed it was a business. Three phone numbers were next, followed by a date from last December. After the date, Pat had penned, "Missing: $30,000, 2 paintings, SS and passport. Timothy Bussy, Peter Loy, Lawrence Craft."

I turned to Charles. "When do the receipts from the five cities begin?"

"Aha," he said, "I knew that was coming." He had a sly grin on his face and pointed to the pile from Atlanta. "January 3."

"Are all the receipts from Atlanta from about the same time?" I asked.

"Yep," he nodded. "Hotels, gas, restaurants, two from pawnshops; all January."

In her ledger she had written "$20,000 (cash!) retainer" after Barlow's phone numbers and immediately under it she had "$9,000 exp./150 hrs. at $60." To the right of that, she had a double line with "11,000 bal."

"So?" Charles asked.

I explained that it would appear that Mr. Barlow had hired Pat and paid her a significant retainer and she had used almost half of it in Atlanta.

"Shee," he said. "We need to raise our C&C Detective Agency rates and find suckers like Barlow."

I ignored his comment about our—his—imaginary detective agency. "Where was she the first two weeks in February?"

Charles looked at me like *how would you know that*, but he didn't ask and began looking for dates in the next four piles. "Savannah," he said.

I told him that she used another five thousand of Barlow's dollars during that period. The bills from her Savannah trip were similar to those from Atlanta.

It took us another hour to piece together that Pat had been to each of the five cities on business for Barlow. She had depleted the retainer in Columbia, and he had wired an additional fifteen thousand. Her trek to other cities had ended in March, when she arrived on Folly Beach, but her expenses escalated. Barlow had wired money each month to cover her fee at sixty dollars per hour. Her Holiday Inn bill alone for the five months she stayed exceeded thirty thousand dollars.

"No wonder she moved in with Mrs. Klein," said Charles.

I had always hated doing paperwork and Charles had never done any, so after spending an absolutely gorgeous afternoon plodding through Pat's box-o-stuff, we decided a gathering of friends was in order. Besides, we had no clue as to what she was looking for in the collection of receipts and ledger notes. Amber had to spend time with Jason on homework, so I knew she wasn't available. I agreed to call Larry, and Charles asked if he could invite Cal, if he could find him. The more the merrier, we agreed. Neither of us suggested inviting Acting Chief King or anyone from the Charleston County Sheriff's Department.

CHAPTER 37

Folly Beach had often been saddled with the difference-between-night-and-day comparison to its nearby neighbor, Charleston. Compared to the stately mansions in Charleston, my house was a dump. But I'll take Folly anytime.

My backyard was small by most standards—a true blessing. Yard work was right up there with cooking, exercise, and sumo wrestling on my to-don't list. The fewer blades of grass, the better. There was room for a wooden, mildewed picnic table that came with the house and two black, plastic lounge chairs I bought on sale from Larry. My neighbor's yard sported a stately, although wind-worn, pine that graciously blocked the late afternoon sun from the yard.

During my few years on Folly Beach, I had learned, with apologies to Las Vegas, "What happened in the backyard, stayed in the backyard." Regardless of how illegal, illicit, or downright salacious, unless the neighbor's activities spilled into your yard, they were overlooked by most everyone, including Folly's finest. I had never had a gathering that would qualify under any of those categories, but it was comforting knowing the possibility existed.

Larry and Charles walked around the house together and said they had met in the front yard. Charles had found Cal, who told him he would join us in a half hour or so, unless he got a call from Carrie Underwood asking him to join her in concert. But, he had confessed to Charles, the chance of that was "on the underside of zero."

We had perfected our instant parties after three years of practice-practice-practice. Larry was assigned to bring the beer and always did. Charles said he would bring the snacks, but never did. And I was to furnish my beverage of choice, wine. I never failed. I also had to have snacks on hand. Charles had told Cal he could bring the musical entertainment.

Charles and I took turns filling Larry in on what we had learned about Pat and our visit to Mrs. Klein. Larry, pulling from his checkered past, reminded us that the contents of the box was evidence in a multiple murder and our borrowing it was, most likely, a felony. We agreed to turn it over to the "proper authorities" tomorrow. "After we make copies," Charles added under his breath.

Cal sashayed around the corner before Larry could enlighten us on the booking procedures before our indoctrination to the state prison system.

"Hey, Michigan, Kentucky, Hardware Store Person," said Cal. "Thanks for the invite."

He wore his signature Stetson, khakis, and a short-sleeve, bright orange golf shirt with the Titleist logo on the front. He had a beat-up guitar case in his right hand and a six-pack of Coors in his left. He looked like Country Club Cal.

Charles formally introduced Larry to Cal while I took the beer to the refrigerator.

On my way back, I heard Cal ask, "Ever been a jockey?" He looked down at Larry.

I cringed. Larry hated horses.

"Never," said Larry, curtly.

"Oh," said Cal.

Charles sensed a lack of instant bonding between the two. "Any murders at your home this afternoon?" he asked, like it was an everyday occurrence.

"Don't think so, Michigan," Cal replied. He had turned away from Larry and looked around like he was missing something.

Larry cleared his throat. "Let me get you a beer," he said.

"Much obliged."

Larry headed to the kitchen, and Cal thanked us again for inviting him. "Tight quarters at home," he said. "But not much to do outside except get plastered and saunter into things I better avoid."

Larry handed him a Coors.

Cal tipped his hat toward Larry. "Thanks. You're a courtin' the cop from my building?"

Larry looked up at Cal, his jaw tensed. "Officer Ash and I are dating."

"Yeah," said Cal, "I seen you around before. She seems nice, real cute-like."

Charles felt the tension and interrupted. "Cal, how was the jamboree last night?"

"Sort of a downer, Michigan," he said, turning away from Larry. "Everybody's getting bummed by the murders. I didn't know her much, but a few of the gals there had talked a lot to Rowland. She'd hung around some; spent most of her time on a stool at the bar. They were crying in their beer." He shook his head. "Folk're staying home—scared. Nearly half the people there were cops. Do they think the killer'll bring his danged crossbow into GB's and start shooting arrows around the room? Don't know what to think; no, don't know what to think."

"What were the police doing?" I asked.

"Trying to look inconspicuous," said Cal. He giggled. "Yeah, inconspicuous. About ninety degrees in there, and you got these guys with burr haircuts, shiny, polished, black dress shoes, armpit-stained sport coats, with bulges barely hiding their guns. Yep, inconspicuous."

"Local or Sheriff's Department?" asked Charles.

"I don't know all the local cops like you do," said Cal. He slowly turned to Larry. "But they didn't look familiar."

"Did Heather sing?" asked Charles.

Cal smiled. "She was there. Stood on the stage. Made noises into the mike. Sing? Wouldn't say so."

Larry had opened a family-size bag of chips and poured them in a large mixing bowl he found in the kitchen—not the bowl's intended use, but I was certain I'd never be mixing anything in it. He went back and brought out three frosty brews and told me I was on my own getting wine. We all sat on the bench seats attached to the picnic table. We touched our glasses together "in memory of our friends from the Edge," said Charles. I thought about Cal singing "Amazing Grace" at the jamboree a couple of weeks earlier.

"Larry," said Cal, "are you worried about Officer Ash living where she does?"

"Why?" asked Larry, much too quickly.

"I was thinking about Heather," he replied as he took off his Stetson and set it on the guitar case beside the table. "The gal can't sing a lick, and she's as strange as a praying mantis—talking about ghosts going bump in the night, divining for goo-goo spirits, and all. But I'd hate to see anything happen to her, living where she does and all. Just thought you'd be worried about your cop gal, that's all."

Larry lowered his head and slowly took a chip from the bowl. I knew he was worried but also knew calling Cindy "cop gal" wasn't wise. Charles was rubbing off on me. "Cal, did you know Travis Green? I hear he's split," I said.

Cal's head jerked toward me and twitched. His mouth barely moved when he said, "The first time I met him, he told me country music was for old farts, sagging-boobed broads, and Democrats." Cal turned to Larry and then to Charles. "That was our longest conversation—if you could call it a conversation."

I saw a slight smile flicker across Larry's face. "Suppose he's not jamboree regular?"

Cal leaned down to his guitar case, took his Stetson and placed it carefully on the ground, and took out his classic Martin. "Speaking in Heather-speak, I'd have to say that the vibes improved a bunch at home when Green, that little toad, hit the road."

"Think he's the killer?" asked Charles.

"He's my bet," said Cal. He hesitated, ran his right hand over the strings of his guitar, and stared at the plywood patch. "If he isn't, the killer could do worse than skewering him."

Maybe we should hold our next fun-filled party at a funeral home, I thought.

Fortunately, a half dozen beers and a bottle of wine later, the mood had swung from depressing, somber, and hostile, to laid-back, mellow, and neutral, and then to giddy, funny, and festive. I don't think it made it to illegal, illicit, and definitely not salacious—perhaps next time.

Even Larry loosened some when Cal told us how he had toured the South for forty-plus years, the last thirty of them in a white 1971 Cadillac Eldorado.

"Bought it in 1973 from a country star who'd gone the same route I took earlier—booze, drugs, cheap-expensive women." Cal strummed the guitar the entire time he was talking. "The poor guy bought the Caddy new for eight grand. The payments came due more often than his checks for singing. The night before I got it, he was saturated and backed it into the only light pole in an empty parking lot at a two-bit bar; put a god-awful dent in the rear." Cal laughed. "The Caddy was about the length of the Queen Mary, so I never got around to fixing the rear—didn't need all that space anyhow." He hesitated, hit a couple of soft licks, and said, "Made parallel parking a hell of a lot easier; never worried about the car behind me."

I could identify with that. All I had to worry about was what was in front of me.

CHAPTER 38

A late summer thunderstorm swept through the Lowcountry Thursday morning. The paper said the rain would move out to sea by midmorning and had mentioned a tropical storm that Florida might need to worry about sometime late next week. They could have it.

I looked out the kitchen window for remnants of last night's party—illegal, illicit, or otherwise. A few stray chips were all that remained. The night had had its ups and downs, but as the hours passed, things improved. Cal and Larry had appeared on better terms by the end of the night. They had put their daggers, barbs, and hostile stares away. We had nudged Cal into a miniconcert. Listening to him pull songs from the Hank Williams Sr. songbook interspersed with tearjerkers from the early sixties, I remember thinking I had been sent back through time to a table behind an old roadhouse somewhere in Alabama—old-timers talking about getting in the cotton crop or talking about the "Commie-led civil rights uproar yonder in Selma." I also remember thinking I should thank God every day for such good friends as Charles, Larry, and maybe Cal—if he didn't turn out to be a killer.

That jarred me back to the present. Sometime during the evening, Charles and I had agreed that I would get Pat's cache copied and turned over to the police. I didn't remember which police or even if we had decided. I did recall that he would staff the gallery so I could take care of that simple task.

Rain or not, it would be a good time to visit Brian, possibly have lunch with Bob, get the papers copied, and then find the nearest police officer to hand the originals to. Would they believe me if I said the box was left on my doorstep?

Traffic was light on Folly Road—the rain was keeping the day-trippers away, and it was after the morning rush hour. That was good since the windshield wipers were working overtime and still not keeping up with the downpour; standing water covered long strips of the roadway.

The rain had eased slightly by the time I pulled in the hospital, but I still had to slop through puddles to get from the parking garage to the covered entrance. My deck shoes were soaked; why had I chosen today to make the visit? I stopped feeling sorry for myself when I waited for the elevator and realized how fortunate it was that I was visiting a living director of public safety and friend.

I forgot my wet feet and water-dripping Tilley when I peeked in Brian's room and saw him sitting on the bedside chair. He was alert, had only one tube running from his body, and was reading *People* magazine. It was a fantastic sight.

We exchanged pleasantries. I asked when he would escape, and he said sometime over the weekend—"unless I kick the bucket before then," he added. A clear sign that his sense of humor was back.

He threw the magazine at the table about five feet from his chair. It missed. More recovery apparently was needed. "So," he said, "I hear the acting chief thinks you and your band of misfits are one step above baby killers and goat thieves."

"He doesn't appear to have your tolerance for community involvement by law-abiding citizens," I said. "Who told you that?"

He grinned. "I have sources."

Every member of the Folly Beach Department of Public Safety had visited their chief, some multiple times, so I didn't know who his sources were, but it would have been a safe bet that each of them wore a badge.

"Any idea about work? It's no secret that the acting King is driving everyone crazy on *your* island."

His smile faded. "Not really; it'll be months, I'm afraid."

"Brian, with your contact in the Sheriff's Department, I suspect you're up on the crossbow thing. Is anyone making progress? I'm worried."

"Why?" he asked.

"Mainly because Cindy Ash lives at the Edge. But since this has started, I've gotten to know a few of the others—Country Cal, Arno Porchini, Harley Something, and even Heather Lee. Any of them could be next. It's scary."

Brian kept alternating his gaze from me to the door leading to the corridor. "Everybody's been trying to shield me from the investigation—keep my stress level down, they say—but according to Detective Lawson, the Sheriff's Department is doing all it can. There's an unusual shortage of leads for such visible crimes."

Brian had always referred to his daughter by her title when work was involved.

"What about your guys?" I asked.

He looked toward the door. "You didn't hear it from me, but they hate their acting chief. He's treating them like head lice, not listening to anything they say; he's pompous, knows it all, and tells his colleagues from the Sheriff's Department how stupid my officers are." He paused; his hands gripped the chair arms. His stare burned into my brain. "And I can't do a damn thing about it—not a damn thing."

A nurse came through the open door. "Mr. Newman," she said with a tone of finality, "time to get back to bed and get some rest." She was about six feet tall and had the bulk of a pro running back. He wasn't about to argue. He stood on his own but kept a tight grip on the bedside table. Before he reached the bed, Nurse NFL turned to me and said, "He *needs* to rest now." She stopped and looked toward the door. No argument from me either. I told Brian I'd see him later. He thanked me for coming. As I headed to the door, he said, "I'm worried, too. Be careful."

CHAPTER 39

I had called Bob on the way to the hospital and got his machine; left a message about lunch, but hadn't heard from him. The rain had stopped, and I was thinking about calling again as I maneuvered around the puddles in the hospital's lot. I changed my mind when I saw Detective Lawson's blue Crown Vic pull into a space two rows from my car.

I was between her and the hospital entrance, so I waited.

She seemed surprised to see me in the lot but covered it well with a smile. She was dressed in her on-duty attire with her hair pulled back. She looked both professional and attractive. "Here to visit Dad?"

I told her I'd already seen him and that Nurse NFL whistled naptime.

She laughed. "She has a way about her. We could use her on the force."

Karen was off duty and stopped before heading home. I stood in the lot and didn't know what to say. She solved that problem when she asked if I wanted to walk with her to Al's—she was starved.

During the short walk, Karen talked about how relieved she was about her dad's recovery. She walked a little peppier when she talked about him. She was worried who would take care of him after he was released, and I tried to reassure her that he was self-supporting and would need little assistance. Besides, I said his officers would be checking on him more than he wanted.

A block before Al's, she reached over and grabbed my right hand. "Thanks for being there for him." She gave my hand a tight squeeze, and abruptly let go. She looked away.

"He's a good guy. I'm glad he's okay."

Al's was nearly full as we crossed the threshold into the bar and went from light to dark.

"Oh, Lordy," bellowed Al when he saw us. "I hope this isn't a raid. First time I've been full in weeks."

Customers at the two tables closest to the door abruptly stopped their conversations and turned to see who had entered. They didn't see battering rams or semiautomatic weapons being brandished by burly guys wearing black vests with POLICE emblazoned on the front, so they went back to their burgers.

Al grinned; his coffee-stained teeth reflected his age and bumpy life.

Karen leaned over the bar, and in her most official voice said, "If I can't get one of your world-famous cheeseburgers in the next fifteen minutes, I'll haul you out of here quicker than you can scream police brutality."

She winked at the aged barkeep/restaurant owner; Al laughed again. I stood back and admired the detective at work.

"Miss lady detective," said Al, "you ain't getting anything to eat until you tell me how your daddy's doing."

Instead of pulling her handcuffs, Detective Lawson gave Al a glowing update.

"Fantabulous," said Al. "You bring him here when he gets out of that hospital. I'll treat him to the biggest, best burger in these here United States." Al turned to me. "I'll send the bill to Bubba Bob."

"Good idea," I said. "What could be better for a heart attack victim than a big, juicy hamburger?"

"Don't forget the double slice of cheese." Al's grin widened, and he continued, "Chill, man can't live on lettuce alone."

Al told Karen that he'd be able to meet her culinary needs, but "Bubba's Booth" wasn't available and the "squatters" in it wouldn't be leaving anytime soon. She said that wasn't a problem and that "just being in your company" made it worthwhile. "That's so sweet," replied Al. The syrup flowed freely.

We were seated on mismatched wooden chairs at a small table near the front window instead of the soft, and broken-down, vinyl-topped bench in Al's only booth. The table slanted toward the blacked-out front window; a stack of bar napkins was wedged under one of the legs to keep the top from looking like a ski slope. The cheeseburgers and fries tasted just as good as they did at the booth.

"Any news on the crossbow killer?" I asked between bites.

"You know I can't tell you anything," she said as she surveyed the diners. As usual, we were the only Caucasians there. Other customers glanced our way. I didn't know if it was because of the pigment of our skin, the attractiveness of a young female, or the transparent nature of her occupation.

She took another bite, looked down at her fries, and said, "Off the record?"

I nodded.

"Our department's throwing all its resources at it."

"Except you?" I said.

"Yeah … that's crap."

"Why not you?"

"It galls me," she started. "I've been the primary on every homicide on Folly Beach for the last five years—you know that, you've been in the middle of most of them." Her shoulders were tensed, her left hand pushed down on the table jiggling the delicate balance provided by the bar napkins. "And all of a sudden, the Sheriff decides that since my father is chief, I couldn't objectively investigate the murders. Crap."

"That's ridiculous," I said.

"He says it's because of Dad's heart attack. Just crap. Now your new acting chief's making it worse. Instead of using the experienced eyes and ears of the Folly force, he's pushing them away."

"That's what I hear. Leads?"

And here I sat with a box of potential leads in the car. Should I tell Karen? Why was I hesitating?

"Other than the victims living at the same place and seeing each other at GB's weekly gathering, there's nothing tying them together."

"Could it be a nut killing for no reason other than they live there?"

Karen looked around the room. Her hand was more relaxed. "Sure, it could; but random killings within such a small target group are rare. There's some tie."

"I hear one of the residents, Travis Green, has skipped. What happened to him?"

"There's a BOLO on his car, but all it takes is a couple of license plate switches to screw up the system. Law-abiding citizens don't check to see if the plates on their vehicles are theirs. Just being gone makes him a suspect."

"What about the others?" I asked. I was surprised by her candor.

"When you throw a bunch of people, some working, some semiworking, in a low-rent boardinghouse on Folly Beach, you can be assured of a mixed bag of backgrounds. We've found a felony, a few misdemeanors, a herd of divorces, more than a handful of DUIs, and bankruptcies galore." She stopped and ate a fry. "Heavens, Chris, we even found a cop!"

"No Olympic crossbow champs?"

She giggled; her eyes brightened even in the dim light. I assumed it was because of my charm, but most likely, it was her second beer. "Well, as a matter of fact, one of the residents, Harley McLowry, hasn't bagged any Olympic medals, but had shot a few deer with a bow and arrow. He doesn't have strong alibis—no witnesses to where he was; said he was at home or out for a ride—but he's passed a lie detector test."

"What next?" I asked.

Rap music—or as Bob calls it, rap-crap—blared from the jukebox, and I had to lean in to hear. I was tempted to contribute a couple of dollars and punch up some country.

"They're battling with a judge now," she said. "They want warrants to search all the apartments and vehicles of those who live in the house, but the tight-reared judge says there's not probable cause. Cindy Ash volunteered her apartment for a search. That happened yesterday; and, of course, nothing was found."

"She's scared," I said.

"Don't blame her. I'd be." Karen stared at me and began to say something.

When she stopped, I asked, "What?"

"You and Charles aren't playing detective, are you?"

"Of course not."

Believe me, believe me, please believe me.

"Remember, you're talking to a highly-trained, skilled, experienced detective."

"We're worried about our friends," I said. "I have no interest in getting involved with a loony killer."

Can I actually fool a highly-trained, skilled, experienced detective?

"Glad to hear it," she said.

I had no training, little experience, and no skills, but still didn't believe her. I felt the Chardonnay turning sour in my stomach. Should I tell her about the box? Wouldn't it be better to turn it over to someone else to keep her out of the loop?

Were Charles and I really trying to find the killer? Was Cindy in real danger? Was Cal? Arno? Heather? Harley? And even Mrs. Klein?

And the more frightening question, was one of them the killer?

I hadn't realized how far my mind had wandered until I heard her tapping on the table.

"Huh?" I said.

"How's Amber?" Karen had finished her heart-healthy cheeseburger and was on her last few fries.

"Oh, fine." I said. *Went out on a limb with that one, didn't I*, I thought.

"She's a lucky lady."

Al finally made it to our table before I could reply. His arthritic knees slowed him more than usual. It hadn't hit me until now that he was the bartender, waiter, busser, cook, and cleaning crew. He said he'd heard about Pat Rowland and asked if we knew who was doing it yet. We both shook our heads no.

Al broke out his best grin and looked over his shoulder toward the jukebox. "Your murderees liked country music, didn't they?"

I nodded.

"Guess that guy sitting at the table in the corner's the one."

Karen and I quickly looked to the corner. The gentleman Al referred to must have been in his nineties. A walker was sitting beside the table. "Why?" we asked in unison.

"He hates country music. Almost got in a fight with Bubba Bob last week when a George Jones song wandered between two blues tunes." Al started laughing, and cringed when his knee began to buckle. "Almost had to take his walker away. Yep, think he's your guy."

I was glad I had resisted the temptation to refine the music selections.

Karen thanked him for the "hot lead" and said she needed to be going. She planned to visit the hospital and see if she could make enough noise to wake her dad.

Had I made a mistake by not telling her about the box?

CHAPTER 40

I stopped at Pack & Mail on the way home to get copies of Pat Rowland's stash of papers. The helpful owner gave me a puzzled look but copied everything without question. She said that stranger items had graced her copier.

Now the hard part. Who was I going to give the box to? I had eliminated Detective Lawson and Officer Ash, and it would have been a mistake of grand proportions to voluntarily approach the acting chief. So I did what no sane citizen would do and drove around Folly Beach looking for the police.

There was more traffic on the island than places to park, so I knew there was a good chance I'd find an overworked, tired, frustrated, and sweaty, officer at the turnaround on the east end—the entrance to the old coast guard station and path to the best view of the historic Morris Island Lighthouse. A dead-end road at one of the most popular spots on Folly Beach during the summer is a guaranteed formula for a traffic jam. Today was no exception.

Two patrol cars were parked driver-side to driver-side in the widest spot in the circular turnaround. Cars were weaving around them in a semiorderly fashion. Officer Ash was in one of the marked cars, so I fell in line with the vacationers and headed back toward town.

The next patrol car I found was parked in front of Bert's. It wasn't quite on the same level of an answered prayer, but finding an officer within a hundred yards of my house was convenient. Bert's lot was full, so I parked in front of my house and lugged the Bonterra Vineyards box to the store. I found Officer Spencer standing in a checkout line that would have been the envy of most groceries. No fewer than nine customers—nine human customers and three dogs—were waiting patiently as the clerk systematically rang up their goods and tossed treats to the canines. Officer Spencer was second in line, so I waited by the double door at the front of the packed store. I stood as close to the wall as possible; I had learned never to stand in the way of a thirsty customer heading to the beer case.

"Delivering for the wine distributor?" asked Officer Spencer as he gingerly stepped between two growling poodles that were approaching each other and leading their masters to the store.

"Not a bad idea," I said. I had backpedaled and was standing beside Spencer's patrol car. "But no." I set the box on the hood and wiped my hands on my shorts to loosen some of the dust from the box. "Actually, this is for you."

"I'm a beer man," he said as he looked at the Bonterra box.

Now that we had established his drinking habits, I explained that Charles had come into possession of the box and that *we thought* it might have relevance to the murders. We wanted to "do our civic duty" and turn it over to the "proper authorities."

I concede to being a senior citizen and, of course, am coming face-to-face with senility, so I forgot to tell him when we came into possession of the box, why we had visited Mrs. Klein, and how we had spent a great deal of time reviewing its contents. It even slipped my mind to mention that we had made copies.

I wasn't certain how much he believed me but knew he would hesitate to challenge my story. He opened the flaps covering the box, looked inside, and turned his gaze back to me and said, "Um hum." He handed me his plastic grocery bag and put Ms. Rowland's box in the backseat of his Crown Vic. "You know I'm going to give this to Chief King, don't you?"

I nodded. "Good."

"And," he continued as he got in, "he's going to want to know how you got it, and when, and more importantly, why."

"Sure," I said.

"And he's not going to believe your story. In fact, he'll scream at me for not bringing you in for obstructing justice, withholding evidence, and ... and, in general, pissing him off."

So much for civic duty.

CHAPTER 41

Twenty miles west of Charleston, I tried to recall why I had agreed to be on I-26 headed to the Horse Capital of the World, Lexington, Kentucky. Charles rode shotgun and was doing everything he could to distract me—no accident, I suspected. As we left Folly Beach, he felt compelled to share that the causeway to the beach wasn't opened until 1920 and that was only to property owners. The next year it opened to everyone, and the lot prices "soared" to two thousand dollars. He told me about the history of the developed areas along the Ashley River, and something about something else—I had tuned him out by then. Besides, his words had been drowned out by the strumming of a Martin guitar and Country Cal in the rear seat singing,

> "... *The next time we met, there were others;*
> *you introduced me to your husband, kids, and world.*
> *You were older, no longer a child but a person;*
> *I saw beauty, strength, a glimmer or our past unfurled ...*"

I vaguely recalled a late-night call from Charles, who said that we had limited *our* search for the crossbow killer to too small an area; we needed to "saunter" slightly northwest a bit. I wasn't paying much attention until he told me "a bit" was nearly six hundred miles. The key to the killings, according to Charles, was Stewart Barlow. That's who had paid Pat Rowland to find something or someone. I recalled telling him that I'd think about it. He said, "Good. I'll be at your car at 6:00 a.m."

Once Charles decided something, it was pointless to try to dissuade him. In my younger, more foolish, years, I might have tried. Maturity, or more accurately, surrender, dictated that I didn't make the effort. Besides, it had been a while since I had been to my home state and, unfortunately, didn't think the public would mind the gallery not being open.

I had packed enough clothes for a few days and opened the front door at Charles's designated time. I would have been shocked if he hadn't been leaning on the car and grinning at me. He was there, so I used my one available shock when I saw Cal standing with him, his beat-up guitar case and olive drab, road-worn, cloth carryall sitting beside it. Rather than seeing Country Cal, I got my first glimpse of Calvin Ballew, wearing navy blue shorts, way-off-white tennis shoes, and a relatively neat, bright blue golf shirt. He was Stetson-less.

I also remembered thinking that Calvin, alias Country Cal, could easily be a suspect as well as Charles's country-crooning buddy. Should I have asked to check his bag for a crossbow?

With the sun rising behind us and Cal pausing after his melodic version of his greatest hit, Charles finally decided that I needed to know why the backseat was occupied.

"Wasn't it great that Cal could get away to go?" he shared.

"Uh-huh," I whispered and nodded. Anything else would have slowed his story.

"When I saw him last night at Bert's, I was afraid he'd be playing at GB's tomorrow and stuck on the beach."

"Nice of Michigan to invite me," chimed in Cal. "He thought that since I lived at the Edge, my life was in danger, and ..."

"Cal," interrupted Charles, "how about staying on a first-name basis instead of state of origin? Chris'd appreciate it."

I knew Charles wouldn't be able to take being called Michigan for twelve hundred miles and no telling how many days. It was kind of him to use me as his reason for the request.

Cal strummed his guitar and looked at the back of Charles's head. "First you tell me I have to dress like a detective and not a rhinestone cowboy, and now you're telling me what I have to call you." He strummed again and then laughed. "A control freak, ain't ya?"

Cal's a quick study. Charles grinned but didn't turn his head from the road. "Yep."

Another strum, and then Cal said, "Okay then, *Charles*, why are we taking this little trip? You told me you'd explain on the way."

Thank you, Cal.

"Simple," said Charles. "Process of elimination. Lester Patterson got himself killed—no reason anyone can figure; and then Arno barely escaped with a bolt in the arm—no reason anyone could figure; and now, Pat Rowland got herself murdered on the streets of Folly Beach; and, lo and behold, Chris and I found a reason ... sort of."

"And it is?" asked Cal.

Thank you again, Cal.

"We've learned from sources I can't divulge, that Rowland is ... was ... a private detective hired by a bigwig in Lexington. She was supposed to find someone. She'd looked in several cities before ending up here."

"And that makes her the key, how?" asked Cal, without a strum.

Thank you, Cal—for not strumming.

"She's the only one living at the boardinghouse with anything we can figure as a reason for murder," said Charles.

"I'm confused," said Cal.

"Welcome to my world," I mumbled.

He continued. "Then how come shoot Lester and Arno?"

"And," I added, "what about Travis Green? It's mighty suspicious that he's disappeared."

"And," Cal jumped on the bandwagon, "why not Harley? He lives there, too."

"And," I added, "why not Heather Lee?"

"Yeah," said Cal. "One more night of listening to her off-key warbling, I'll be shopping for a crossbow myself."

"It's good to hear you don't have one," said Charles. "Didn't think your bag was big enough."

So far, no one had mentioned Cindy Ash or Mrs. Klein as suspects. No need for me to stir the confusion.

"Fellas," said Charles, "I don't have it all figured out. That's why we're heading to the birth state of A. Lincoln; sorry I don't have an appropriate quote for your proper edification."

"Thank the lord," said Cal.

"Want to hear my theory or waste time being jealous of my brilliance?" asked Charles.

The only sound was the car engine. Charles took it as an apology and continued. "I think Pat Rowland was following the trail of someone for Stewart Barlow who, as Cal and his country-compadres would say, had 'done him wrong.' The trail led to the cities that we found the receipts for and ended at Folly Beach." He paused and then said, "Yep, I think that's it. Somehow she suspected that the person, or persons, *who done Barlow wrong* lived at the Edge, but she didn't have enough proof. She moved in to get closer."

"And then … then, someone shoots Lester, Arno, and Rowland?" asked Cal. "I'm not following, so …"

Charles interrupted. "My theory's not quite foolproof, and I'm getting hungry." He looked out the side window as the exit zoomed by. "Don't you ever stop?"

We were on the outskirts of Columbia, and I did need a coffee break. Charles's analysis hadn't quite put me to sleep, but it didn't help me stay awake. I stopped at a Starbucks just off the interstate west of the state capitol. The freestanding, shoebox-shaped coffee shop was typical Starbuck's. The multilevel and multicolored hanging ceiling panels looked like hovering spaceships, and the air vents like baby ships. The multicolored theme was carried through with the pendant lights, and poor quality, but colorful, oil paintings dotted the gallery wall near the restrooms. Soft jazz played in the background. We joined the line waiting to order—a line of construction workers mixed with businessmen in suits and retirees killing time.

We corralled a rare, unoccupied table in the corner. Coffee cups, laptops, and newspapers occupied the rest.

Under the bright lighting, I noticed that Cal's blue eyes were fading to gray from age and hard living. He sipped black coffee and stretched his long legs out into the aisle. He'd told the barista that she'd better not put any of that latte, or green or purple tea, or whatever else they use to poison a good cup of Joe in his cup. His grin said the coffee had met his standards.

"A few years back," he said to no one in particular, "I played a couple of bars over on Broad River Road." He pointed toward the interstate.

"Never thought the world would come to looking like this at a coffee house. Nope, never did."

"You must have done quite a bit of traveling," said Charles. He blew on his steamed, extra hot, hot chocolate to cool it enough to drink and leaned on the small table that separated him from Cal and me.

"Yep," said Cal, "played about every small town between here and Missouri." He hesitated and stared out the window. "Drove that old Caddy about seven zillion miles; lived out of the backseat most of the time."

Charles took a sip and a bite of coffee cake. Crumbs dotted his University of Kentucky long-sleeve T-shirt. "How'd you get bookings?"

Cal laughed. "A one-man show." He fiddled with the plastic top on the coffee and looked at the writing on the cup like he was studying Egyptian hieroglyphics. "In the mornings, I'd drive from small town to small town, look for an old high school gym or bar, even some colleges. I'd find someone around who looked official and said I'd play a concert that night for tips and a chance to sell my records and 8-track tapes out of the trunk."

"Guess it worked," I added.

"Most of the time," said Cal. "Remember, that was a while back— no cable TV, MTV, CMT, music in everyone's ear with MP3 players, computer games ... hell's bells, no one even had a computer. In the small towns, I was a combination of a traveling circus, medicine man, live entertainment, and celebrity. All free." His stare drifted to the window again, memories flashing past. "By the afternoon, everyone in the town knew about the *big*, free *concert*."

"Good crowds?" asked Charles.

"Occasionally," said Cal. "To be honest, for a one-hit wonder, trying to kick a drinking, drugging habit, I got what I deserved." He shook his head, and I noticed his fingers tapping nervously on the table. "On good nights, had a hundred or so folks; sold enough records to buy gas to the next town; people were generous enough to buy me a couple of hot dogs and ... and, every so often, someone offered me a real room to stay in. The Caddy's seats were large, but I'm larger and don't fold comfortably." He stopped and gave us a big stage grin. "Every once in a while, the person offering me the room was a lady, if you know what I mean."

We did.

CHAPTER 42

My passengers slept between the Starbucks and where I switched to I-40 near Asheville. I wasn't much more awake than the sleeping beauties around me, so I stopped at the sign of the golden arches to stretch and got lunch. The word food roused my fellow travelers. Cal said he was having a Big Mac attack and thanked me for stopping at his favorite restaurant. Charles asked where we were. He was disappointed that we weren't in Lexington—in his dream world, things are what he wants them to be.

"Chris," said Charles, his mouth half-stuffed with fries, "isn't Amber from around here?"

"Uh-huh," I said. Amber had told me her life story, which began within thirty miles of where we were sitting, but she hadn't shared it with anyone on Folly Beach. I wasn't comfortable telling Charles anything other than confirming what he already knew. He was miffed that I wasn't more forthcoming, but had learned that sharing personal information wasn't my strength.

Cal had listened patiently—or simply devoting his full attention to devouring his Big Mac. "So, what's it with you and Amber?" he asked. Perhaps he had been listening. "I hear she's mighty smitten on you."

"Smitten!" said Charles. "She'd move in with my smooth-talking, charming friend at the drop of an Easter egg; I don't know why, but she would. Go figure."

Enough, I thought, and looked at Cal. "Have you been married?"

"Pretty sure I had a couple of wives in the sixties. One was named Katty ... Katty Lefler ... not a bad country singer in her day. She and her sister, Kathy, had a duet act—Katty and Kathy. They played up and down the east coast—North and South Carolina, some Georgia and Florida. Our days overlapped for a while until she smarted-up and left me somewhere between the gutter and rehab. Didn't blame her an iota." He stopped and looked at Charles. "How about you?"

"Nope," said Charles. "What about the other one?"

"Other what?" asked Cal.

"Other wife; you said you had two."

"Nothing worth talking about," said Cal. "It didn't last much longer than this trip. We met at a bar I was playing outside Knoxville; got all kissy-faced and plastered—not sure which first. Next thing I knew, I was in a wedding chapel in Gatlinburg, eating chocolate and pecan fudge and saying 'I do.'" Cal took another bite of Big Mac, slurped a Coke, laughed, and said, "Monday rolled around, and she rolled out. Never got divorced, so if we really got married, I still am. Damned good fudge, though."

"Ought to be a song in there," said Charles.

I nodded in agreement.

"Speaking of a song," said Charles. He turned his attention from Cal and focused on me. "Seems like Karen Lawson would like to play a duet with you, lover boy."

"Don't know what you mean." I became increasingly anxious to hit the road.

"I suppose you haven't noticed her coming around more, asking people about you, wanting to give you updates on the chief's condition only a couple of days after you'd seen him. I suppose you haven't seen her eyes increase their wattage when she's around you. And I suppose you didn't notice the near Amber-Karen feline-fight in the Dog."

"Charles," I said, "all I've noticed is that she's worried about her dad and has thanked me for being there. Period."

Charles rolled his eyes and looked at Cal, who leaned back in his chair and had a wide grin on his face. "Cal," said Charles, "I think you'd better drive the rest of the way. My friend here's done gone sightless."

"Time to go," I said and pushed away from the table, hoping no one noticed my red face.

Cal got coffee to go and asked Charles if he wanted any.

"As President Reagan said, 'I never drink coffee at lunch—I find it keeps me awake in the afternoon.'"

I hoped sleep would come quickly to nosy, pushy, president-quoting Charles.

The conversation on the winding mountain interstate from Asheville to Knoxville was more benign—hardly any talk about the crossbow murderer or my love life. Every thirty miles or so, Cal would say something like, "Clyde, North Carolina—played an old school there once," or "Maggie Valley—fell off a mule after a concert; stood on a hay wagon when I was singing," or "Newport—don't remember what happened there, but my left foot hurt for days."

"What's the story behind your *big hit*?" asked Charles.

Cal stared at the landscape speeding by. "I was about fifteen; lived in a trailer park in Lubbock. The cutest little girl I'd ever seen lived behind us." He paused and continued to stare out the window. "Name was Leslee."

"And …?" asked Charles.

"And … and we spent hours hanging out. Rode our bikes all over the area … explored creeks, found little ole snakes and nearly scared her to death with them, and … well, anyway, I fell as much in love with her as a fifteen-year-old could."

Cal continued to stare outside and didn't say anything for the longest time. Charles was smart enough (this time) not to interrupt the silence.

"It ended like most teen love stories," Cal finally said. "Leslee was discovered by the star football player. I was about as athletic as a beach umbrella and didn't have a chance. She was a year older and in the next grade." Cal finally turned his attention back inside the car. "The last time I talked to her, I remember telling her I'd always be there for her. She said, 'I'll catch you later.'"

"What happened to her?" I asked.

"Don't know. I heard she moved to France, and then someone told me she had gone to medical school."

"Ever try to find her?" asked Charles.

"I'd love to. I don't know her last name now," said Cal. "Know how many Leslee's there are in France or docs in the U.S.?"

"Not offhand," said Charles.

"Me either," said Cal.

I suspected we were at the end of the story.

Somewhere just north of the Kentucky state line, Charles asked Cal if he ever got tired of being on the road.

"Yep," he said. "Somewhere in the eighties I hung up my guitar strap—symbolically, of course; I didn't have a wall to hang it on. I decided to enter the paying world of work."

He paused a little past Charles's comfort level of silence. "What'd you do?"

"Became a long-haul trucker. Good money; job security."

Cal didn't notice anything strange about getting off the road by becoming a long-haul trucker.

"What happened?" asked Charles.

"Rolled the truck on a curve near Little Rock. Decided singing was safer."

Safer unless you were Les Patterson, Arno Porchini, and possibly Heather Lee if Cal found a crossbow.

CHAPTER 43

Folly Beach to Lexington was five hundred fifty miles—or in Cal-speak, nearly seventy-five cities where he had sung. I stopped at a Sleep Inn near Hamburg Place on the outskirts of the city late afternoon, rather than challenge downtown at rush hour. Charles swore he had never been to Lexington but said he knew we had to be in horse country when the name of the street we took off the interstate was Man o' War Boulevard.

I was providing the transportation, gas, room, and food money, so I pulled rank and took a single room and told Charles and Cal they'd have to bunk together. Cal said if Charles snored as much as he had talked the entire way, he'd sleep in the car.

I wasn't real familiar with Lexington but had been there enough to find my way around. Cal had played a few honky-tonks in the area but said it had been before the turn of the century and he didn't recognize the new office buildings, big-box retailers, and branch banks near the hotel.

"Now what do we do?" asked Charles. He and Cal had invaded my tiny room. He sat in the only chair, leaving Cal to fend for himself. The crooner slowly lowered himself to the floor and used the wall as a backrest.

"I thought you'd have it figured out," I said.

I was looking at Charles, but Cal responded. "I checked the brochures in the lobby. There was one about something called the Kentucky Horse Park, and one on Shaker Village of Pleasant Hill." He reached toward his head like he was going to push his Stetson back before realizing it hadn't made the trip. "I didn't see any that mentioned crossbow school."

I thought it was a joke, but I didn't say anything in case it wasn't.

Charles ignored him and nodded his head like a plan was forming. "The Stewart Barlow fellow has an address on Main Street—wherever that is; true?"

"Yeah," I said.

"And you said that must be a business. So, we need to head there in the morning."

"And do what?" asked Cal.

"Detectin'," said Charles, like *duh*, we should've known that.

Cal pushed Charles enough to where he admitted that Mr. Barlow just "might not" confess to killing anyone, having anyone killed, or having hired Pat Rowland.

I tuned out their discussion—generously using the word *discussion*—and found the phone book in the bed stand. In my previous life with a health insurance company, I occasionally had contacts with some of the mega-agencies in Central Kentucky and had become friends with Steve Dewrite, one of the owners of the Dewrite-Allen Agency. Insurance agents were uber-nosy by trade, so I thought Steve might know Stewart Barlow and took a chance and called him. Charles, whose nosy level would put him in good stead with insurance agents, stopped talking and listened as I dialed the agency.

Dewrite was still in the office and agreed to meet me for an early supper. He said he was surprised to hear from me but didn't question the out-of-the-blue invitation. I told Charles and Cal I could get more information if we met one-on-one. Charles opened his mouth to argue, immediately shut it, and frowned.

Cal noticed and said, "Good. Who wants to have supper with a stuffy ole insurance man?"

Charles grudgingly agreed and then began bemoaning how he and Cal would starve since the hotel didn't have a restaurant. I looked out the window and rolled my eyes. "Come here and see if you can find anywhere to eat."

Charles elbowed me away from the third-floor window. "Not much," he said, "just McDonald's, Pizza Hut, Wendy's, Waffle House, Taco Bell, Arby's, KFC."

"Sure hope they have vending machines here," said Cal. "We might starve." He smiled.

I gave Charles two twenties to seal the deal.

Dewrite said the easiest place to meet was at Harry's Bar, part of the larger Malone's Restaurant complex within walking distance of the hotel. The restaurant was closer than I had anticipated, so I arrived ten minutes early. The oversize bar was in a new building and about as much like Al's as a cricket was to a giraffe. The bar was packed with happy-hour patrons—most Caucasian and nattily attired in suits and coats, with the ladies wearing skirts and miserable-looking high heels. The walls were dotted with large, flat-screen televisions tuned to more sports channels than I knew existed. A smiling, college-aged hostess showed me to a bar-height round table for two. A glance at the menu told me that Harry's had about 713 items more than Al's. I took a deep breath and thanked the food gods that I'd be going home to Al's.

I was lost in thoughts about wanting to be back in South Carolina, when I heard Steve's booming voice. "My God," he said, yelling above the buzz of the full bar, "I haven't heard from you in ages."

Steve was nearly a foot taller than I and weighed an additional hundred pounds. To say he was rotund would be kind. I hadn't seen him for three years, but he looked at least a decade older than what I remembered.

We shook hands, and I pointed toward the empty seat. His suit cost more than some cars, but it was tight in all the wrong places. His shirt had lost its morning starch, and his rust and brown Hermes tie would have appeared quite dapper on most of the males in the bar; on Steve, it looked exhausted.

He motioned for a waitress and ordered a Blanton's and water. He caught his breath and turned to me. "I heard you'd retired and headed for the good life somewhere in the south. Think I'm envious."

I gave him a capsule summary of my last three years but chose to leave out the parts about nearly being murdered by a crazed killer seeking revenge, or the time I was saved by my strange best friend who was stuck in the hotel a few blocks away. I didn't think it would be prudent to tell him about arguing with the police about whether someone committed suicide and then getting in the way of the person who actually killed the "suicide" victim. Truth be told, I could easily have been the murderer's next victim. And he never would have understood me hanging around with Country Cal, Larry, the retired cat burglar, and Charles, whatever one could call him. Steve felt obligated to moan about staffing problems in his agency, how the economy played shambles with his business, his budgeting woes, and his multiple hernias and aching bunions.

He was babbling about another health issue, but I caught myself staring at the large, flat-screen television I could see over his left shoulder, and missed the diagnosis. I realized that I was paying more attention to the baseball game than to Steve. And I'm convinced that watching baseball on television is about as exciting as watching paint dry—oil-based paint; water-based dries quickly and is more exciting than baseball. The last fifteen minutes banished any doubts I may have had about retiring.

I nodded a couple of times and said "that's too bad." I had no idea what Steve had been talking about, but the look on his face told me it wasn't good.

I decided to get to the reason I was here before Steve started showing me his prescription bottles or photos of his grandkids and grandpets. "A friend works for the police and is investigating a strange case." I hesitated and took a sip of Chardonnay. I realized how absurd my story would sound if I told all of it. *A little late to be worrying about it*, I thought. "Well, there's no need to go into all the details, but the name of a man from Lexington came up. I told my friend that I was going to Louisville and would stop here and see if I could learn something about the guy. I knew you know everyone who's anyone. So, here I am." A little ego-stroking went a long way with my self-absorbed former colleague.

"So, who is he?"

"Name's Stewart Barlow."

"He in trouble?"

I wasn't ready to share. "I don't think so; my friend said it was a routine investigation; a name he came across."

Steve glanced down at his drink and grinned. "I know Barlow. And your friend isn't telling you everything. If Barlow's involved, there's trouble."

"How?"

"Barlow's got a business down on Main Street, the Bluegrass Gallery. He was a client of mine for years, up until May." Steve was looking around the room. "This all confidential?"

I nodded.

"Barlow filed a claim saying some of his paintings were stolen. It sounded fishy to our investigator. Barlow huffed and puffed and, quicker than a flash, withdrew the claim. We didn't go to the police but should have." Steve shook his head. "We dropped his account—should've done it sooner, I might add."

I didn't think Steve had said anything to hang my hat on. I used Charles's technique. "And …?"

"This is only rumor, okay?"

I nodded again.

"The word is that Barlow deals in stolen art, forgeries, and no telling what else. I hear we're talking mucho bucks—maybe millions. But I don't know that for sure—none of my business."

Amber had been trying for months to get me to eat healthy foods. I watched Steve wolf down three Mini Bacon Cheeseburgers and a double order of fries. I saw his stomach push his oversize shirt to the max; Amber had a point. Of course, I was eating a Pepperoni and Sausage Pizza as I watched him.

I asked Steve several questions between bites, and he talked for fifteen more minutes about Barlow, but all it did was reinforce what he had said earlier, "… *don't know that for sure.*"

I suffered through several more insurance-related stories before telling Steve that it had been a long day and I needed to get back to the hotel. We walked out together.

"Your police friend isn't telling you the whole truth," he said as we turned to go our separate ways. "If Barlow's involved, there's trouble. Another rumor is he's laundering a boatload of money. Be careful."

Not unfamiliar advice.

CHAPTER 44

I walked toward the Sleep Inn's elevator but was distracted by the familiar sounds of a Martin guitar and Cal coming from the breakfast area off the lobby. He was standing in front of two commercial-grade waffle makers on the counter against the far wall. He had one foot in a chair with his guitar resting on his knee. He was sharing his version of "Help Me Make It Through the Night" with Charles, two middle-aged women wearing Sleep Inn name tags, and a teenage boy dressed in shorts down to his ankles.

Charles was sitting at a small table farthest from Cal. He shared the table with two large cups from Wendy's, empty wrappers from McDonalds and Taco Bell, and a large box from Pizza Hut—the remnants of my forty dollars.

Cal nodded in my direction but kept singing, so I walked to Charles's table. I shrugged my shoulders and pointed at Cal. Charles grinned and said, "By popular demand."

"Popular demand?"

"Yep," said Charles. He looked toward the table with the two hotel employees. "They asked Cal if he was a singer, and one thing led to another—you just missed four construction workers—big George Jones fans, if you're interested."

"Why'd they ask if Cal was a singer?"

"He was sitting in here strumming his guitar. Guess they eliminated ballet dancer."

As Kenny Rogers would have said, "You've got to know when to hold them, know when to fold them ..." I took a deep breath, sat back in the chair, and enjoyed the miniconcert.

Cal had "established rapport" with his audience. He began regaling stories of meeting Porter Wagoner, having drinks with Billy Walker, arguing with Jim Reeves, and teaching Don Gibson the words to "End of Your Story." Cal was clearly more comfortable drifting back to 1962.

The lull in the strumming gave me a chance to whisper to Charles what I had learned about Barlow. I spared him the update on Steve's bunions.

Charles raised his chin and smirked. "See, I told you so," he said. "Barlow's the killer or knows who is."

I wasn't certain about that but couldn't dispute what he said, so I was almost relieved when Cal began Patsy Cline's "I Fall to Pieces." I smiled to myself and wondered what Steve Dewrite would have thought if he could see me now.

Cal finished the classic and leaned the guitar against the breakfast bar to the right of the "stage." He turned serious, or perhaps sad, and began telling his new fans about being at Tootsie's Orchid Lounge in 1961 when he heard about the serious automobile accident his "good friend" Patsy Cline had been in. "The wreck was terrible, but nothing like how I felt when Patsy and the others were killed in the plane crash in '63." He nodded his head. "So sad, so terribly sad." He was almost whispering. After his moment of silence, he looked at the two ladies and smiled. "I knew Hawkshaw pretty good but only met Cowboy Copas once." He was still smiling but shook his head. "Sure don't know when your time's up, do you?" He paused so the "crowd" could put their hands around his story, and then put his guitar back on his knee and slowly strummed "Sweet Dreams."

Tears were running down the cheeks of one of the ladies. The skeptical me wondered how many times Cal had told that story to audiences, both big and small. And how many female fans felt the need to comfort him after hearing his heartbreaking remembrances from events that happened more than forty-six years and God knows how many cities ago.

The applause had died down—at least, as much applause as four hands could make (the teenage boy had snuck out when Cal started talking about people who had died years before his parents were born)—and Cal looked at the wall opposite his temporary stage. "I see the clock on the wall telling me it's time to go. Thank you." He reached up to tip his Stetson, the one resting more than five hundred miles away, and bowed.

I wondered if Cal and I were the only people in the room to notice that there wasn't a clock.

CHAPTER 45

The Bluegrass Gallery was in an old building on Main Street between the Lexington-Fayette County Courthouse and, according to Lexington residents, the world's epicenter of basketball, Rupp Arena, the home of the University of Kentucky Wildcats. The gallery's storefront was a cross between a charming, historic structure and a not-so-gracefully aging edifice in need of expensive repairs.

Charles and I had adjourned to my room after Cal's miniconcert and discussed how we would get anything helpful out of the gallery owner/thief/forger. Cal had said he "might be in a tad later," something about having to discuss the history of the Nashville Sound with some fans. Charles told him, "Whatever." The history lesson must have been quite detailed; he never showed.

On the walk from the parking garage around the corner from the gallery, we tried to remember how we were going to approach Barlow. Cal made it clear not to ask him since he was occupied with other interests and missed our brilliant planning session. Charles stopped in the middle of the sidewalk and held his cane horizontally out to his side, blocking Cal and me from proceeding. "Don't worry," he said. "I'll do the detecting here; follow my lead."

"Don't worry," hah!

Saturday might be a busy day at the Bluegrass Gallery; but if so, the customers slept late. The gallery was empty, as a subtle chime beside the door announced our arrival. I could identify with an empty gallery. The morning sunshine hadn't made it into the gallery, but the interior was illuminated by a series of daylight-balanced spots suspended from tracks from the ceiling. The walls were painted snow-white and proudly displayed large, elaborately framed art. Charles drifted to the wall on our right and glanced at the tag, inconspicuously attached beside a large painting of three horsemen chasing a fox through a richly-detailed, plush meadow. He gave a muted gasp, turned to me, and mouthed "thirty-seven thousand."

The similarities between Landrum Gallery and the Bluegrass Gallery ended with each having four walls, a ceiling, a floor, and a door opening to the sidewalk and street.

A male voice from the back of the gallery startled Charles out of sticker shock. "Good morning, gentlemen. How may I help you?"

We turned toward an extraordinarily well-attired, middle-aged man. He looked like he had stepped out of a Brooks Brothers' catalog—he was trim, about five feet eleven inches tall, had razor-cut, gray-flecked black hair, and his smile revealed teeth out of a toothpaste ad. His charcoal gray suit had subtle light-gray pinstripes. His shoes were polished so well that a speck of dust would have been embarrassed to land on them.

Charles, good at his word, stepped forward, put his cane under his left arm, and extended his right hand to the "GQ" model. Our front man's detecting immediately discovered that he was shaking hands with Stewart Barlow, the proprietor of the Bluegrass Gallery. Mr. Barlow— the *proprietor*, not the owner, or "Hi, I'm Stew"—pronounced his first name in a manner that I could only describe as snooty and old-money, and it was THE Bluegrass Gallery.

I cringed, thinking that Charles was going to introduce me as proprietor of THE Landrum Gallery, or Cal as THE Country Cal. I exhaled when Charles simply said I was Chris and my tall, thin friend, Cal.

After one formal and three Follylike introductions, Stewart returned to his original question. "And how may I help you?" He left out "gentlemen."

Charles was still directly in front of the proprietor. "We arrived last night from Charleston, South Carolina," he said in his best stuffy voice. "Chris is from Louisville, and we're on a business-pleasure trip to the Derby City."

Stewart nodded like that made sense—he was a good salesman— and said, "Yes."

"And," continued Charles, "a close friend of ours is the police chief of a small town near Charleston—Folly Beach. Have you heard of it?"

Stewart raised his eyes to the ceiling, studied the question, and said, "Believe so. Go on."

"Well," said Charles, "our friend is investigating a series of strange deaths and, completely by accident, came across your name and the Bluegrass Gallery's address in some papers of one of the victims. Our friend didn't think it had anything to do with the killing but thought that since we were heading this way, we might stop and ask if you knew anything about the poor victim."

"That's terrible," said Stewart. "Who was the unlucky person?"

"Her name was Pat Rowland; she ..."

"Oh, my God," said Stewart. This was the first real emotion I'd seen from the plastic proprietor.

He looked like his knees were going to buckle and slowly walked to a black leather chair in the corner. He slowly lowered himself onto the heavily padded seat. Charles and I moved closer to him. Cal remained across the room. Detecting didn't appear to be his thing. I felt awkward looming over Stewart but, other than sitting on the floor, we didn't have any choice.

"You knew Ms. Rowland?" asked Charles, an understatement after Stewart's reaction.

"Yes ... yes," Stewart replied. "She's a private detective—a good one, I've heard. I hired her a year ago."

"Mind telling us why?" I asked.

"I've got a house out Paris Pike," he said and waved his hand toward the northeast. "Last year I had it remodeled—had to rent another house to live in because of the mess. Well, after the work was completed, I discovered that some things were missing. There were a dozen contractors working on the house—men in and out all day. No way to know who took my property."

"What'd they get?" asked Charles.

"Some valuable family pieces and some cash."

We waited for him to elaborate. He didn't.

"What'd the police say?" I asked.

"Hah," he smirked. "Nothing useful. Sure, they took all the information down and said they would contact pawnshops. None of the items had serial numbers, so they doubted anything would come of it."

"So that's why you hired Ms. Rowland?" asked Charles.

"Yes. At least she would try."

By this time, Cal had moved closer to the action.

"Did she find out who it was?" I asked.

"Don't think so. She gave me regular reports, sent me a bunch of invoices. Traveled all over the South following leads. The last six months or so, she said she was on the island you mentioned, Folly Beach."

"Did she report from there?" I asked.

"She said she had a good lead. She moved out of a hotel into a fleabag rooming house, but didn't say why. Said she had to find out more before she'd tell me."

I was surprised to hear Cal's voice from behind me. "When was that?"

Stewart appeared surprised, too. He looked over my shoulder at Cal. It was as if he had forgotten Cal was there.

"Two or three weeks ago—on a Sunday. She called me at home; that was unusual."

That was around the time the murders started, I thought. "No other hint?" I asked.

"Not really; she was hyper, said not to get my hopes up."

"Any ideas?" I asked.

"Not a one." He smiled. "She did say that if I ever wanted to get away from the real world, she would highly recommend Folly Beach."

"So, you've never been there?" asked Cal.

Stewart looked around the gallery. "I haven't been out of here since I got back from France last Wednesday."

"Buying trip?" asked Charles.

"Selling trip. I had some pieces I recently acquired and had a potential buyer in Deauville."

"That sounds exciting," I said. "Oh yeah, I almost forgot, the chief wanted me to ask you if you know Timothy Bussy, Peter Loy ..."

His face turned a lighter shade of white than the gallery walls. He interrupted, "Uh ... no, no, I don't think so." He hesitated and regained his composure; he looked at me suspiciously. "Who're they?"

"No idea," I said. "Just asking."

We talked a few more minutes and realized that if he knew anything, he wasn't going to tell three strangers. Charles said we would tell the chief what we had learned and that he might be getting in touch with Stewart.

We were heading to the door when Cal stopped and turned to Stewart. "How valuable was the stuff that was stolen?"

Why hadn't I asked that?

Stewart hesitated. "Oh, not real valuable. Maybe, oh, twenty-five, thirty thousand. Some of it had sentimental value."

CHAPTER 46

"Charles," I said, "thanks for not asking if the paintings were forged."

"Or if he had a crossbow," added Cal.

"Would have, but figured he wouldn't fess-up," said Charles as he snatched a fry from Cal's plate. "Did almost ask if a *proprietor* was anything like a snooty owner."

We were sitting in a small restaurant a couple of blocks from the Bluegrass Gallery. Charles said all that detecting had made him hungry, and especially thirsty—beer-thirsty.

Cal slapped Charles's hand as he reached for another fry. "I'm new to this detecting business, but I've spent all my life around words—writing them, singing them, being cussed out by them, trying to figure out the best ones to use in songs." He offered his best stage smile to summon the waitress. "Miss, could you get my friend here an order of *his own* fries? Much obliged." He turned back to me. "What I heard him say was: 'some things' were missing, 'took my property,' 'some valuable family pieces,' 'items,' and 'some cash.'"

"And ...?" asked Charles.

"And," Cal replied, "the only thing I understood was cash."

He looked to me and back to Charles. "Wouldn't a normal, forthcoming, honest person have said something like, 'some of my grandmother's antique, porcelain bird figurines,' or 'a valuable painting by the French impressionist Frou-Frou,' or even 'fifty thousand dollars and some bank CDs'?" Cal nodded. "The boy's lying through his capped teeth; he's hiding something."

"Cal's right," I said. "Let me tell you something that's bothering me. Rowland had racked up bills and fees that we know exceeded thirty-five grand, and I'd bet much more. That's to find some items that were worth 'twenty-five, thirty thousand dollars' according to Barlow."

Charles was watching the television in the corner, ignored what I was saying, and pointed his cane at the set. The sound was off, but the images were of heavy rains and wind sweeping boats out of the water and across nearby, narrow roads. The closed captions said something about Hurricane Greta and Guadeloupe.

"That's what we need," said Charles. "Another hurricane."

"I don't know where Guadeloupe is," said Cal as he turned to the screen. "Never sang there, but pretty sure it's not near Folly Beach."

True. We went back to dissecting Stewart Barlow.

Cal tapped his fingers on the table. "You know," he said, "if Barlow was in France last week, he couldn't have killed Rowland."

"And why," asked Charles, "should we believe an art thief and forger about where he was?"

"Good point," I said. "But it'll be easy for the police to check."

Cal continued to tap his fingers on the table. "Okay ... okay, I'm confused," he said. He stopped the tapping and turned to Charles and then to me. "We know Barlow hired Pat Rowland. She was supposed to find out who stole some stuff from his house."

We nodded.

"So she bops across several states following people who worked on his house and may have absconded with his stuff?"

"I think so," said Charles.

I nodded again.

"So," said Cal, "she tracks someone to Folly Beach and gets herself killed for the effort. Follow?"

I was beginning to get lost, but nodded my head again.

Cal looked at his empty fry plate, then at Charles's empty beer bottle, and then to me. "Now remember, boys, I'm not the detective here, but I'm confused. Why would Barlow have anything to do with killing Rowland if she was working for him? And what's with a crossbow? And ... and this one really confuses me, why shoot Lester and Arno, and what's happened to Travis?"

"Cal," said Charles, "buy me another beer, and I'll give you my theory ... maybe more than one."

"More than one beer or more than one theory?" I asked. This was getting interesting.

"Not sure," said Charles.

Cal's high-wattage smile worked again on the waitress. Two beers and one glass of wine were cheerfully delivered.

"Theory uno," said Charles after a long swig from the bottle, "Barlow's behind the killings. Something much more valuable than a few things were stolen from his house. He hired Rowland, paid her a bunch of money to find the thief. Then …"

"How would …" interrupted Cal.

Charles put his right index finger to his lower lip. "Shhh. Let me finish."

"Sorry," said Cal.

"Rowland finally caught up with the thief on Folly. It took her five months to find him, and when she did, she moved to where he lived—your building, Cal."

I could tell that Cal wanted to say something, but wasn't ready for another "Shhh." I knew to let Charles talk himself out.

"Rowland told Barlow who the thief was, and since Barlow is a dirty, rotten, forging, stealing scoundrel, he knew that she knew too much about his business and what was really stolen. He had someone kill the thief and Rowland to keep her quiet. Did you see his reaction when Timothy Bussy and Peter Loy's names were mentioned?"

"Yeah," I said. "I was afraid to bring up the other name we found—afraid he was going to have a stroke after the first two."

Charles nodded and didn't scold me for interrupting. He continued, "He's responsible for the killings; that's theory one." He picked up his cane from the floor and pointed it at Cal and then me. "Don't say anything. Let me spit out theory two before I forget."

The pointing worked; Cal and I remained mute.

"Theory dos. Starts the same as uno: Barlow hires Rowland to find the thief. She finds him, and the thief figures out that's why she moved into his building. The thief kills her; end of theory."

Cal raised his hand, proving why the early years in elementary school are the formative years. "Can we ask questions now?"

Charles laughed. "Easy ones," he said.

Cal looked at his hand and wiggled his fingers. I could almost hear him mentally counting questions. "If theory one is correct and Rowland found the thief," said Cal, "why did Barlow have someone put arrows in Les and Arno, and where's Travis—isn't that overkill, almost overkill, and maybe overkill?"

"Because ..." said Charles.

This time Cal interrupted. "Whoa, hold it a second; let me get all my questions out."

Charles's half-open mouth closed.

"Now," said Cal, "in theory two, let's say the thief found out that Rowland was after him and he killed her; why shoot Les and Arno?"

I could stay silent for only so long. "Misdirection."

That got their attention. "If only Rowland was killed, either by someone Barlow hired or by the thief, the police would have focused only on her. That would have led directly to Barlow." I hesitated, had a vague thought, and then lost it. "Barlow would have told them about the thief, and with only one murder, all the cops' focus would have been directed toward Rowland."

"So," said Cal, "you're saying some friggin' idiot actually killed innocent people to misdirect the police." He shook his head. "That's sick ... that's damn sick."

"If you think that's sick, he used a crossbow," said Charles.

It was already midafternoon, so we decided to stay in Lexington and get a fresh start in the morning. I suspected that Cal had his mind set on another miniconcert and becoming reacquainted with his new Lexington fans. The older I got, the less excited I was about long drives, so I agreed that another night at the Sleep Inn was fine. We retired to our respective rooms after Charles agreed to let me buy them supper. He was generous like that.

I called Karen Lawson to see how her dad was. That was the reason, wasn't it? She was at work and couldn't talk long, but was excited and told me he was doing better than the docs had anticipated. She knew he was on the road to recovery when he started griping about not being at work and began asking everything about the crossbow killer. She asked when we were heading home, how Charles was handling the big city, and if Cal was with us. She closed by saying that maybe we could get together when I got back—something about "hankering" for one of Al's burgers. I said sure, closed the phone, and wondered why she asked about Cal.

No one answered at Amber's. She didn't have an answering machine, so I'd have to call later.

I met Charles and Cal in the lobby. More accurately, I met Charles. Cal was leaning over the check-in counter in deep conversation with the clerk, who coincidentally had been 50 percent of his concert crowd when the clock on the wall said last night's show was over. After a couple of loud "hmms" by Charles, Cal broke away from his conversation and walked with us to the car.

"Negotiating frequent guest points?" asked Charles. Cal smiled and folded his long legs into the backseat and we headed to Logan's Roadhouse. For the next two hours, we enjoyed a scrumptious, unhealthy steak meal—loaded baked potatoes, yeast rolls, salad with non-fat-free dressing—and split their famous big and chewy hot fudge brownie. And washed it down with Milwaukee's finest suds.

Crossbows, the Edge, Barlow, Rowland, Les, Arno, Travis, a near-fatal heart attack, and Acting Chief King never entered the conversation. They weren't missed.

CHAPTER 47

"Name's Trigger."

That was the first Charles and I had heard from Cal since his head hit the headrest as we pulled out of the hotel parking lot. He had slept through Kentucky and across the Tennessee state line. We were near Knoxville. Before we left the hotel, he said something about getting too old for too much fun. Not even Charles asked what that meant.

Charles had been fiddling with the dial on the radio, trying to get updates on the latest hurricane, but had given up and switched the XM radio I had given to myself as a treat before moving to Folly. It was always tuned to the country channel, Willie's Place.

"Roy Rogers's horse—the stuffed one?" asked Charles, finally responding to Cal's comment.

"A stuffed horse? Huh?" asked Cal.

"Never mind," said Charles. "Who's Trigger?"

"Not who, what," said Cal.

"Okay," said Charles. I heard Charles's mounting frustration. "What's Trigger?"

"Willie's guitar," said Cal.

Please let it go, Charles, I thought.

"Willie Nelson?" asked Charles.

"Duh. Know another Willie with a guitar named Trigger?"

And I thought Dude was from another planet. I could physically feel the tensions from my work-life leaving my body as I headed back to my home at the beach and listened to the semi-incoherent, nonsensical conversation between my carmates. Having supper with Steve Dewrite brought back too, way too, many memories.

Cal was awake and ready to talk. "Did I ever tell you about Willie and ..."

"Yes," interrupted Charles.

"You don't know what I was going to say," said Cal.

"Here's a Charles's rule of thumb," said Charles.

I wasn't aware he had rules; I perked up.

"Anytime," he began his rule, "someone starts a sentence with, 'Did I ever tell you ...,' they had; so stop them before you have to suffer through it again."

This was fun. "Cal," I said, "you haven't told me; what about Willie?"

Charles rolled his eyes. "Shee!"

That made my morning.

"I was in the alley between the Ryman and Tootsies enjoying an adult beverage with a couple of Opry sidemen," said Cal. "One of the musician-followers—groupies in modern lingo—came out of Tootsies and said that Willie was slightly under the influence of firewater and depressed; said he had decided to kill himself. He had walked out onto Broadway and plunked himself down in the middle of the road, waiting for a car to help him meet his maker." Cal laughed loud enough to shake the seats. "By the time I got my legs under me, Willie's wife de jour grabbed a couple of hefty guys and pulled him out of the street." Cal had stopped laughing and stared out the window. "Sure miss the good ole days."

"Yeah," said Charles.

Cal cocked his head toward the XM box. "Met that guy once," he said.

"Willie? You already told us that," said Charles.

"No, the guy hosting that radio show, Bill Mack."

"And he is...?" asked Charles.

Cal squinted in Charles's direction. "How can you think you know everything and not know who the famous Bill Mack is? That boy's been country music's biggest DJ since the sixties. And one of its best songwriters and a good singer to boot."

"Guess I listened to the wrong radio stations," said Charles.

My guess was that Bill Mack had never been president.

"Bill lives down in my home state; must like it more than I did." Cal shook his head. "He's still there. He even let me visit his overnight radio show a couple of times. Anyway, he's a nice fellow."

Charles wasn't overly impressed; he turned the XM off and continued to fiddle with the radio. He finally found a station that had more understandable words than static. The announcer said something about Greta, but that's all I caught.

"What'd they say about the hurricane?" I asked Charles.

"Something about it growing strength and expected somewhere along the coast late in the week." He turned and looked at Cal. "The Bill Mack fan club was so loud, I missed it."

I drove another half hour before I realized that the only words from the backseat came from the radio.

The silence was broken when the nasal-sounding voice from the rear said, "Cal to front seat ... Cal to front seat."

I looked in the rearview mirror; Charles turned toward Cal.

He had our attention and leaned forward, "I've been thinking."

I inwardly tremble when Charles says that, but didn't know Cal well enough to know how to react.

"And ...," said Charles.

"People expect to see me decked out in a fancy, rhinestone-covered coat, cowboy boots, and a cowboy hat. I play to what others want to see and think I am." He hesitated, waiting for who knows what. "Well, to be honest, I'm more comfortable in this golf shirt and shorts than all that other stuff. It ain't misdirection like you were talking about yesterday, but it's deception—creating an image. Reality don't really play into it; it's a front, you could say."

"Makes sense," I said. I bit my lips not to say *so what*. Cal was trying to tell us something, something important.

He sat back and picked his guitar up from the seat beside him and held it like he was going to break out in a tune. "No doubt that Barlow's a fraud, trying to put on airs, be something he ain't; yes, no doubt. But there's someone at the Edge doing the same thing. Charles, I'm not trying to shoot down your theory about Barlow being the killer; after all, you're the detective. But I think there's a killer at the boardinghouse, and we're only seeing what he ... or she ... wants us to see—seeing what we expect."

"Want to tell us who?" asked Charles.

"Nothing'd give me more pleasure," said Cal. He began strumming his guitar. "But I don't have a clue."

"Speaking of rhinestones," said Segue Charles, "how long have you had your outfit you wear when you sing?"

"Longer than I've had sobriety; several decades. The Stetson's so full of hair grease, you could fry hamburgers in it. The coat's on its umpteenth re-stoning."

"Eeyou, to the hat," said Charles. "Where do you get rhinestones?"

That's the kind of trivia Charles feasts on. The words *who cares* are not in his vocabulary.

"Used to order them from a little company in Nashville," said Cal. "It's out of business. Now I get them at Claire's."

"The kids' store?" asked Charles. He forced back a giggle.

"Yep."

That's a good example of seeing what we expect to see, I thought. All we have to do is see what we aren't seeing. And I thought finding the killer was going to be difficult.

CHAPTER 48

My heart nearly stopped as I turned on Arctic Avenue in front of the Holiday Inn. Two Folly Beach patrol vehicles were parked a block up at the boardinghouse—one on the berm, the other in the parking lot. We had pulled back on the island, and I was taking Cal home before running Charles to his apartment. Had there been another murder? Was Cindy okay? Had someone been arrested? My mind raced.

"Don't guess they're here to welcome us home," said Charles. A statement both ironic and prophetic.

I pulled into the lot beside the boardinghouse and was relieved to see Cindy safe and sitting in the car parked at the street. She didn't appear as happy to see us. Officer Spencer was in the car beside me. He waited for Cal to unfold his oversize frame from the backseat and grab his traveling bag from the trunk. Charles and I were standing beside the car when Spencer approached my door.

"Everything okay?" I asked.

"Yeah, fine … sure," he said. His left foot shuffled in the sand, and he didn't make eye contact with us.

"What's up?" asked Charles. He had walked around the car and joined me leaning against the Lexus.

"Take the car home. I'll follow," said Officer Spencer. He was almost whispering.

I nodded and then waved bye to Cal, who awkwardly stood outside earshot. He thanked us for the weekend and opened the door to the house. I drove the short distance home and watched the patrol car following close behind.

"I hate this," said Spencer. His eyes darted between Charles and me. We were standing beside my car in front of the house. Cindy had parked behind Spencer but stayed in the car. "You're under arrest."

Charles looked at me and then at Spencer. "What the …?"

Spencer held up his hand to stop Charles before he finished his question. There was no doubt what he would be asking. "I've been ordered by *Acting* Chief King to take both of you into custody. We knew you were out of town and waited for you to get back."

"What charges?" I asked. I felt like I was in a television show.

"Remember," Spencer continued, "I told you *he* would be pissed when I gave him Rowland's papers?" A couple of cars whizzed by, and he looked at them. "Let's go on the porch."

We moved to the porch—less conspicuous than standing by the road—and Spencer said, "He was more than pissed. I thought he was going to burst a blood vessel. He turned red, asked me a bunch of questions I had no answers to, pointed toward our holding cell, and told me he wanted the two of you in it. In it now."

"What charges?" I tried again.

"Obstruction of justice, tampering with evidence, and the *acting* chief's favorite, meddling and screwing with *his* investigation." Spencer's expression was a cross between a snarl and a smile. "Sorry, guys, I told him you gave me the papers after you saw what they were. He didn't believe me."

During my first sixty years around the block, I had never been arrested. But I couldn't imagine how an arrest could have been more polite, more apologetic, and stranger than this. Spencer asked us to join him in the cruiser. He apologized for having us sit in the rear—the prisoners' seat behind the barrier that protected him from the wild and crazed arrestees. He drove to the salmon-colored, contemporary combination city hall, fire and police department, and holding cell. Charles shook his head. I stared ahead and reevaluated if I had been too hasty retiring from the boring life of a health care administrator.

Spencer opened the heavy steel cell door like a bellhop at a four-star hotel. He waved for us to enter the room, excuse me, the cell and said he would bring us a cordless phone. He suggested—highly suggested—that we call a lawyer. In his words, the charges were pure BS. I'm not an expert on police procedures, but suspected he had broken a half dozen of them since he greeted us at the Edge. I almost expected him to hand us a menu and ask if we wanted appetizers before supper. Instead, he handed me a cordless phone and the Charleston phone book.

Charles removed his Tilley and set it on the steel ledge that served as a bed in the small cell. Officer Spencer had taken his cane when we entered the building. I asked if he wanted the phone book. He shook his head and fiddled with the secret pocket in the crown of the hat, and fished a folded piece of notebook paper from the pocket.

"Hey, Sean," said Charles, after he punched in the number from the paper. I assumed he had called Sean Aker, of Aker & Long, attorneys-at-law. Sean was a skydiving buddy of Charles and partner at one of two law firms on Folly Beach. I had met him a few times over the last couple of years and had used his services to start Landrum Gallery.

"Yeah, it's Charles ... oh, just fine; you?" I assumed Sean was more or less than fine since his answer took longer than Charles's. "Chris and I ... yeah, that Chris ... uh-huh; yeah, we may need a little of your help. We're in the Folly Beach hoosegow ... yes, Sean, jail ... oh, something about obstructing justice, yada, yada, yada, and pissing off the acting chief of police."

Charles rolled his eyes and held the phone away from his ear. "Yes, Sean, yes ... I know you're not a criminal attorney. That's why I called you; we're not criminals. Okay, okay ... yeah, call on this number and ask for Officer Spencer. If someone named Chief King answers, hang up.... Okay, thanks."

I gave him a chance to say something and then finally asked, "So?"

"Said I was an idiot for calling him; I needed a criminal attorney; and then said he'd make a couple of calls and see what he could do."

Spencer opened the door. He had been watching through the small window in the cell door.

"Can I get you anything?" he asked.

A key to the cell; a ride off the island; wake me up from this nightmare ... "No. Thanks anyway," I said.

Spencer returned a half hour later with the phone and handed it to Charles.

"Yeah, Sean ... okay ... they can do that?" Charles's voice grew louder with each word. He glanced at Spencer, who was standing as far from the cell door as he could and still be in the corridor outside the room. "Yeah … and *happy dreams* to you, too!"

Charles handed Spencer the phone. The embarrassed officer took it and asked if there was anything else he could do. Charles asked, "What's for supper?"

Spencer shrugged and closed the door.

"Guess where we get to spend the night?" said Charles as he looked around the tiny space.

"Ritz-Carlton?" I asked.

He simply shook his head and sat on the steel bed attached to the wall. A toilet and, for some strange reason, a shower were on the opposite wall. Charles looked around the room like he was on cootie patrol; he studied each corner, crevice, and the floor from edge to edge. "Think the room's bugged?" he asked, and continued to look.

"I doubt it—that would violate some constitutional right or something," I said.

He asked me to sit beside him on the bed and leaned closer. I wondered if Mrs. Klein was right about our relationship.

He whispered, "If *Acting* Chief King is this mad after we turned the papers over to the police, what's he going to do when he finds out we were in Lexington interrogating a key player in *his* case?"

I was so shook about being thrown in jail—albeit a nice, clean, almost sterile-looking, jail—I hadn't thought that far ahead. My initial reaction was to come clean with the chief, tell him everything, and pray for the best. My second reaction was that I knew any self-respecting lawyer (if there was such a thing) would gag on that approach.

"Let's wait and see what Sean says in the morning," I said. "I'm about at the end of my rope on this. We seem to be losing." My head was splitting from ear to ear, I was hungry, and I was ready to crawl into a ball and fall asleep—on the floor.

"Chris, Chris," said Charles. He was slowly shaking his head. "As my least favorite president, Tricky Dick, once said, 'A man is not finished when he is defeated. He is finished when he quits.'"

Then I quit, I thought. But decided not to tell Charles—I didn't need a prison riot.

CHAPTER 49

"Wake up." Someone was shaking my shoulder. I thought—hoped—it was Amber. The room was illuminated by a low-watt bulb outside the cell. Reality oozed into my caged-in brain. Charles was rudely shaking me from a sound sleep. A blurred look around told me that I wasn't where I wanted to be, and the total silence around me combined with my stuck-shut eyes, told me roosters were still asleep.

"What?" I asked, not even pretending to be polite. I stretched my legs and sat upright. I felt like I'd been carrying fifty-pound bags of potatoes on my head; a shooting pain ran down my back. Every bone in my body ached.

"Ready to break out of this joint?" he asked. A wide grin covered his shadow-covered face. "Just kidding—always wanted to say that."

Now polite was in my rearview mirror. "You woke me to tell a joke!"

"Of course not," he said, feigning hurt. "It just came out. Sorry."

My eyes were growing accustomed to the low light. "So, why?"

Charles had moved back to his steel bed and stared at me. "I wanted to wait until morning to talk to you, but couldn't."

He continued looking at me as I rubbed my eyes with my wrist. I nodded and looked at my watch—3:15.

"I've been on Folly Beach for nearly a quarter of a century." He looked down at the fingers on his left hand. "During that time, I've never been on a payroll. I worked some here and there, earned a few dollars under the table; been considered a bum by a few; been 'that's ole Charles' to others. I know some see me as a joke, a worthless, but harmless, inconvenience." He looked at the floor. "I know a flock of folks, but none would consider me a close friend." He looked up; his eyes were red. "Until you came along. You treated me like a person, taught me photography, paid for some stuff you knew I couldn't afford."

"Charles ..."

"No," he said, "please let me finish. I just memorized this a few minutes ago. You became my best friend. Sure, you make fun of me sometimes." He smiled. "For good reason usually; but you treat me with respect, and when you opened the gallery, you gave me real responsibility. You gave me purpose ... a purpose. If you close the gallery, it'll pull that out from under me. I don't want you to lose money, but I don't want you to close *our* gallery." He hesitated and looked toward the door. "There, now I've said it. Go back to sleep—pleasant dreams."

"Whoa," I said. "You didn't wake me out of a dream—a very good one, I might add—and lay this on me and then go beddy-bye." I was humbled and touched, but needed to lighten the mood—not the easiest thing to do sitting in a jail cell at 3:15 a.m.

"Okay," he said, "now that you're awake and I've said my piece, let's talk about the murders."

"Why not?" I said. "My head's killing me, and my back feels like it should be in a pretzel bag. What about the murders?"

"We agree," he began, "it must have something to do with the Edge."

"Yeah."

"And we've eliminated Lester, Arno, Pat, and Cindy."

"Since Lester and Pat are dead, Arno almost was, and we both know Cindy—yeah, I guess."

"Then that leaves the missing Travis Green, songbird Heather Lee, Harley Harley, old Mrs. Klein, and ... and Cal."

"Assuming it's someone living there."

"Okay, for the sake of argument, let's say the killer was someone who worked on Stewart Barlow's house and is a guy."

"I'm not sure that's accurate," I said. "But go with it."

"That eliminates Heather and Mrs. Klein. Harley's a plumber and knows his way around a bow and arrow, has a weak alibi, but passed the lie detector test—so he's probably out."

"Those tests aren't foolproof. Another weak assumption, but okay."

"That leaves Travis Green and Cal. And," said Charles, "since Travis drives a Volvo, he couldn't be the killer."

I smiled as I thought of Dude's proclamation. "Knocks him right out of the running," I said.

Charles appeared not to see the humor. "So," he said, "did we spend the last three days with a cold-blooded killer? A crooning, Hank Williams-imitating, cold-blooded, psycho killer?"

All my adult life, I had found that things seemed at their worst in the middle of the night. This moment was no exception. "To be honest, I don't know."

"Me either. Dream away."

*   *   *

Things didn't appear much better when 7:00 a.m. rolled around—especially when the next sight my weary, sleep-filled, eyes saw was Acting Chief King yanking open the door to the room where Charles and I were sleeping. His burly body filled every cubic inch of his uniform shirt and slacks; his scowl was magnified by the scar over his eye.

He rammed his open palm into the steel door. I saw it coming and wasn't startled; flesh on steel jarred Charles out of his sleep. "What'd I tell you when we met?" growled King. "What'd I say about your damn meddling? Where'd I tell you you'd end up if you didn't pay attention?"

I assumed his questions were rhetorical and didn't speak. I wasn't sure Charles could; his eyes were still trying to focus. We were exactly where he said we would be.

"Don't even try to explain," he said. "Your freakin' lawyer is out there to talk to you." He waved us out of the room and motioned us down the narrow corridor to a battered, wooden table and four chairs in another tiny room. "We'll continue this later." He spun and stomped out.

Charles's faux grin emerged. "Something to look forward to."

I heard muted conversation from outside, and then Sean Aker came in and greeted us with a smile.

"Pleasant night?" he asked. He was dressed in Folly Beach attorney-casual, wrinkled khakis, a bright orange polo shirt, no socks, and scuffed, dusty, deck shoes.

We were short on humorous comebacks, so we stared at our attorney and waited for him to sit.

"I had a nice, pleasant conversation with your new best friend, Chief King," Sean began. "Before I tell you what we discussed, tell me everything you know about *finding* Pat Rowland's papers and anything else about the murders."

"Well," started Charles, "we ..."

"Hold it," interrupted Sean. "If you did anything illegal, you may want to skip it when telling me what happened. I'm *not* a criminal attorney." He paused and glared at my cellmate. "But I know I can't knowingly lie to the police."

We spent the better part of an hour telling Sean everything we knew about Pat Rowland, what we had learned from the box of papers, and our trip to Lexington and talk with Stewart Barlow. He asked a few questions but spent most of the time shaking his head and running his hands through his thick crop of hair. "Happy camper" wouldn't describe his stare.

We finished and leaned back in our chairs. Sean looked at each of us and down at the notes he had taken. He then pushed his chair away from the table, stood, and walked to the door. He hesitated and then returned to the table.

"Okay, here's where we are. Other than gross meddling, the chief doesn't have a whit of spit to hold you on. You turned over the papers—maybe not as quickly as you should have—but you turned them over. The trip to Lexington is a bit problematic. It was more than gross meddling; it could have impeded a police investigation, but it still won't stick."

"What next?" I asked.

"We ask the chief to come in, give him our best smiles, and grovel."

"Gee," said Charles, "we're paying you for that advice?"

"First," said Sean, "you know you won't be paying me a dime. Second, the chief knows he doesn't have anything on you. Third, I talked to the Charleston County police this morning, and they're frustrated with our acting chief and he knows it. He's in no position to make a big deal out of two meddlers in the middle of the largest murder investigation in eons."

"Concerned citizens," said Charles.

"Meddlers," said Sean.

Sean had my vote.

"Now," said Sean, "are you going to listen to me, or argue semantics?"

Charles huffed and puffed, took a deep breath, and then we listened to what Sean had to say.

"Bring on the chief," Charles said.

Charles could spread BS better than a farmer could spread its namesake, so he was our spokesperson. Sean made sure to sit in knee-kicking distance. Charles began and shared how he had been having a pleasant conversation with his *friend*, Mrs. Klein, and how she had accidentally let it slip that Pat Rowland had left a box in the storage locker. Of course, according to Charles, we knew that the box would be of great value to the police, and so we had asked Mrs. Klein if we could take it to give to the *proper authorities*. He forgot the part about copying the documents. Acting Chief King was sitting back in the fourth chair around the table; his arms were folded in front of him. He wasn't believing a word from my tale-spinning friend.

Charles then told the acting chief that he wanted to see where his good friend, Chris, had lived in Louisville and convinced me that we should take a long weekend and visit Kentucky. Lo and behold, Country Cal wanted to go with us, and coincidentally, during the trip, I had remembered the name Stewart Barlow from the papers we had turned over to the *proper authorities*. Since we were driving right by Lexington, Cal thought it might be a good idea to stop and see Mr. Barlow. If we learned anything, we could tell the *proper authorities*, thus saving taxpayers money and the police time by not having to go all the way to Lexington.

I was touched by how conscientious and concerned we were about taxpayers' money.

Our noncriminal attorney figuratively stepped in and held up his hand to Charles. "There you have it, Chief. My clients have been forthcoming." He turned to me, "Chris, did you learn anything from Mr. Barlow that could help Chief King with solving these heinous crimes?"

Sean wanted to steer past the fact that we failed to get within eighty miles of Louisville, had rooted though the papers enough to learn about Barlow's address, and the time lag between when we found the box and when we turned it over to the police. Thank you, Sean.

I reached for my most sincere voice and told the chief how distressed Barlow was when we told him that the investigator he had hired was dead. I also told him how unhinged he had appeared when we mentioned two of the names we had accidentally seen in the box of papers from Pat Rowland—Timothy Bussy and Peter Loy.

Acting Chief King surprised me when he asked what it meant.

"I'm not sure," I said. "But it shook him. We simply asked if he knew them, and he reacted like a dark secret had been uncovered."

"Hmm," said King.

"He also said he was in France the week before," I said. "If that's true, he couldn't be Rowland's killer. That should be easy for you to verify."

"Fellows," said Sean as he pushed the chair back from the table, "let me talk to the chief a minute. I'll be back."

Like we had a choice, I thought.

Sean and the chief left, and the minute turned to an hour. We stayed at the table. We must not have been considered a flight risk since we were not escorted back into the cell.

Sean opened the door and stuck his head into the room. "Let's go."

I looked at Charles. "No argument from me," he said.

CHAPTER 50

"Yo, Bonnie and Clydster," yelled Dude. He was sitting at his regular table in the Dog and waving a copy of *Astronomy* magazine over his head for us to join him.

"I'm Clydster," I whispered to Charles as I tried to be invisible and hurried toward his table along the far wall. Moments earlier, we had "escaped from the big house," as Charles had proudly put it. More accurately, we had walked out of the small holding cell in the city hall, but I agreed with Charles's glee. A celebratory breakfast would help us adjust back into freedom. I should have known that rumors traveled faster than our feet carried us the three blocks.

We passed the table where the two city council members held their daily meet-and-greet sessions and were subjected to Councilmember Salmon's off-key humming of the theme from "Cops." He made Heather Lee sound like Tammy Wynette. "Hide the silverware, they're out," came from someone at the table closest to the counter, but by the time I turned to see who it was, the three men and one woman at the table had their heads buried in menus. Charles grinned, and I kept walking.

"Couldn't keep the striped shirts, huh?" said Dude. He was enjoying himself far too much.

"Nope," said Charles with a straight face. "Had to give the saw you sent back too; the acting chief enjoyed the cake."

"You should've vegged in the clink for the big-blow," said Dude. His grin had faded. "Jail be safe when Greta visits. She ain't no Gidget heading our way."

I knew I'd regret it, but blundered ahead. "'Gidget'—the movie?"

Dude rolled his eyes—one of these days he'll learn he's dealing with a landlubber. I looked to Charles for a translation.

He didn't disappoint. "Gidget's a contraction for *girl midget*, a small female surfer. Right, Dude?"

"Well, yeah," said Dude. "Of course! Dude to Chris; Greta's going to be a big-butt-blow."

Now that we were on the same page—okay, same planet—I asked Dude when and where they're saying Greta will hit.

"Fish day; where we unloaded my boat to that sucker last year," said Dude.

"Friday at Murrell's Inlet," said Charles.

"Charles," I said, "I got it—I was there, remember?" Murrell's Inlet was about ninety miles north of us, but I also remembered that Hurricane Frank was supposed to hit Savannah and it decided to visit my front door instead. How can experts tell the exact time of sunrise in the year 2941 and screw up where a hurricane will hit by a hundred miles? I knew better than to ask Dude or Charles.

"Enough big-blow jabber," said Dude. "That be somebody else's bad. Who be bumping off bods?"

I didn't see an upside to sharing our theories with Dude, so I shrugged and asked him if he had heard anything else about his friend, Travis Green.

"Still be gone," he said. He shook his head; his long, gray hair waved freely following his head. "Think he be croaked … yeah, he be croaked."

Charles asked why he thought that.

Dude looked toward the door to the front patio and then back at his glass of water.

"Intestines." Dude looked up from the water glass and alternated his gaze between the two of us and repeated, "Intestines." He abruptly stood, took his magazine from under his napkin, and left.

Charles and I were in no position to argue. I prayed Dude's gut—intestines—was wrong.

We were almost finished with the breakfast that Amber had stealthily slipped in front of us while we were talking to Dude. Charles remembered that it was Tuesday and decided that we needed to go to GB's for the country jamboree. He also decided that the *we* should include Larry, Cindy, Amber, and anybody he could "pick up" between now and then.

I was pleased when Amber said, "Sure, Jason's doing homework and spending the night with Samuel." Our luck ran out when a call to Pewter Hardware resulted in Larry laughing at me. He was in "hurricane's a-coming" mode and needed to overfill the shelves with screws, plywood, generators, pumps, and batteries. He also said that Cindy was working the second shift and might drop by GB's later. I wished Charles good hunting on his quest to find a date and walked home to take a nap.

A night in the hoosegow was exhausting; who would've thought?

CHAPTER 51

Age and a growing paunch took much of the pleasure out of walking, but I knew parking anywhere near GB's would be near impossible. Amber's apartment was only a block from the Tuesday night happening, so I met her at her door for the short walk to the bar.

I continued to be amazed how fantastic she could look after an exhausting day on her feet smiling at customers like she truly cared how much extra syrup they wanted for their pancakes or how glorious their day at the beach was going to be. I was amazed and pleased. I gave her a "hello" kiss that lingered to the point where I almost suggested that we skip the jamboree and spend a quiet evening in the apartment—kitchen and living room excluded. The sweet smell of bath powder, the touch of her slightly damp auburn hair, and the cute dimples in her cheeks when she smiled were hard to resist, but I knew if we didn't show up at GB's in the next fifteen minutes, Charles, his date, if he managed to find one, and no telling who else, would be knocking on the door interrupting any privacy we could muster.

"About time you got here," said Charles before our feet had cleared the threshold. He had pulled two of the round tables along the wall opposite the bar. Seven chairs were already situated around the tables. Charles, Country Cal, Arno Porchini, and Heather Lee occupied four of the chairs, and seven beer bottles occupied the tables.

Cal was in his stage outfit. I saw his rhinestone coat in a new light; I smiled to myself when I thought about the supplier of his fine jewels. He saw Amber and stood, tipped his Stetson, and pulled one of the three vacant chairs out for her.

"Ah," she said, "one gentleman in this dive."

Cal beamed and waved to the waitress. Amber ordered a Miller Light; I asked for GB's finest white wine. They only had one, so it sounded more lavish than it was—Chris, the connoisseur.

It was early, but there was only one empty table. The strong smell of onions on the grill and the stale smell of beer were in the air. I recognized a few of the patrons, but several had the sunburned glow of vacationers. I wondered how long it would take them to figure out that Garth Brooks wouldn't be dropping by.

Charles sat closest to the wall, and Heather perched cross-legged on the chair next to him. She wore the same yellow sequined blouse and wide-brimmed straw hat I'd seen on her each Tuesday. She had on slacks instead of the billowy skirt. There were two beer bottles in front of her—one half empty, the other ready for the recycle bin.

Arno was in the chair to the right of Charles. His sling was showing wear; streaks of dirt covered the area under his elbow, and someone had tried to sign the side. It was still wrapped around his shoulder, and he grimaced every time he lifted the beer bottle. He already had two empty bottles in front of him. The grimaces should subside shortly.

"How's your shoulder?" asked Amber. She had taken the first sip of her drink and was turned facing Arno.

"Killing me," he said and took another swig. "Go to the doc next week; damned pain pills ain't doing a thing."

One of Charles's friends, Jim Something-or-other, came over to the table. Jim worked at the Holiday Inn, and I'd had several pleasant conversations with him during many of my coffee runs. He said hi to Arno, Amber, and me, and then leaned down to Charles. "Hear you spent a night wasting my tax money," he said and laughed. "Does you right. When're you going to give up on this country music and get a good music education over at the Bluegrass Society?"

Jim was one of the organizers of the Folly Beach Bluegrass Society and their popular Thursday night bluegrass jam at the Rock and Roll Rolling Thunder Roadhouse—called the Roadhouse Café by the locals. Charles said something about Thursdays were his night to get a facial and he couldn't work bluegrass into his schedule. Jim looked at Charles and waited for a follow-up comment. Charles looked at him and grinned. I choked on my wine—Charles, a facial!

"Funny," said Jim, who turned and started back to the bar, but hesitated. "Remember, Charles, country music comes and goes; bluegrass is forever."

"So are death and taxes," said Charles, but Jim was already across the room.

GB tapped on the old-fashioned mike and cluttered the airwaves with the electronic equivalent of fingers scratching a chalkboard. "Testing, testing," screeched his smoke-clouded voice. He welcomed "friends, good buddies, and vacationers from afar to a night of music you'll never forget." I wasn't sure where he put Jim in that mix; after all, he was trying to recruit patrons away from GB's to forever bluegrass.

Heather reached behind the chair for her guitar, told us that she was first, and then bounded toward the raised wooden stage. GB had started her introduction. Cal leaned over to me. "I've told him; I've told him. I've told GB not to start with Heather—the customers aren't drunk enough yet."

I tried to be polite but couldn't stifle a little laugh.

As a prelude to her terrible singing, she honored her fans with the nonmelodious sounds of her tuning the guitar. I heard Arno ask how Charles liked his accommodations last night and if he was any closer to catching the killer. Cal told "North Carolina," known to me as Amber, that if she ever got tired of "boring ole Kentucky" she was hanging around with, he was "available to soothe all your aches and pains, give you new dreams, and make you feel eighteen again."

She said "eeyew" to experiencing eighteen again but would remember his kind offer. She reached around me and pulled me closer and kissed me on the cheek. I was beginning to relax despite Heather's best efforts to destroy my hearing. She was singing a cockatoo's version of "I Fall to Pieces."

Heather had finished her quota of one song, and GB was telling his friends and good buddies that "World-Famous Recording Artist, Country Cal" would be on a little later and to drink up. I looked at Cal and mouthed, "World-Famous."

He sat back in his chair and grinned. "Ain't GB the best?" he asked.

I flashed back to my days in the world of work and remembered how my company would give someone a fancy title instead of a raise.

GB would have fit in well. I also flashed back to the middle of last night when Charles and I had decided that the killer was either the mysterious, missing, Volvo-driving Travis Green or my friend, the world-famous Country Cal. *Please let it be Travis.*

Cal noticed two unattended females at the bar and excused himself to "make proper introductions." Amber excused herself to visit the ladies' room. I moved two chairs over and butted into the conversation between Charles and Arno.

Charles was telling Arno that he didn't think the killer would come after him again. "Chris and I," said Charles, "have figured that Pat Rowland was the target. It had something to do with some stolen stuff in Kentucky."

Arno did a double take at Charles and then turned to me. "Then why'd the killer murder Lester, shoot me, and, God forbid, maybe Travis?" He paused like he had a thought. "Or is it Travis?"

"To confuse the cops," said Charles before I could respond. "I think you're safe."

"Easy for you to say," said Arno. His voice was getting louder, and he was becoming more agitated. "You weren't the one with the damned arrow in you." He took another long swig. "I'm scared ... thinking about leaving this godforsaken island. Even rough-tough Harley's getting spooked and talking about skipping."

"I don't think you're in more danger," said Charles. "Besides, we told the cops most of it, so it shouldn't be long before they catch him. Hang in here." Charles continued to whisper. "Besides, where would you go?"

Amber had returned and saw we were in deep conversation. She quietly sat on the other side of the table.

Arno smiled at her and turned his attention back to Charles. "I'm a good carpenter. I could get a job anywhere."

Charles laughed. "True," he said. "I remember those carpenters over on Sea Crest at that remodel job getting mad at you when you built that sawhorse-like-thingee that held one end of that eight-foot-long two-by-four so you didn't need someone to hold the other end while you nailed it to the wall."

Arno smiled. "Yeah, I remember," he said. "The contractor fired one of them; told him he didn't need him. Thought the guy was going to punch me out. Ah, the good old days."

Once again, Charles was able to turn someone's terrible, frightened mood to laughter.

Cal returned and looked at each of us. "They look like lesbos to you?" he asked.

Charles lowered his head and rolled his eyes up to look at the two ladies still sitting at the bar. "Not until you walked over."

Cal glared at Charles. I laughed. Arno moaned. And Amber slowly lifted the bottle to her lovely lips.

Heather had stopped at a table of vacationers—given away by their stop-light-red complexion—and shook hands with each of them before moseying back to our table.

"Fine job, Heather," said Cal as he tipped his hat to her.

"Nice," said Amber.

I simply nodded.

Charles took his hat from the back of his chair, put it on, and then, not to be outdone by Cal, tipped it toward Heather. "Really good," he said.

Heather beamed and then hugged Charles. He almost fell out of the chair.

She repositioned her chair and moved closer to Charles. *Hmm*, I thought.

The next singer, a younger, heavier, and less talented—much less talented—version of Randy Travis was working his way through "1982," but few in the standing-room-only bar could hear him. The group at each table had to talk louder to be heard over the voices coming from the adjacent table. Instead of yelling across our table, I talked to Amber—my preference anyway. Out of the corner of my eye, I could see Charles leaning toward Heather; both were laughing. And Cal and Arno were deep in conversation. The more Arno drank, the less he grimaced when he moved his arm. Apparently, his doctor had prescribed the wrong painkiller.

Was this the calm before the storm?

CHAPTER 52

I did something Wednesday morning I had been determined not to do since I retired. I turned on the radio to hear the weather. I wished I hadn't.

The harried weatherman was recounting the top story and telling the early-morning listeners that Hurricane Greta was now a Category 4 storm, with sustained winds exceeding 140 miles per hour. It was located off the coast of Florida and projected to hit landfall Friday somewhere between Charleston and Georgetown.

I stared at the radio. What we had talked about for several days was only talk. Now Greta was being spoken of in the same breath as Hurricane Hugo, one of the worst storms ever to hit the area, and I was sitting a few miles from where it was projected to slam ashore.

The weatherman had passed the mike to a newscaster, who reported that mandatory evacuations would be imposed—possibly as early as in the morning from as far south as Savannah and as far north as Myrtle Beach. It didn't take a geography degree to know that Folly Beach was dead in the center.

I looked down; my hands shook. In two weeks: two hurricanes; two murders, maybe three, one attempted murder; a failing business; a night in jail; being subjected to Heather's "singing"; and a headache to cheer the heart—and wallet—of a neurologist. I also realized I was hungry; my total food consumption at GB's was fries swiped off Amber's plate. I threw on my I-live-here-and-can-wear-what-I-want clothes and headed next door to Bert's to grab some junk food. Others must have been listening to the weather alarmists; the line of customers was longer than for a Miley Cyrus concert—shelves that normally held bread, milk, beer, and batteries were empty.

I had no interest in fighting the herds and turned toward the Holiday Inn. I didn't want my friends at the Dog to see me in my current state; the nice, pleasant, hot, and predictable breakfast at the hotel sounded better with each step.

Breakfast was not to be. A white, City of Folly Beach Crown Vic patrol car pulled beside me before I crossed Arctic Avenue to cross the hotel's parking lot. Cindy Ash lowered the window, looked around, and asked me to hop in. Hop in didn't sound like a formal command, so I walked around the cruiser and slid into the front seat instead of behind the partition.

"What's up?" I asked.

She continued to look around. "Hold on," she said; her voice cracked.

She drove about three blocks past her apartment and pulled into one of several small lots available for beach parking.

"The Sheriff's Department arrested Cal."

I was stunned. "Huh … when, why? I was with him until late last night."

"They kicked his door in around four." She slurred *they* into an obscenity. "Took about twenty of them to arrest one sleeping cowboy singer. Happened right over my room. Sounded like a herd of buffalo stampeding across Wyoming. Woke everyone in the building." Her voice grew louder. "Nearly gave Mrs. Klein a heart attack. Idiots!"

"What charge?"

"Two counts of murder; one of attempted murder."

Charles and I had discussed Cal as a suspect, but I was still shocked. "He say anything?"

"Hell if I know. I rushed out of my room when I heard the commotion. One of the deputies grabbed my arm; said, 'Now get back in your room, missy' … missy! He knew I was on the job but treated me like I was seven."

"Evidence?"

"I headed to the station," she said. "No way to go back to sleep. Wasn't scheduled to go on duty until seven, so I hung around the station until then."

I knew she had heard my question; I waited. She was fidgeting less and not looking around to see if she was being watched.

"One of the jackass sheriff's deputies bullied his way into the station about five—all puffed up and cocky like he'd caught Osama Bin Laden. He lowered himself enough to tell a couple of us stupid local cops that his office received a call telling them that Calvin Ballew was the killer and that the crossbow was in his room."

"Was it?"

"Sure was; wrapped in a mangy beach towel under his bed—surprise, surprise."

"Trace the call?"

"Prepay cell phone; no way to trace."

"Convenient ... convenient and fishy," I said.

"Not fishy enough for the brilliant detectives," she said. "They hauled him off to the county jail."

Cindy jumped out of the cruiser and began walking toward the beach. I followed. She kicked the sand and cursed under her breath. I had no idea if Cal was the killer; could make a good argument either way; but the dead fish smell in the air matched my comments about the helpful—fishy—tip.

Cindy took a couple of deep breaths, and we stood side by side and looked out to sea. I listened to her wax profanely in her east Tennessee twang.

I felt helpless.

"Got to get back on patrol. My day could only get worse if *Acting* Chief King caught me talking to you." She finally smiled and offered to take me back to the hotel. I told her I needed a walk. She thanked me for listening to her rant.

I was having trouble catching my breath by the time I made it to the hotel. It wasn't that far, but the humidity must have been 700 percent. My food-stained golf shirt was sticking to my skin. I entered the side door and plopped my less-than-trim body onto one of the new, green, cushioned chairs in the corridor overlooking the pool. I sat for a moment to let my heartbeat settle and stared at the new glass-covered columns as the high-tech lighting changed colors to give the effect of the changing sea. I even resisted a cup of "complimentary" coffee.

I tried to remember anything significant from last night. Charles, Heather, and Cal had been soaking up the ambiance of GB's when I left around eleven. Arno's Milwaukee-produced medication had worn off, and he left before I did. Harley even stopped by around ten and had a beer. Charles introduced him to the others before he said he had to get his hog home.

The sun was shining brightly; hardly a cloud was in the sky; the sea was no rougher than usual. And I sat here knowing that one of the largest hurricanes in decades was churning a few hundred miles away, preparing to wreak havoc on us. The beautiful calm sea was filled with vacationers from all over the country; the same sea that hid sharks, riptides, and other unseen dangers—and a new friend was either a gruesome killer, or there was someone smiling and getting away with murder. Irony flowed as powerfully as the tide.

I called Charles. He probably had already heard about Cal since Cindy said that the commotion woke everyone; Heather may have called her new "fan" with the news.

Charles didn't own a cell phone, so if he failed to answer, the only way to contact him was to ride around the island until you found him. After seven rings, I was afraid I would have to enter the September sauna. His groggy, last-second "hello" saved me.

"Heard about Cal?" I asked without preamble.

"What about him?" He was more alert.

I gave him a thirty-second sound bite about the arrest and asked him to meet me on the pier. He hesitated, which surprised me. He was usually ready to go at the drop of a Tilley. He hemmed and hawed before saying he would be there in a half hour. That was fine; I was finally getting comfortable, and my shirt wasn't sticking quite as tight to my back.

Jim stopped by the chair to make sure I'd survived a night of country music and to encourage me to "see the light" and convert to bluegrass. I said I'd think about it. I then asked Diane, the night clerk, if she had an update on Greta. She didn't but said she was heading as far away as she could get when she got off. She had already requested vacation time for the rest of the week and had relatives somewhere near Greenville. She told me to get out, too.

As we were talking, I saw Charles pedal up to the front of the hotel on his trusty Schwinn. He parked it to the left of the main doors. He had on a long-sleeve, white, Arizona State Sun Devils T-Shirt, faded jeans, and his hat.

I pointed at his shirt. "To scare off Greta?"

We walked toward the east end of the hotel and then across the parking lot to the steps leading to the pier. To his credit, he didn't start peppering me with questions until we were halfway out the pier and settled on one of the many wooden, stationary benches that lined the impressive structure.

"I thought maybe Heather would have called you; Cindy said the cops made enough noise to wake everyone."

"Umm ..." He paused and looked toward the boardinghouse. "Nope."

I turned toward Charles and saw a rare sight. He blushed. "Yeah," I said, "maybe she wasn't close enough to hear the commotion."

"What else did Cindy say?" His changing the subject answered my unasked question.

I told him about the anonymous tip, the untraceable cell phone, and the crossbow under the bed.

He slammed the point of his cane on the wooden deck of the pier. "That proves it."

Proof was the last thing I heard in my recounting Cindy's story. "Proves what?"

"Travis Green's the killer. Heather told us."

"Yeah, but ..."

"We knew it was Cal or Travis. Remember?"

"Suspected."

"Chris, you know Cal. He's managed to hobo around this country for more than forty years; lived by his wits; made a few bucks when he needed to; knew how to do what he had to do. See?"

"Yes."

"Does he strike you as stupid?"

I was getting a little tired of playing twenty questions. "No—so?"

"So," he said, "I'll tell you so what. Cal's smart and has street smarts to boot—he's too danged smart to leave the murder weapon under his bed. Come on, I could show you a zillion places on Folly Beach to hide it and never get caught. And, get real, an anonymous tip from an untraceable phone? I'll bet my Saab that they don't find prints on the crossbow. And when they don't find prints, does it sound like Cal to wipe the prints off the weapon and then put it under his bed for the crossbow fairy to find?" He stood and pointed his cane toward the Edge. "What more proof do you need? Cal didn't do it."

I'd hate for Charles to be Cal's lawyer, but he was right.

CHAPTER 53

"Hi, Mrs. Klein," yelled Charles. He and I were walking along the dune line between the boardinghouse and the beach. "Remember us? I'm Charles, and this is Chris." Once she noticed us, Charles veered away from the beach and to the steel steps that led to her terraced yard.

"Of course I do, young man." She leaned on the shovel she was holding and gave Charles a stern look. "I'm old, not senile. And don't ask, I'm still not going to rent to you boys."

"We've already found a place, Mrs. Klein. We were just walking down the beach and saw you and wanted to say hello."

Just walking down the beach, I thought. Charles made me sit on the pier for the last hour waiting for Mrs. Klein to appear. I told him she had probably evacuated. When he saw her come around the corner, he did a Ray Charles bob with his head and said, "See?"

"Sorry, boys," she said. "I'm a little cranky. Up all night; police stomping all over the place; arrested one of my tenants."

"We'd heard something about that," said Charles. "Terrible."

"Come sit a spell," she said. "I recall you two are a bit wimpy and have to be in the shade." She slowly headed to the table where we had gathered on our first visit. She wore the same faded, print dress.

"Ready to head inland?" I asked.

"Lordy, boys," she said and looked toward the high, puffy clouds on the horizon. "Joseph and I sat right in this house during Hurricane David in '79; Joseph's spirit and I welcomed Hugo in '89; others came and went through the years; and wasn't it just the other day that Frank came a-calling?" In a move that must have given Charles a thrill, she lifted her shovel and jabbed the business end in the air to the east. "It'll take more than a damned old wind to get me out of this house—put money on it!"

I looked at the cracks in the wall that she had pointed out during our first visit and would have sworn that the entire second floor leaned toward us.

Charles asked if she had someone to take her off the island in case she decided to leave.

"Didn't you hear me, boy?" she yelled, her normal voice. "Let me tell a story."

She dropped the shovel beside the table and lifted her head toward the sun. She took a cigarette from a pack that was already on the table, lit it, and took a long draw.

"My dear husband, Joseph, worked for the Ringling Bros. and Barnum & Bailey Circus from '36 to '41." She had told us that more than once, but I didn't interrupt. "Back around '38 or '39, can't remember which, the circus was playing small towns in northern Florida; ocean side, not the gulf. Yep, Atlantic. Well, a humongous old hurricane was supposed to hit smack-dab where they had their big tent. The weather experts told them they had less than twelve hours to head-em-up and move-em-out." She took another puff and stared off to the horizon. "In those days, most of the performers were foreign—especially the high-wire acts and the fellows with the big cats. Names and countries I couldn't pronounce. Well, with the threat of wars and problem with all the countries, a lot of them snuck into the good old US of A on forged passports. Seems the government was looser then. Government—now don't get me off on that subject."

"We'll try not to," shouted Charles. "Go on."

"Joseph said those fake passports were worth more than any amount of gold; said until his dying day that illegals could do anything they wanted with those fake documents. Well, it backfired. They got the train loaded and moving, and along came the hurricane—some man's name. I can't remember what." She hesitated. "No, can't remember its name. Anyway, two of the cars were blown off the tracks just as the train was crossing a bridge. Joseph always said it was meant to be. Well, fifteen of those illegals were killed when their train car was trapped under the bridge. They drowned." She hesitated again and stared at the ocean. "Terrible, terrible."

"That's horrible," I said. "Was Joseph okay?"

"Yeah, he was in the front car; didn't know anything had happened until the train jerked to a stop."

"How did the fake passports backfire?" asked Charles.

"No one ever found out who the men were—all their names were wrong." She shook her head. "They buried the entire group in a rundown cemetery in Florida, smack-dab in the middle of nowhere. The golden passports became fool's gold. So sad." She looked up from her memories and looked at her house. "Safer to stay, boys. Mark my words, safer to stay."

"Be careful, Mrs. Klein," said Charles. "We don't want anything happening to you."

"Worst thing that'd happen is I'd end up dead," she said as she pulled another cigarette out. "Lordy, it's about my time anyway—maybe past time. Not like what's happening to my tenants." She lit the cigarette and started playing with the polished chrome Zippo lighter. "You boys don't think Cal did it, do you?"

"No," said Charles.

"Good. He thinks the world of you two. Told me your trip to Kentucky was the best time he'd had in decades. He didn't do it."

"Who then?" I asked.

"Hope it's Travis Green—he's done split. I thought he was a nice young man, but you never know." She took another puff. "No, you never know. Don't look past Harley. He smokes, you know. One thing my dear husband, Joseph, always said was, you can't believe what's right in front of your eyes. He learned that from the con men in the circus; he always kept talking about misdirection, deception, all circus and magic tricks. To be honest, boys, I never really understood what he meant, but it didn't stop him from saying it, over and over, and over."

She flicked the cigarette butt toward the surf, pulled herself up using the shovel for support, and grinned. "Time for a nap. Watch out for stray hurricanes." She laughed until she coughed.

*   *   *

I walked to the gallery, and Charles headed off to retrieve his bike from the hotel. He asked if I needed help, and I told him no. I didn't expect customers with Greta looming but wanted to make sure everything was off the floor and secure in case wind or water found their way in.

The phone was ringing as I unlocked the door. I picked it up and made the mistake of holding it near my ear.

"When in the hell were you going to answer? The cows have already come home to roost."

"Hi, Bob, want to buy a photo?"

"You know damned well I don't. Since you're being a smart-ass and not a recording, I'm deducing you're still in the middle of Hurricaneville."

"Where are you?" I asked, still trying to sound like a professional shopkeeper.

"My wonderful and wise wife has me handcuffed to the front seat of the car as she drives to a wonderful, luxurious hotel in Asheville, North Carolina—the Grove Park Inn or something like that."

I could hear Betty laughing. I was constantly amazed that Bob had found someone who appreciated him and even thought he was humorous.

"A vacation?" I asked.

"Why, hell no," he sounded exasperated. "She told me I didn't have enough sense to come in out of the rain, much less a hurricane, and she's dragging me off for a few days of sun, sumptuous sweets, and sultry sex."

"Ha!" Betty exclaimed in the background.

"Before she sticks a gag in my mouth, here's why I called. I've got a client who has an old, four-bedroom farmhouse just north of Prosperity—you've had trouble finding prosperity, so this one's about thirty-something miles west of Columbia, just off I-26. Anyway, he called and said the house was empty and asked if I wanted to wait out Greta there. Betty already had her salacious plans, so I thought of you."

Another "Ha!" in the background.

It was irritating when Bob did something nice—screwed up his chi and made it harder to stay mad at him.

"I may take you up on that," I said. "Sounds like it'll get scary here."

Between yelling at Betty for driving too slow and then too fast—not like he would drive—he finally told me exactly where to find the gift house and key.

"Smart move," he said. "You shouldn't look a gift house in the mouth."

I thanked him and let him go, so he could keep Betty from getting them killed—or so Bob thought.

CHAPTER 54

"Did you know Hurricane Hugo was the biggest hurricane ever to hit the United States Atlantic coast above Florida?"

I was sitting in the Planet Follywood with Amber, Jason, and Samuel, listening to Jason share his newly acquired knowledge. I vaguely remembered when I was in school, we had tornado drills; I suppose coastal kids learned about hurricanes, sharks, and riptides. Planet Follywood was Jason's favorite restaurant. It was the night before the mandatory evacuation, and the restaurant was nearly empty. Most of the residents had headed west, not in wagon trains as their ancestors did, but in minivans, Dodge Ram pickups, and a dying breed, things called *cars*. Vacationers had wanted to get in every minute at the beach before being run out, so they were still at water's edge or in their condos and houses packing for the trip home from an abbreviated vacation.

"Yeah," added Samuel, "weirdest thing; it started over a zillion miles away near Africa. Can you believe that?"

I had met Samuel on my first trip to Folly Beach. He was a bright, inquisitive young man who had provided a key clue to solving a murder last year. Additionally, he was in Jason's class, and the two of them set the academic bar sky-high for their fellow classmates.

"Chris," said Amber, "the old-timers still talk about the big Atlantic House restaurant that sat out over the beach near where the hotel is now. Hugo wiped it off the map."

Hurricane trivia was a good diversion for the boys; strangely enough, it took their mind off the arrival of Greta. It wasn't working as well for me. During my short time on Folly Beach, I had heard story after story about the devastation Hugo brought to the area. Bob had told me that

80 percent of the homes on Folly Beach had been destroyed—a boon to Realtors and builders, although they had to pretend being distraught. The tides that had reached more than twenty feet above normal flooded areas that weren't destroyed by the 160-mile-per-hour winds. Greta wasn't expected to be nearly as big. I was still scared. I looked around the restaurant and wondered how high we were above sea level; my gallery was about the same elevation; my humble cottage was even closer to the ocean and sea level. It had survived Hugo; I prayed it would laugh at Greta.

With Bob's offer of a house, I had called Charles and formulated our evacuation plan—a plan that grew along with the intensity of the storm. I had invited Amber and Jason, who quickly accepted. Charles's invitation list was more complicated. Larry agreed to come but would drive separately so he could get back to his store as soon as possible. Then, in a moment of who knows what, Charles invited Heather. He hadn't told her she couldn't bring her guitar, but I wouldn't be disappointed if it was left behind. Finally, in the spirit of love, concern, good vibrations, brotherhood, and stupidity, Heather invited Arno and Harley. Harley had accepted if he could drive his hog. Space was already at a premium, so Charles agreed to his "demand." Cindy was forced to decline—Acting Chief King told his officers that come "hell, high water, or hurricane" they were going to stay on Folly Beach. After hearing King's latest failure to "win friends and influence people," I called Brian Newman to make sure he had an escape plan. Karen answered and seemed genuinely pleased that I had called. She was taking the next few days off and was moving her dad to a hotel about seventy miles inland. She wanted him to be closer to the hospital in Charleston if something happened. She said I was welcome to join them, and I mumbled something about having to help some others and thanked her for the offer. "Please call each day to let me know how you're doing," she said, and then rang off.

Samuel's family was leaving at sunrise for the safe confines of his aunt's house in Columbia, so he needed to get home early; *early* translated as no dessert. Jason, the gentleman he was, escorted Samuel four blocks to his home. I, still working on my skills as a gentleman, walked Amber to her apartment, gave, and received, a warm, extended hug, and said I'd see her in the morning.

I went to the pier instead of going home. The sun had already set, but I could still hear the eerie, sharp, pounding sounds of hammers and nail guns filling the air. They were attaching plywood sheets over windows and other glass surfaces. The pier, like Planet Follywood, was nearly deserted. The temperature must have been in the mid-eighties, with the humidity out the roof. I walked far enough out the pier to where I could see the infamous boardinghouse and then sat on the nearest wooden bench.

What would Folly Beach look like when I returned? Would my house and gallery still be standing? Was Travis Green the killer? If not Green, who? Harley? Why not Heather? Were Charles and I wrong about Cal? What was so valuable to kill several people over? When would Chief Newman return to work? If my house survived, was I ready to ask Amber to move in with me; was I ready for an instant son? What's with Charles and Heather? What's with Karen and me?

CHAPTER 55

Our unlikely band of evacuees began gathering at 9:00 a.m. the day before Greta was expected to change the Lowcountry landscape. I opened the front door and found Charles sitting on the step wearing a University of Tulsa Golden Hurricanes long-sleeve T-shirt, black shorts, old tennis shoes, and his hat. His handmade cane leaned against a tattered, olive drab, Army surplus backpack.

He remained seated and looked back over his shoulder at me. "About time," he said. "Only ten minutes early."

I looked at him, groaned, and carried my suitcase past him to the car. He followed. We had agreed that we would get Amber and Jason and then head to the Edge for the rest of the herd. Amber was always prompt, so I wasn't surprised to see her and Jason waiting at the top of the steps at their second-story apartment.

The group at the boardinghouse didn't share Charles and Amber's promptness gene. Charles muttered something about needing to cattle-prod someone, buy them watches, and getting on the stick—all said before he got out of the car and headed to the door. Five minutes later, he came out lugging a bright orange suitcase and Heather's straw hat. Heather followed a step behind and was rubbing her eyes. There was no guitar case, proving prayers could be answered. Larry pulled around the corner in his new red Chevy pickup, the Pewter Hardware logo prominently displayed on the driver's door. Arno appeared next. His arm was still in the sling, and he grimaced as he lifted his old valise into the back of Larry's truck. Harley was the last out. His evacuee possessions were in a cloth bag with an uncanny resemblance to a pillowcase. He threw the bag in the back of the truck without the glimmer of a grimace. I suspected he could have thrown Arno in with as much ease—a reminder why I wouldn't want to tangle with Harley.

We were ready to pull out when a City of Folly Beach cruiser blocked the entrance. It was Cindy, and she was alone. Harley had already mounted his namesake, and the distinct, deep rumble of the engine drowned out all conversation. Cindy nodded her head toward the front of the building, and Charles, Larry, and I followed her away from the bike.

"I wanted to tell you before you headed out," she said as she scanned the area. "We found Travis Green around midnight. He ..."

"Dead or alive?" interrupted Charles.

"Dead; arrow in the chest."

"Bolt," said Charles.

"Whatever," said Cindy.

"Where?" I asked.

"At the end of East Huron, down over a bank. From the looks of it, he's been there for days."

"Who found him?" chimed in Larry.

"A guy out there; don't remember his name; his dog had been barking up a storm, and he finally let it off the leash and followed it. He's pretty shook."

Who wouldn't be, I thought. "What about Travis's car?"

"Good question," said Cindy. "It was in the carport three houses from where the body was."

"Hadn't you been looking for it?" I asked.

She shook her head. "Yeah—we blew it," she said. "It was backed into the carport so far you wouldn't normally notice it; it was under an old vinyl car cover. It looked like it belonged to the owner of the house—a couple from Maine. They're only here in the winter.

Heather skipped around the corner and looked at the four of us gathered in a tight group. "Are we going or what?" she asked.

Cindy smiled at her and turned back to us. "That's all I know; I'll call Larry if I hear anything." She looked around one more time, decided that the entire population of Folly Beach wasn't looking, and gave Larry a hug and a long sloppy kiss on the cheek. "Take care," she whispered, and then turned to the rest of us. "You, too."

Dark, heavy, storm clouds were beginning to roll in; rain couldn't be far behind. We needed to hit the road—especially Harley's Harley.

Our minicaravan crossed over the bridge that separated Folly Beach from the rest of the country. I glanced in the rearview mirror and wondered what *my* island would look like when we returned. Traffic through Charleston was bumper-to-bumper and moved at about a half mile per hour faster than a turtle's pace. I had hoped when we reached the interstate on the other side of town, it would change. It did; our speed improved to fifteen miles per hour. Unfortunately, most roads that led to the evacuation route funneled onto I-26, and the term bottleneck was an understatement.

Heather had fallen asleep in the backseat with her head resting on Charles's shoulder. I caught a glimpse of him in the mirror; he saw me look and winked.

We had traveled all of fifty miles along the pine tree-lined I-26 when Heather got her second wind and offered to sing some tunes to "help ya'll relax." Charles conveniently fell asleep that same moment, and I whispered, "Maybe later; don't want to wake him." I saw Charles's left eye wink.

An hour later, and still an hour or so from our destination, everyone was awake and mumbling about a bathroom break. I pulled off the interstate, followed by Larry and Harley. A steady rain had been falling for the last thirty miles, and I figured Harley needed to get under roof and dry off. Many other evacuees had had the same idea, and the lines to the restrooms snaked out the door of the minimart.

We were in no hurry to get to our temporary home in Prosperity. Our rush was to get away from the beach, and we had slowly achieved that. Larry, Harley, and I stood outside under the canopy. The others were still in line for the restroom or to buy drinks. I smiled as there were as many people in line to buy liquids as there were in lines to deposit liquids.

Water dripped from Harley's helmet—a helmet that looked like it belonged on a soldier in World War I. "I can tell you one thing," he said, his voice matching his burly frame, "I'm danged glad to get out of that apartment building—not sure it'll make it through another storm."

"Why?" asked Larry. "That building's about as sturdy as anything on the beach—concrete block foundation, brick, stucco."

"Foundation ain't going anywhere," said Harley, "First floor might hold out. But the second floor's bad; it's wood covered with thin stucco; looks solid, but it ain't."

Herding the evacuees in our party was no simple task. Charles and Heather were standing in the candy aisle, seeing who could guess how many different color M&Ms were in a Trail Mix package. Jason was standing nearby with his arms folded, shaking his head.

"And they're adults, Mom?" he asked.

To her credit, Amber simply smiled.

Arno was reading the front page of the Columbia newspaper and playing with the near-tattered sling holding his wounded arm.

"Okay," said Harley, "I'm dry. Let's get back in the rain."

None of us volunteered to pilot his motorcycle the rest of the way in what was now a downpour.

Bob wasn't kidding about our temporary digs being a farmhouse. We followed his directions: "Hang a left when you leave your worthless, empty life of poverty and reach Prosperity. The manse will be a quarter mile on your right." Since it was the only house we had seen since "hanging a left," we pulled in the long, rutted, gravel drive and stopped in front of the two-story, wood frame house that could have been the cover photo on a rural electric magazine. A covered porch spanned the front.

We were greeted by three sleepy-eyed goats sitting on the porch and pondering life. Rain was getting more intense. All three goats wore collars and looked like they were as much a part of the porch as the hanging wooden swing on one end and the two rocking chairs on the opposite side. The goat that drew both Charles and Harley's attention was at the step with its head cocked and a quizzical expression on its bearded face that said, "Don't recall seeing you before—friend or foe?" His collar had a belt buckle attached that displayed the distinct bar-and-shield Harley-Davidson logo. It wasn't the logo of a university, but Charles was still impressed. Harley beamed like he had found his long-lost cousin on the sheep side of the family. Arno was less infatuated and walked around the house admiring the carpentry and workmanship that went into the farmhouse.

Charles and Harley distracted our welcoming committee while we cautiously entered the house. We were met with the musty smell of a closed-up space, but the rooms were neat, well-appointed, and dust-covered. The living room was as large as Amber's apartment; truth be known, the house was probably larger than all our living quarters combined. Jason checked the rest of the rooms. I heard him say "cool" and "wow" as he walked around. The rest of us began exploring and staking out bedrooms. The sleeping arrangements were not my first choice, but Jason's presence made the decision easier.

Charles, Amber, and Heather made a food run to a small grocery we had passed on the way in. Jason went to make sure "adult foods" were not the only things bought.

Harley talked about his home at the beach and his concern that it wouldn't be there when he got back. He said it was about the best place he had ever lived and that he was glad Mrs. Klein was leaving. Harley, Arno, and I were sitting on the front porch watching the rain, along with the three guard-goats and a large, gray cat that had pranced around the corner letting us know that it was his house.

"You sure she left?" I asked. "She told us that nothing would get her out of there."

Harley absently petted the head of the Harley-goat. "I didn't see her leave," he said, "but I think that's what she said."

"Where would she go?" asked Arno. "She doesn't have family."

"I sure as hell hope she left," said Harley as he stared off into the rain. "If she didn't, we'll never see her alive again."

That put a damper on an already saturated day.

The mood lifted when the food gatherers pulled in the drive. Charles edged the Lexus as close to the front porch as possible without flattening the small row of shrubs that lined the drive. Heather, Jason, and even Harley kept the supper talk lively and humorous—Heather with stories of mishaps along the way on her dual career as a massage therapist and country "star."

Harley surprised us when he shared that he had an earlier career as a hypnotist. He had a stage show where he hypnotized audience members to cackle like geese on a verbal command. He said he could train the mind to believe anything.

Both Jason and Charles asked him to hypnotize us. Amber put an end to that "brilliant" idea with an emphatic "No!"

Jason, to our relief, changed the subject to his adventures exploring Folly Beach with Samuel, his "best friend in the whole wide world." Amber's smile was strained during some of the stories; I'd bet this was the first time she'd heard some of his more risky antics. I felt sorry for her having to endure the minuses of child-rearing as a single mother.

The television's signal came from an old-fashioned, rabbit-ears antenna. Jason laughed at the contraption until his mom told him we could only get two channels. The weather reports were interspersed with regular programming—I was never a fan of the Weather Channel, but missed it now. The best we could figure was that Greta would be hitting the coast around noon tomorrow; the eye was expected to hit north of Charleston; and, the most scary part, it was still classified as a Category 4 storm—the next to worst possible.

Amber and Jason headed to their room first. The rest of us broke open a box of Doritos Charles had snuck into the grocery basket while the health-conscious ladies were trying to find fruit for breakfast. I told Charles what Harley had said about Mrs. Klein leaving. We hoped he was right, but Charles said it didn't make sense. She had "weathered the storm" many times without leaving, and he didn't see that she would change her ways now.

CHAPTER 56

"Chris, Chris ... are you awake? Chris ..."

The less-than-melodious voice of Charles jarred me from a rock-solid sleep—a habit I was not getting accustomed to. It was a relief not to be in jail this time. I didn't know what time it was, but knew that I couldn't have been asleep long. The strange room, combined with the storm outside, combined with Charles's bed-rattling snoring, kept me awake well after midnight.

"I'm not awake! What time is it?" I shook my head trying to push the sleep aside.

"Nearly four. Get up, let's go."

"Stop," I said. I was sitting on the side of the strange bed looking out the window at solid black—no lights, no sunshine, no nothing. Rainwater was rolling down the window glass. "Go where?"

"I've been thinking while you were enjoying your beauty sleep," he said without mentioning his snoring. "We've got to get Mrs. Klein."

I knew I wasn't dreaming—Charles had seen to that—but I couldn't believe what I was hearing. "She might not be there. Why don't we call the police and have them check on her?"

He smiled. "Ahead of you again, my friend. Used your phone and tried Cindy, no answer; then called the Folly Beach cops, phone's out." He raised his left hand and put it in front of him, palm facing me. "Before you say it," he said, "I called the Charleston Sheriff's Department, and the phone wasn't dead—would've gotten a better response if it had been." He hesitated—the smile was gone—and then threw my phone on the bed. "The jackass dispatcher said something like, 'Haven't you heard; there's a hurricane coming. I'm sure she's safe; nobody's that stupid to stay on the island.' He took her name and said he was busy and had to go ... jackass." He leaned over, picked up the phone, and yanked the sheets back. "Get dressed; time to go to the beach—bring a kite; good wind." He turned and headed to the door.

A few choice words, a few yawns, and one stumped toe on the bedside table later, I was dressed and joined Charles in the living room. Somehow, he had rustled Arno and Harley out of bed and into his adventure into the eye of the storm. Larry sat calmly on the couch. Charles had assigned him to stay and provide a "male presence for Jason and the lasses." Charles had also decided that it would be best not to wake Amber, Jason, or Heather; "wouldn't want to ruin their sleep," he said. That was a courtesy he hadn't extended to the adult male population. Besides, he didn't want to bring down the wrath of a female hurricane if Amber and Heather knew where we were going. Lucky Larry would get to tell them.

Charles's plan sounded benign when he outlined it at the house: We would drive to Folly Beach; we would arrive at the roadblock keeping people off the island around eight—hours before the eye of the storm kissed shore—and tell the police that we thought Mrs. Klein was still in her house. They would thank us and send someone to retrieve her; and, if necessary, we could bring her to Prosperity until the island reopened.

Simple enough—but not to be.

*   *   *

Traffic flowing inland on I-26 was lighter than I had expected. Clusters of vehicles passed us on their way to safety. There was hardly anyone on our side. Things changed drastically as we passed Columbia. The line of cars heading toward us intensified. A ribbon of headlights was nonstop. There were numerous fender benders between Columbia and the outskirts of Charleston. Way too many people were in too big a hurry to escape Greta's wrath. And, like all good Americans, they had waited until the last second to leave.

To kill time and keep me awake, we talked about the crossbow killer and bemoaned the fact that our sole suspect had been the recipient of a deadly arrow. And Charles and I were convinced that it couldn't be Cal. Arno and Harley were not as sure. They were quick to point out that Cal didn't have any alibis, no one knew that much about him, and—drum roll—the police found a crossbow under his bed. That was hard to argue with, but Charles and I did anyway. Why the crossbow was the weapon of choice was as big a mystery to me as the killer's identity.

The unanswered questions didn't stop Charles from proclaiming that we were going to figure it out. One of my unachieved goals in life was to be as confident as Charles, especially about things I didn't have a clue about.

The rain had stopped by the time we exited I-26 at Charleston and wiggled our way through the city to Folly Road, the last leg on our mission of mercy. There may have been a pause in the rain, but the winds were ferocious. Palmetto trees were bent in unnatural shapes; shingles from some of the older buildings were flapping, and many had already dislodged and were blowing across the road. The large signs at two drugstores were blown out, and one had fallen through the sunroof of a Mercedes parked nearby. Traffic coming toward us was at a standstill. How many people could be left to evacuate? A Shell station tow truck was in front of us, and I could only see one set of headlights in the rearview mirror.

Before we got to the strip center anchored by the Piggly Wiggly, we saw an onslaught of flashing emergency lights—fire, police, and EMS vehicles blocked the road. A late model, white SUV was upside down in our lane, and two minivans were off to the side of the road, their windshields shattered into thousands of pieces. It was bad.

Traffic leaving the beach was being rerouted through the shopping center. I took that cue, turned right into the center and continued through the parking lot until it exited onto a small side street, and then turned right on Folly Road. Charles was twisted in the seat counting the emergency vehicles. "Looks like every official car from Folly and James Island—maybe even the CIA, FBI, and Homeland Security," he said.

Cindy had told us the police would be blocking the island at Mariner's Cay Drive, a hundred yards or so from the bridge leading to the island.

There was nothing there—no police, no stanchions, no roadblock, nothing. I suggested we go back to the wreck and tell someone about Mrs. Klein; Arno and Harley both had worried looks on their faces and nodded agreement. The torrential rains had begun again. Three to one was no match for Charles. He grabbed his cane from the floorboard and pointed it toward the windshield. "That way, driver. Mrs. Klein is waiting."

The rain was coming in solid sheets; the windshield wipers didn't have the power to keep up. Brush along the road was ripped out of the ground by the winds and swirled around us; a wooden light pole from the development on our right toppled and landed less than a yard from our hood. Water from the Folly River rippled across the road. And we continued like we were on a sunny, calm drive to the beach.

I was shocked. We were unchallenged as we drove down Center Street toward the Holiday Inn and the ocean. The sun was up but hidden by layer upon layer of ominous black clouds. I didn't think it was possible, but the rain intensified; the tide had already washed over the walls separating the beach from the front row of buildings on Arctic Avenue. The parking lot at the hotel was under water, as was Arctic and a portion of Center Street. The palmettos that lined the normally calm and attractive streetscape were tilted at forty-five-degree angles and barely hanging on. Three had already been torn from the ground. Rita's Restaurant's recently built patio was covered with dark seawater. We were still more than a block from the beach.

If we were going to make it to Mrs. Klein's place, we'd need another route. Instead of challenging the rising tide, I backed up and turned at Folly's only stoplight—or it was when the electricity was on. The city was dark—no stoplight, no streetlights, no lights from the nine-story Holiday Inn. Electricity had evacuated with the residents. It was eerie.

Colorful rooftop tents on the restaurant on the corner had been yanked from their mooring and whipped in the wind; one had already sailed across the street. The sounds of the hundred-mile-an-hour winds screamed through the trees, overgrown vegetation, and man-made obstacles; it sounded like a hundred freight trains racing past.

"Whoa!" said Harley from the rear seat as I swerved to avoid a large trash dumpster that slid across the street like a steel tumbleweed. I could see a lake of salt water to the right—a spot that was usually a dry, public parking lot. Power lines dangled from the few remaining poles and blocked part of the road. We were the only vehicle moving on Folly Beach, and could weave wherever necessary to avoid victims of Greta.

The double glass doors at Bert's Market, the store that prides itself for always being open, were covered with plywood. The word *Closed* was crudely spray painted in red on the temporary wooden barrier. I stopped in front of my house and gave it a quick glance. It was standing. But two of the six, rustic, wood posts holding the rope handrails were twisted at strange angles; the remaining four posts were nowhere to be seen.

I couldn't imagine how much worse the storm would be by noon; I certainly didn't want to be around to see. I hurried the others out of the car. We weren't dressed for a heavy rain, but by this time, it didn't matter. Fortunately, it was warm.

Waves were closing in on my street, two blocks from Mrs. Klein's home. Wind was pushing the rising tide inland, sparing nothing in its path. The blacktop road leading toward the beach was our quickest and safest way to the Edge. The stop sign catty-corner to our destination was still standing, but water was nearing its top. The octagon-shaped sign whipped back and forth. We shouted to be heard.

I knew what we had to do, and we had to do it now. We left Folly Beach yesterday to get away from the wrath of Greta—now we were going to walk right into it.

I didn't see how things could get worse.

Someday—if I live that long—I'll learn not to think that.

CHAPTER 57

We're too late, I thought. Charles, Arno, Harley, and I waded across Arctic Avenue in front of the boardinghouse. We grabbed each other's arms to keep from being washed away by the turbulent current pushed by windswept waves. Harley, being the strongest by far, led our group. The water was thigh-deep at spots and swirling around us like a ball of snakes in a feeding frenzy. Water lapped the windowsills. The five windows at the side were broken, with water rolling through the openings.

I lost my footing, slipped under the tide, and swallowed a mouthful of cold salt water. Charles grabbed me around the waist. He held on until I regained my balance. Harley and Arno struggled to keep Charles afloat.

An uprooted palmetto tree blocked the door—its trunk was the diameter of a telephone pole. The roar of the wind and tide made it impossible for us to hear each other. Harley slowly worked his way to the far end and pointed for the rest of us to grab the top of the tightly-wedged tree. We fought the current and managed to move the tree only two feet; but that was enough to get to the door. Charles and Arno braced the tree so the deadly sea wouldn't ram it back against the door or me. I managed to grab the door handle and forced it open about eighteen inches. I squeezed in. Water was to my knees. It took all my strength to keep it open long enough for Charles to follow me. Both of us pushed against the door, and Arno let the tree drift back to the house. His sling was swept away by the current. The door held, and Arno got around the tree and slipped through the opening. Harley followed.

I was exhausted. I leaned against the soaking wall, gasped for breath, and looked around. The entry hall was a disaster. Furniture, which never looked great, was trashed. It bobbed in the knee-high water. Glimmers of muted light streamed into the room from two windows. Charles had his hands on his knees; or I guessed that was where they were, since his knees were under debris-strewn seawater. Harley and Arno were in much better condition and weren't even breathing hard. Harley looked around the room and shook his head. Arno's arm was dangling free. His sling was probably blocks away.

"Well, that was fun," yelled Charles. He looked around the room. "I'd love to sit ... wade ... here in the parlor with you guys, but we have work to do."

It took both Harley and me to open the door from the entry into the hall. The door to Mrs. Klein's apartment was directly across from us—and was already open, pushed by the rushing water. Her apartment was darker than the entry parlor. The only sounds I heard were wind whistling through the jagged glass in the broken front window and Charles yelling for Mrs. Klein.

There was no answer. I looked at Harley, and he shook his head and started to push the bobbing furniture around so he could see in each corner. I started on the opposite side of the room and pointed to the kitchen area for Charles and Arno to search. I didn't want to find Mrs. Klein in her apartment—if we did, she'd have breathed her last breath. The search took what seemed like an eternity—especially for such a small apartment. We shuffled our feet along the floor—in Charles's case, his cane—to probe every inch. The water was muddy and litter-filled. The smell of salt and the wet drywall made the task all that more difficult. Sweat stung my eyes. She wasn't in her apartment. I said a silent prayer.

There was a chance she'd evacuated like all other intelligent life on the island. But we had to be sure. We'd never get the rest of the house searched if we stayed together. It was still nearly impossible to hear each other; listening to a freight train speed by from three feet away would have been quieter. Arno and Harley were stronger than Charles and I, so I motioned for them to work their way through the rising water and the rest of the first floor. I pointed to Charles, to myself, and then at the stairs; we would search the second floor. Amazingly, everyone understood the hand signals. The second floor was far from the water's reach, so I thought if she hadn't evacuated, she would have headed there to avoid the rising tide.

The threadbare carpet on the stairs was soaked and slick. I slipped in the water that was beginning to cascade down the steps, but managed to keep my balance. Charles and I were three steps from the second floor when I noticed it. The horrendous sounds of Mother Nature were terrifying, but a new sound shook my faith. The reverberation of wood cracking and snapping came from above us. Light filtered through the roof. A waterfall of rainwater poured through the fissure a few feet in front of us. The Edge was collapsing—we had minutes at most to find Mrs. Klein and get out.

The room on the right at the top of the stairs was Cal's. The door was locked, but Charles rammed it with his shoulder and it flew open. We could finally hear each other talk. I told him I'd take Arno's room on the left. I was luckier than Charles; Arno's door was unlocked. I yelled for Mrs. Klein. No answer; but I searched the room anyway. It looked more like a workshop than a bedroom. There was a bed, but it was surrounded by a makeshift wooden workbench holding two saws, a hammer, a vise, and several pieces of hardwood. There was a wooden contraption about the size of a photoprinter with clamps on two of the sides. It looked like it was made to hold something.

Could it be? *It'll wait; now focus.* Where's Mrs. Klein?

I heard Charles yell that he was going to Lester's room. It faced the beach. I hurried from Arno's room and started toward Harley's, also on the front across from Lester's.

I pushed his unlocked door and saw the exterior wall buckle. The roof was pulling loose at the side wall, and the wall facing the beach was accordioned by the collapsing roof.

Time was up. I turned toward the hall and was face-to-face with Arno.

"Did you find Mrs. ..." I said before he stopped me.

Arno was out of breath. "Where's Charles?"

"Is she okay?" I asked.

Arno looked at the roof behind me. He had his good arm behind his back and a three-foot-long 2x4 in his right hand, his bad arm. "Charles?" he shouted.

Charles came out of Lester's room. "She's not in there," he said and then saw Arno.

Arno slipped around me. Charles and I were now between him and the stairs. The floor on the second story of the dying house began to shake. I looked down at the vibrating floor, looked at Charles, and then found myself staring into the barrel of a pistol.

"Shit," said Charles.

CHAPTER 58

The gun was small, no larger than twenty-five caliber, but as deadly as an atom bomb. Arno pointed the board toward the stairs and growled, "Go!" His eyes were as black and intense as Greta. In the beam of light coming from the deteriorating roof, I saw blood dripping off the 2x4. Harley?

Charles was at the top step. Without warning, Arno swung the board and caught Charles on his right temple. He never saw it coming. His legs buckled, and he tumbled, headfirst, down the stairs. His cane and Tilley followed him down.

Arno stepped behind me and shoved the board in my back. I was at the top step. His face was contorted. A sinister grin distorted his lips. "After you," he said.

I flinched and closed my eyes before he raised his arm holding the board; I stumbled over the edge of the first step and grabbed the handrail.

Plaster from the roof began falling in surfboard-size chunks; water pelted down. My left arm was wrapped around the railing. Then Arno crashed into me. I opened my eyes and saw a yellow broom handle ramming into his back—a broom held by Mrs. Klein.

Arno's momentum carried both of us down the stairs. My head bounced off the wall, and I hit the water, back first. Arno landed on me. If there hadn't been three feet of seawater, the fall would have killed me. Arno's weight pressed my lungs. I couldn't breathe. The gun flew out of his hand when he hit. He tried to grab it before it sank in the opaque, swirling water. He still had the deadly board in his hand but made the fatal mistake of thinking I was unconscious. My head was barely above water; I had swallowed a mouthful of salt water before I regained my balance and stood.

The table that had held old photographs of Joseph in better times was floating between Arno and me. He was facing the window and trying to stand. I braced my foot against the bottom step and, with every ounce of energy I had left, shoved the table into his back. I was nearly out of energy; my arms stung, my breathing was labored. It took him by surprise, and he lunged forward. He stumbled, and his head rammed into the windowsill. A five-inch shard of window glass sliced into his neck. He tried to stand and slipped. He grabbed at the sill and the glass but missed. His eyes rolled upwards; his body went limp. Blood from the gash spewed against the wall and went from bright red to pink as it was diluted by the rain running down the surface.

I turned away from the gruesome sight. His eyes were wide open, but he didn't see anything in this world. Greta was no longer his concern.

Mrs. Klein was on the steps just above water level. She still had the broom in her hand. "Oh, Lordy," she said and put her other hand to her mouth.

I gasped for breath. I hesitated and then waded over to the steps and asked if she was okay.

She shook her head no; rainwater and tears were running down her cheeks. "I'm alive."

"Sit on the step; I'll be right back."

Where was Charles … Harley? Were they alive?

More of the roof collapsed; water continued to sweep down the stairs and almost carried Mrs. Klein with it. The sound of chaos was deafening. My back was killing me; bouncing down the stairs had taken its toll. My breath was slowly returning.

Where were they?

Hope came from the most unlikely sentence, "Hey, Mr. Photo Man! I could use a hand."

Charles was in the hall outside Travis Green's room. The water was up to his waist, blood from the wound over his left eye ran down his face, and he was cradling Harley's head. As soon as Charles had hit the water after tumbling down the steps, he heard the ceiling beam fall with Harley underneath. Harley's nose was barely above the rushing water. I waded toward him and through the near-darkness saw the problem.

Harley was conscious, but his left arm was pinned under a ceiling beam. If Charles tried to move the beam, Harley's head would go under. Could he ever use a hand.

Water rushed through the windows. In no time the entire first floor would be submerged—assuming the second floor's collapse didn't kill us first.

"Arno?" said Charles.

"Dead," I said. I had grabbed one end of the beam and, aided by the buoyancy of the water, was able to shove it off Harley's arm.

"Good," said Charles.

"Damned good!" said Harley.

That was the first I'd heard from him.

"He smacked me with that damned board ... caught me off guard," said Harley.

His pride was hurt as much as his head. "You okay?" I asked. He wobbled to his feet.

"Headache," he said. "Did you find Mrs. Klein?"

"She's okay," I said. "On the stairs."

A loud crashing sound came from overhead. "Can you walk?" I asked Harley.

"Sure," he said. "No headache ever stopped me from walking."

"Let's get out of here," said Charles. He looked up at the drywall buckling. A two-foot square of it fell on my shoulder. Charles ducked as another large piece splashed beside him.

We waded to the front stairs. Arno's body was floating face down and was pressed against the wall by the rising water.

"Hi, Harley," said Mrs. Klein. A body was floating in front of her, her house was being destroyed piece by piece, memories were cruelly being washed away, and she was calmly sitting on the steps like just another day.

"Enough chitchat," said Charles. "How're we going to do this?"

"First, we have to get out of here." I looked back down the hall toward the ocean. Water was at least a foot higher on the wall than when I found Charles and Harley. I knew I'd be lucky to carry myself, and Charles didn't look in any better condition. "Harley, can you carry Mrs. Klein?"

"I can walk," she huffed.

"Sure," said Harley as he looked at her frail body on the stairs. "If you can't walk the whole way out, I'll help."

She'd be no match for the turbulent tides outside her door, but Harley had spared her pride.

"Then what're we waiting for?" asked Charles. He turned and waded toward the door, pushing a floating chair out of the way.

The palmetto that blocked the door had been pushed across the street by the fierce tide. Water was nearly chest deep, and the rolling tides raised it several inches with each incoming wave. Mrs. Klein took one look and said "maybe" she'd need a "little help." Harley grabbed her before she changed her mind and hefted her over his head. Charles pushed her dress over Harley's head so he could see.

"Don't get fresh, young man," she said and tapped Harley on the top of his head.

He winced. "Where's my helmet when I need it?"

The closest path to dry land was directly up the street toward Bert's and my house.

A small wooden storage building was floating across the street. "Traffic's a little light today," yelled Charles. We were wading up the middle of Arctic Avenue.

Ripples of pain shot through my back when I laughed. Mrs. Klein smiled—no simple task with her house destroyed behind her.

CHAPTER 59

There wasn't a speck of dry on us when we stumbled in my door. The interior smelled damp and stale. I looked up and was impressed with my roof repairs. Water was running under the door but was easily contained. Hurricane Frank had taught me to stuff towels at the bottom of the door from the outside to at least slow the tide. Everything else appeared dry. Dry and sweltering—no power, the windows closed, no air circulated, and in the mid-eighties outside, much hotter inside. I found an old bathrobe and offered it to Mrs. Klein along with the privacy of the bedroom. She refused at first, but finally accepted it. Water was slowly rising on the street and, in another hour, it would reach the wheel well of the Lexus. Charles sprawled out on the living room floor, and Harley slumped in a kitchen chair. We did a visual inspection of each other to make sure there weren't any serious wounds needing immediate attention—minor cuts and bruises were everywhere, and my Band-Aid supply was depleted quickly. Tetanus shots were in our near future.

I had grabbed the cell phone from the car on the way in, but it read *No service*. We were trying to figure out the best way to tell the police what had happened when a pounding on the door solved the problem.

Acting Chief King stood on the step decked out in rain gear and a frown. Cindy Ash was standing behind him.

"What's it about 'Everyone Must Evacuate' you don't understand?" he snarled. He elbowed his way in the door, pushed the rain hood off his head, yanked off the coat, and shook it on the enclosed porch. Cindy meekly followed him into the living room. "We saw you damn fools in front of Bert's," he continued.

Mrs. Klein opened the bedroom door and walked into the living room, dragging the bottom of the robe on the floor.

"Oh, Mrs. Klein," said King. His tone mellowed a tad.

She glared. "*Acting* Chief King," she said in a schoolteacher's tone, "these three young men just saved my life." She walked to within six inches of King, continued to glare, "and … and solved the terrible murders that you and your incompetent collection of public servants couldn't do. Now you just shut up; stop your bullying. Shut up and listen!"

I took the lead. "Chief, if we could gather in the kitchen, I have a lot to tell you."

"Shouldn't we get off the island first?" asked Harley. He was standing at the window watching the rising water.

"I've got a high-riding four-wheel drive and can get us off in a little while," said King. "They say the eye's moved farther north than expected. This should be the worst of it." He nodded toward the kitchen.

That was the best news I'd never heard.

Charles, Harley, and I limped to the kitchen; Mrs. Klein strolled with renewed energy. I stood, as did Cindy. The others sat. Considering the circumstances, I didn't offer refreshments or drinks.

"Chief," I said without preamble. "Arno Porchini is the crossbow killer."

"Wrong," he said. "Have you blasted idiots forgotten he was shot?"

"Victim and perpetrator," I said. "He shot himself, Chief," I said. "I'll explain in a minute. Let me finish."

"Yes, *Acting* Chief, let him finish," yelled my enforcer, Mrs. Klein.

I paced around the room. Moving eased the pain in my back. I noticed that Cindy had her notebook open. Chief King sat with his arms folded; a frown dominated his face. I began leading the chief through our day, beginning with Charles's middle-of-the-night wake-up call. Charles beamed when I said the time. King tried to interrupt, but a "Hmm" and a glare from Mrs. Klein silenced him.

Cindy stopped taking notes when I said Porchini was dead. I briefly shared what happened after that, but I could tell the chief was getting frustrated, so I stopped. "Questions?"

"You sure he's dead?" asked King.

"Deader than Lincoln," said Mrs. Klein. "I saw it all." She pointed at me. "That young man told you exactly how it happened. If he didn't stop Porchini, we'd all be dead, and everyone would think it was because of the damned hurricane."

"Why didn't you call the police about Mrs. Klein?" asked the chief.

"Tried," said Charles. "All the phones were dead."

"Then why not tell us when you came back?"

"You were busy with the wreck out by the Pig," said Harley. "It's not our fault the cops were too incompetent to block the island."

The chief glared at Harley, but let it go.

Cindy had been silent until now, but jumped in, "How'd you know it was Porchini?"

"I began to suspect it when we evacuated, but didn't know for sure until I went into his room."

"Huh?" asked Charles.

"Cindy, Chief, Charles, Harley," I said and looked at each of them. "Why a crossbow?" I had their undivided attention. "That's bothered me from the beginning." I turned to Mrs. Klein. "You gave me one huge clue, and I missed it," I said. "Misdirection—in the circus, in magicians. Give us something to believe what we already want to believe."

"Explain!" barked the chief. He had begun to listen, though. He leaned back in his chair, and his eyes followed my movement around the room.

"Okay," I said. "It shouldn't be hard to prove."

Charles smiled; everyone else stared at me. "Arno was a carpenter on a big house remodel in Lexington, Kentucky. Somehow during the job, he found a stash of passports, money, maybe some jewelry, other paintings, valuables, no telling what else, and stole it. What he didn't know was that the house belonged to a crook—an art forger and thief who runs a legitimate business. The forger, Stewart Barlow, couldn't go to the police with the truth since the passports weren't real, but they were worth hundreds of thousands of dollars to Barlow. I suspect he bought, stole, and laundered using the other names." I took a breath and looked at Mrs. Klein. "Remember when you told me how valuable forged passports were to the circus performers?"

"Sure do," she said and smiled.

"The three names we found in Pat Rowland's papers?" asked Charles.

"Yep," I said, "all forgeries."

"Go on," said King.

"So Barlow hired Pat Rowland to find the thief. He knew that whoever stole the stuff could use it against him, possibly blackmailing him or sending it to the police—trouble either way." I looked around the room. "Arno may never have done anything, but Barlow couldn't take that chance."

"And she tracked him down?" asked Cindy.

"Unfortunate for her, she was a good detective. She tracked him down, but it took her looking in several cities and spending thousands of Barlow's dollars. Somehow she found out he was on Folly Beach, and when she finally suspected the thief was one of the guys living at Mrs. Klein's place, she rented a room."

"Such a sweet girl ... sad, sad," said Mrs. Klein.

The rain continued to pelt down on the tin roof.

"How'd she find him?" asked the chief.

"Great question," I said. "Don't know for sure, but suspect it was at the Tuesday night jamboree at GB's. He was there every week, but so was Country Cal, and occasionally Harley, and Lester Patterson. She began attending shortly after arriving and narrowed it down but didn't know for sure. Remember, Les, Arno, and Harley were in construction, and Cal had a history of being nearly everywhere in the country. And then it got dicey." My headache was worsening, and I slowly lowered myself to the floor.

"Arno figured out she'd moved into the Edge for more than being closer to his charms?" asked Charles.

I looked directly at the chief and said, "How does Porchini kill Rowland without drawing suspicion to himself? Everyone else who lived there would be a suspect, and intense digging into his past could point suspicion to Porchini. Remember, he didn't have any idea how much she knew or had documented."

Chief King stared at his hands leaned against the table, and said, "So you shoot yourself to lead suspicion away."

I looked at him. "No gunshot residue; no way to tell how far the alleged killer was from Porchini. Al, a friend of mine, threw out another clue I missed. He said that our military actually trained soldiers in the use of the crossbow for that reason. With no sound, the enemy couldn't tell how far, or near, the enemy was. It could be six inches or sixty yards."

"Hmm," said King. He looked at Charles and then back to me.

I continued, "Instead of a suspect, Porchini became a lucky—a very lucky—sympathetic victim of a crazed killer. All he had to do was rig something to hold a crossbow near his arm, shoot the bolt into the flesh where he knew it wouldn't be fatal, collect his own blood to smear in the boat, and head out to the marsh where he could pull near the road and yell for help."

"And," added Charles, "put the crossbow under Cal's bed and call the police. Case solved!"

"All that Lester Patterson and Travis Green did wrong was be in the wrong place at the wrong time," I said. "They were tools of misdirection. I think Arno even covered Travis's Volvo so you'd think he was the killer and split; again, more misdirection." I paused when another thought popped into my head. "And it would give him time to skip. He told us he was thinking about leaving the other night at GB's. Harley, he said you were leaving, too. That way, if he had to get rid of you, you'd be the likely suspect."

"I never said I was leaving," said a clearly agitated biker.

Mrs. Klein was silently shaking her head. She looked smaller in my robe than her already petite frame. "Why ... why my house?" she asked, barely above a whisper.

"I'm afraid Pat Rowland drew attention when she moved in," I said. "Porchini could have framed Harley instead of Cal."

Harley finally spoke. "I screwed up that plan when I took the lie detector test. I passed, didn't I, Chief?"

"Yeah," he said and turned back to me. "You found the crossbow stand he used to brace it to shoot himself, didn't you?" asked the chief.

"That's what I saw in his room," I said. "I thought that was what it was, but I was intent on finding Mrs. Klein. There wasn't time to think about it ... and, and I just remembered there was a receipt from Folly Road Self Storage on his workbench. It seemed strange, since he didn't own much of anything."

Chief King stood and looked out the backdoor. "We'll check it out. Anything else?" he asked without turning back to us.

"Yeah," said Charles. "Spring Cal."

"Get us off this island," said Harley.

"Get me a cigarette and build me a new house," said Mrs. Klein. She laughed—not a giggle, but a full-throated laugh.

I had gained new respect for one of Folly's oldest residents—without doubt, one of its most stubborn residents.

"One more thing, *Acting* Chief," said Mrs. Klein, "these here men are heroes. They saved my life and solved your crimes. Get that poker out of your behind and thank them."

Before King responded, or shot her, Charles butted in, one of his great strengths. "Once upon a time, someone asked President John Kennedy how he became a hero. Kennedy responded, 'It was involuntary. They sank my boat.'"

CHAPTER 60

The Monday issue of the Charleston *Post and Courier* reported that the bridge to Folly Beach was opened late Sunday for residents to return. No one else would be permitted to enter the island devastated by Hurricane Greta until most of the cleanup was done and the utilities restored. Several homes along the beach were completely destroyed, and many others suffered serious damage. But the most serious damage occurred north of Charleston County.

The front page of the local section said the Folly Beach police had recovered the body of Arno Porchini, the alleged crossbow killer. The police, citing self-defense, were not pressing charges against the person responsible for Mr. Porchini's death, Mr. Chris Landrum, of Folly Beach.

The national section of the paper reported that in Lexington, Kentucky, an art dealer was arrested for forgery, international money laundering, and a handful of lesser charges. The acting chief of police of the Folly Beach Department of Public Safety was credited with developing tips that led to the arrest and finding forged documents and paintings in a storage locker.

In even smaller print, the paper announced that Gregory Brile, owner of GB's Bar, was hosting a special Tuesday night edition of his weekly country music jamboree. He was quoted as saying, "The lights ain't back on, but we have candles; we'll open the door, and, if I work it just right, the insurance company will pay for the beer—now don't quote me on that last part."

*   *   *

I didn't know who was paying, but since it wasn't me, I didn't care. The beer was flowing freely by the time 9:00 p.m. rolled around at GB's. Our attention was turned to the bandstand as we listened to the last couple of verses from Country Cal's *greatest hit.*

> *"I'll catch you at the end of your story;*
> *I'll be there when life starts to fall.*
> *I'll catch you at the end of your story;*
> *and we'll be together through it all."*

"Thank you, thank you," he said as he finished his set. His mouth was inches from the silver microphone even though it was still out with the rest of the power in the bar. "As some of you know, I just finished a limited engagement in the Charleston County Pokey. Am I glad to be back home!"

The reference to the pokey was greeted by applause.

He nodded toward the four tables in the back corner we had commandeered. "I especially want to thank a few folks. First, my new best buddy, Bob Howard, for finding me—and the rest of the residents of Mrs. Klein's place—a fine, cheap, place to hang my Stetson. Meals are not included like they were where I just came from, but I'm not complaining. Thank you, Bob."

Bob and Betty were on the other side of the table, and he stood and took a bow. Bob also waved a *Bob Howard, Realtor, Island Realty* card in the air—subtle, my friend, subtle. Bob's aunt, Louise, was sitting next to her friend, Mrs. Klein. Both were sipping on some pink drink GB had concocted for them.

GB kept looking at his watch, but Cal wasn't about to give up the dead mike. "And a big GB's thanks to Officer Cindy Ash for hightailing it over to the jail in the middle of Greta to break me out."

Larry was next to Cindy and gave her a hug for all to see. She was off duty and hugged back.

Cal had taken his Stetson off and carefully placed it on the floor. "Before I close," he said, "I'd like us to all stand and join in a moment of silent prayer for Lester Patterson, Travis Green, and Pat Rowland—ya'll know why."

GB's was quieter than any moment the bar had been open. My head was bowed, but I still glanced around the room. I wondered if anyone was praying for Arno Porchini.

Cal broke the silence with the first verse of "Just As I Am." Before he finished, tears were rolling down my cheeks—tears of relief, sorrow, and joy. Mine weren't the only tears in GB's.

Cal finished and simply walked from the stage. No faux encore; all his thanks had been given.

Cal worked his way to our table as GB encouraged us to give a big hand for "a cute, little, girl singer, Miss Heather Lee." She had been sitting beside Charles and waiting her turn to "entertain." Cal let her borrow his guitar since hers was washed away with the rest of the Edge. She jumped from her seat, and wearing her trademark straw hat and big smile, bounded toward the stage. Charles stood and began applauding. Taking the cue, a couple at the bar joined in.

Amber was sitting to my right. Her apartment on the second floor was barely touched by Greta, and Jason was spending the night with Samuel to help clean his house that didn't fare as well. I offered to get her another drink when I saw Karen Lawson come in the door. She was followed by Chief Brian Newman. This was the first time I had seen him out since his heart attack. He walked slowly, but with confidence. His back was straight, and his head held high. I walked over to greet them; Karen gave me a tentative hug, and Brian shared a weak handshake.

There was only one extra chair at our tables, so Charles—the consummate party planner—surveyed the room and spotted one unattended table. He nodded to Cal, and they quickly grabbed the vacant table and carried it over to our grouping.

Karen took the seat closest to Amber, and they began talking in whispered tones. Brian walked around the tables and hugged the ladies, much to the delight of Mrs. Klein and Louise, and shook hands with the guys before he settled down in the chair beside his daughter. He took a deep breath. I took their drink order and headed to the bar.

Heather had conned GB into letting her sing a second song and was finishing it as I walked back to the table, a beer in each hand. Bob tilted his head toward the stage and stuck out his tongue and rolled his eyes like he was gagging. I think—hoped—I was the only person at the table to notice his review of Heather's unique vocal styling.

The table was full of empty bottles, so I judged the evening to be a success. Heather returned to our table of liars and was complimented on her fine singing. Honest Bob grinned at her.

Amber and Karen were still whispering and patting each other on the arm. Occasionally one would laugh or roll her eyes and then the other. I was curious what they were talking about but didn't ask. At least they weren't throwing knives at each other—or at me.

We were in no hurry to leave GB's insurance-company-reimbursed party since none of us had electricity at home.

Somewhere around midnight, we had another visitor. Acting Chief Clarence King strolled through the door, took a professional police gaze around the room, and then walked toward us. Charles and I saw him coming; I considered slithering under the table, but didn't. In fact, we had one vacant seat at our grouping of tables, so I stood and offered it to our visitor. To the surprise of most of us, he accepted. He was off work and figured we would be at GB's. His chair was between Bob and Amber. The *real chief* was sitting behind him.

He pulled the chair to the table and looked at me. "Mr. Landrum," he began, "I hope I never have to see you again professionally, and if you ever meddle in police business, I may shoot you myself." His stare was frightening. "Oh yeah, one more thing, thank you." He then broke into the closest thing I'd seen to a grin from his stoneface.

Brian Newman had been taking in the conversation, and added, "Chief, you're wasting your breath about Landrum and meddling. Drink up."

"Amen to meddling," came the strong voice of Mrs. Klein.

Larry, Charles, Louise, and Bob all stood, and raised their bottles in my direction.

"Amen!"

Printed in the United States
By Bookmasters